# KITT

# KITT

K. YUKI

KITT

Book Cover by K. Yuki
First edition 2026

ISBN 979-8-9947146-0-7 (paperback)

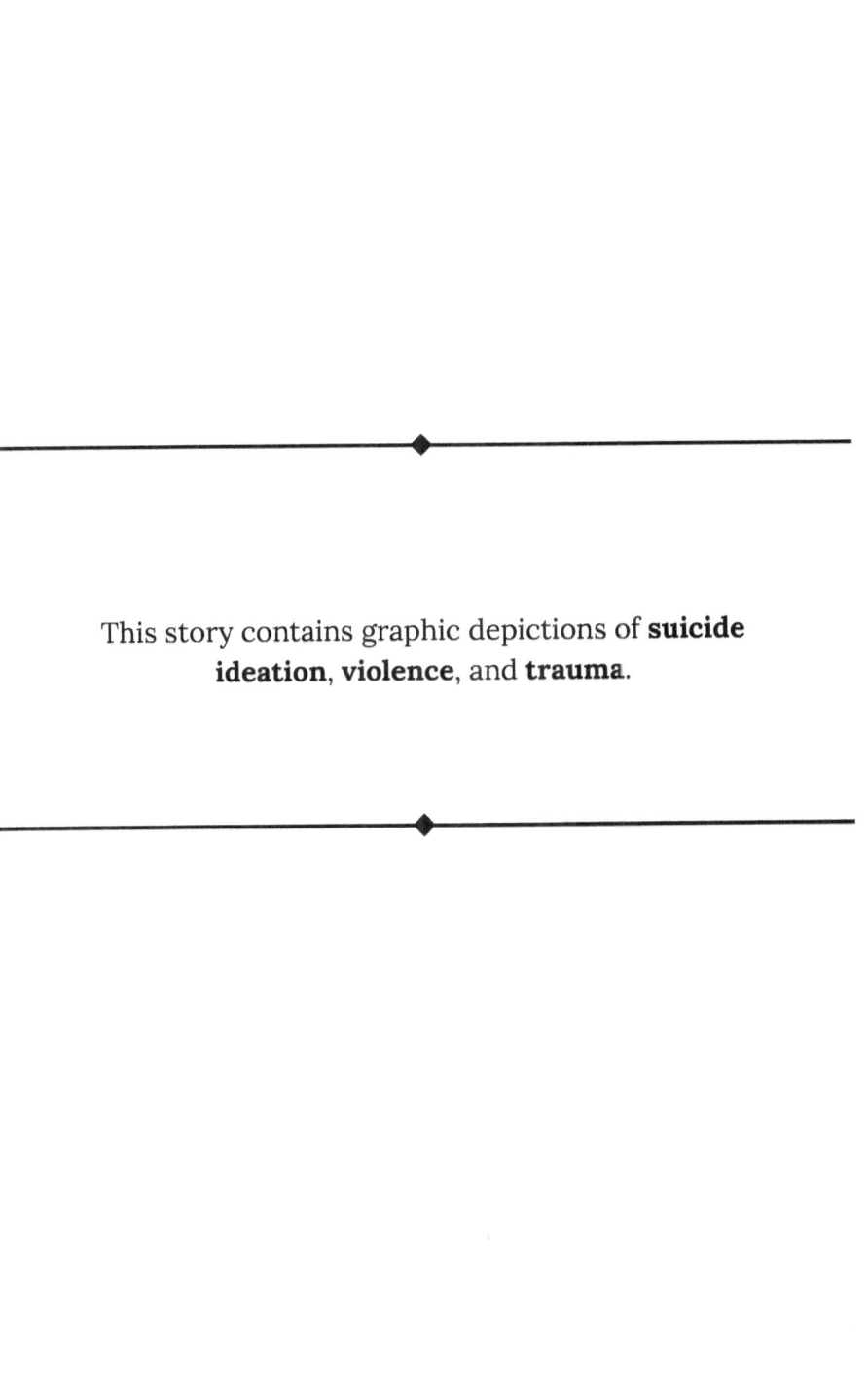

This story contains graphic depictions of **suicide ideation, violence**, and **trauma**.

# SALT & PINE

---

## CARNAL WANTS
### CHAPTER I

Another expedition is leaving Krandor today.

I've been at this window since dawn, watching them gather in the square below. Solis has barely risen—her smaller disc climbing ahead of Astaris the way she always does, the scout-moon racing the sun. The soldiers are mostly human, though I spot two Felidae among them, their ears swiveling as they check equipment. Rare in Orenia. Dad used to say they were more common the closer you got to Celtor.

They say it's just a diplomatic escort. Boring treaty stuff. But I know better. Any journey beyond our walls has to involve some kind of excitement, right? Monsters to fight. Mysteries to solve.

Then a messenger comes thundering through the gates, his horse white with lather. He leaps down before fully stopping, shouts something to the captain that I can't hear from up here.

Everything changes.

The soldiers abandon the careful loading routine. Now they're grabbing weapons first, supplies second. The captain stabs his finger at a map while his officers nod tersely. I press closer to the window, trying to read the symbols on the new crates they're loading.

A red sun falling beneath waves.

*Sekiyō no Ochi.*

I know that name. Dad mentioned it once—one of Orenia's warships, powerful enough to challenge any vessel on the Celtian Sea.

This isn't a diplomatic escort anymore.

My pulse quickens. I find myself gripping the windowsill so hard my knuckles go white. I imagine myself down there—asking what's wrong, offering to help. I've read every tactical manual in our house, studied every famous battle. I could be useful. I know I could.

Before I realize what I'm doing, I'm halfway to my dresser, reaching for my traveling clothes instead of my school uniform.

"Still watching them pack?"

Mom's voice behind me. I freeze, hand inches from my travel cloak.

"You're terrible at puns," I say automatically, because she hasn't made one yet but I know it's coming.

"I didn't make a pun."

"You were going to."

I turn around. She's standing in the doorway,

leaning against the frame like she needs it for support. She's thinner than she was last month. I keep noticing that—the way her collarbones show now, the way her dresses hang looser.

"Lunch is on the table," she says. "You've been up here for hours."

Hours. I glance at the window. The sun has moved. When did that happen?

"I was just—"

"Getting ready for school?" She looks at the travel clothes in my hand. "That's not your uniform, Kitt."

I don't have an answer. She doesn't push for one. Instead, she moves to the windowsill, looking down at the soldiers. Her hand goes to her apron pocket—that automatic gesture I've seen a thousand times. Her fingers are trembling as she fumbles with the cap. She shakes one into her palm, swallows it dry. A moment later, her hands go still.

"For the headaches," she says, though I didn't ask. She always says that now. Like she needs to explain. Like she's defending herself against an accusation I haven't made.

The label is facing away from me. She's never turned it away before.

"Mom—"

"Your father and I used to sit right here." She

touches the windowsill. "Arguing about whether the Celtian Sea smelled like salt or pine. We never found out. We were going to visit someday. See it together."

Her voice drifts. She's looking at the window but I don't think she's seeing the soldiers anymore.

"Mom?"

She blinks. Comes back. "Sorry. What were you saying?"

"I wasn't saying anything."

"Oh." Her smile is a reflex, nothing more. It hasn't reached her eyes in weeks. "Well. Lunch is ready. Don't let it get cold."

She starts to leave, then stops. Turns back.

"Kitt, you know I love you, right?"

The question comes out of nowhere. Too sudden. Too serious.

"I know."

"Good." She nods, like she's confirming something to herself. "Good. That's... good."

She leaves. Her footsteps on the stairs are slower than they used to be.

I find her in the kitchen twenty minutes later, standing at the counter. Not cooking. Not cleaning. Just standing there, one hand on the counter like she forgot what she came in here to do.

The pill bottle is out again. Open this time. She's staring at it.

"Mom?"

She startles. Closes the bottle quickly, shoves it back in her pocket.

"Lunch," she says brightly. Too brightly. "I made your favorite. The eggs with peppers."

I look at the table. There's bread. Cheese. No eggs.

"I thought I made eggs," she says, following my gaze. Her brow furrows. "I was going to make eggs. I had them out. I..."

She trails off. Looks at the counter. There's a carton of eggs sitting there, untouched.

"It's fine," I say quickly. "I like bread."

"No, I'll make them now. It'll only take—"

"Mom. It's fine."

She sits down across from me. Doesn't eat. Just watches me tear off pieces of bread, chew, swallow. Her hands are wrapped around a cup of tea that's gone cold.

"I worry about you," she says.

"I know."

"The way you look at those soldiers. The way you talk about adventure, about being part of something grand." She pauses. Takes a breath. "War isn't grand, Kitt. It's not a story."

"I know that."

"Do you?" She leans forward. There's something in her eyes now—not the drifting absence from before, but something sharper. Desperate. "Because your father knew. He knew, and he went anyway, and—"

She stops. Her hand goes to her chest, pressing flat against her sternum.

"Mom?"

"I'm fine." But she's not fine. I can see her fighting something—tears, maybe, or something worse. "I just need you to understand. People die out there, Kitt. Not heroically. Not meaningfully. They just... stop. And the people who love them have to keep going, have to keep waking up every morning and making breakfast and pretending the world still makes sense when it doesn't. When nothing makes sense. When you're so tired you can't—"

She cuts herself off. Reaches for the pill bottle again. Her hands are shaking badly now.

"Mom, how many of those have you taken today?"

"Don't." Her voice hardens. "Don't ask me that."

"I'm worried about you."

"I said don't."

We stare at each other across the table. The bread sits between us, half-eaten.

"I just want to matter," I say finally. Quietly. "I want to be part of something. Not stuck here, safe and bored and watching everyone else live while I—"

"You matter to me." Her voice cracks. "Isn't that enough?"

The question hangs there.

I should say yes. I should tell her of course it's enough, she's my mother, her love is everything.

But something in me—something small and terrible and honest—doesn't say that. The right answer is yes. I know the right answer. I've known it my whole life. I open my mouth to say it—

"I don't know," I whisper.

Her face does something complicated. Pain, yes. But also something like recognition. Like she understands exactly what I mean. Like she's felt it too.

"Go to your room, Kitt."

"Mom—"

"Please. Just... go."

I go. Behind me, I hear the rattle of pills in a bottle. The sound of her breathing, ragged and wrong.

I climb the stairs to my room and close the door and stand there in the dark, and I don't know why I said what I said, and I don't know how to take it back.

I can't understand any of that yet.

I just know that I want to be somewhere else. Someone else. Part of something bigger than this house and this mother who's falling apart and this feeling in my chest that I can't name.

I lie in bed and dream of adventure.

I fall asleep smiling.

In my dreams, someone sees me. Someone needs me. Someone reaches out their hand and says: *you belong here, Kitt. You're exactly who we needed.*

# ORDINARY

◆

### CHAPTER II

The pill bottle is on the kitchen counter again. Fuller than yesterday. She refilled it. When did she have time to refill it?

I see it before I see Mom. Small. Green. The label half-peeled from moisture, though I can still read **OXYCODONE ½ gr—one tablet every six hours** in black letters. It's open.

Mom stands at the stove, her back to me. She's stirring something in a pot. The motion is mechanical—around and around, the same rhythm, like she's forgotten she's doing it.

"Morning," I say.

She doesn't turn. Just keeps stirring.

"Mom?"

I almost reach for her hand. Almost. My fingers twitch toward hers and then I catch myself, and I don't know what I was going to do if I'd actually touched her. Don't know what that gesture was supposed to mean.

"Hmm?" She blinks, looks at the pot like she's surprised to find it there. "Oh. Breakfast. I made... I was making..."

Her other hand is in her apron pocket. I can see the shape of the bottle through the fabric. She's carrying it with her now. Room to room. Like she can't let it out of reach. Looks at the pot again. It's empty. She's been stirring an empty pot.

"Toast?" I offer. "I can make toast."

"Toast. Yes. That's what I meant to..." She sets down the spoon. Her hand hovers over the pill bottle for just a second before she grabs the butter knife instead. "Toast."

I watch her spread butter on bread. The strokes are uneven—thick on one side, barely there on the other. Her hands are shaking again. They do that in the mornings now, before her first pill. Sometimes between doses too.

She slides the plate across the table. I eat without tasting. Through the window, I can see the expedition gathering in the square below. They're almost ready to leave. Armor catches the morning light—a knight checking his sword, the blade so bright it hurts to look at.

My chest tightens.

"Kitt?" Mom's voice pulls me back. "You're going to be late."

"I know."

But I don't move. Just watch the soldiers loading the last of their supplies. Watch the way they move with purpose. With direction. With somewhere to be.

Mom follows my gaze. Her expression does something complicated.

"They're just people," she says quietly. "Same as us."

"They're doing something."

"So are you. School. Learning. Growing up."

"That's not—" I stop. We've had this argument. It goes nowhere. "I should get ready."

She nods. Doesn't push. Just picks up her tea—the cup shaking slightly in her grip—and turns toward the window herself.

I leave the half-eaten toast on the table.

School is twenty minutes away if I walk fast. I walk slow.

The streets of Krandor are already busy—merchants setting up stalls, guards in red and gold making their rounds, the ordinary machinery of a city that doesn't know anything is wrong. Because nothing is wrong. Not officially. Not in any way anyone can see.

Mom is fine. She's just tired. The pills are for headaches. The weight loss is stress. The drifting, the forgetting, the way she looks at me sometimes like she's memorizing my face—that's all normal. That's all fine.

I believe this because I have to.

The school building rises ahead—gray stone, narrow windows, the Orenian banner hanging limp in the still air. I'm late. Master Takeshi will give me that look, the disappointed one that's worse than actual anger.

I slip into the classroom as quietly as I can. It doesn't work.

"Miss Kitt." Master Takeshi doesn't look up from his notes. "How kind of you to join us."

"Sorry, sir."

"Page forty-seven. We're discussing the Founding Wars."

I find my seat, pull out my book, try to look attentive. Master Takeshi is young for a teacher—mid-twenties, with a leather journal always tucked under his arm. Sometimes I see him writing in it between lessons, hunched over the pages like they contain something important.

"—and Queen Kitt Reelseda raised the first unified banner in Vestperia, uniting what would become Kurune," he says. "Though scholars debate whether the unification was diplomatic or—"

My name. The queen has my name.

Dad used to joke about that. "Our own little queen," he'd say, then laugh when I rolled my eyes. "Though she founded a nation and you can barely keep your room clean."

I'm not paying attention.

Through the window, I can see the courtyard. Younger students are on their break, running and shouting and playing. A girl with brown braids is bouncing a ball against the wall. She's maybe eight, full of that energy that doesn't know how to stay still. Her tail swishes behind her—short and fluffy, marking her as half-Felidae. She misses a catch and the ball goes rolling. A boy, probably her brother, grabs it just to keep it from her. She squeaks in protest, chasing him.

They're laughing.

I watch them the way I'd watch birds. Movement. Pattern. Sound. Sometimes I practice caring. I look at the children playing and I think: *feel something about this.* It never works. But I keep trying, which probably means something. I just don't know what.

"Miss Kitt?"

I snap back. Master Takeshi is looking at me. So is half the class.

"The significance of the Celtorian Banner Reform?"

I have no idea what he said.

"It was... significant?"

Someone snickers. Master Takeshi sighs—not angry, just tired—and moves on.

I sink lower in my seat.

Outside, the girl with the braids is teaching her brother a hand-clapping game. *Clap-clap-clap.* She keeps messing up, dissolving into giggles. He starts over patiently.

An elderly Felidae couple sits on a bench nearby. Heads close together. Just existing. Just being.

I should feel something, watching that. Longing, maybe. Warmth. The desire for connection. That's what the stories say. That's what Mom always said about Dad—that being together was enough.

I don't *feel* it.

I watch them the way I watch the children. Objects moving through space. Patterns to observe.

Maybe something's wrong with them. Maybe their happiness is performance.

Or maybe something's wrong with me.

The bell rings before I can finish the thought.

Lunch is in the courtyard.

I find a spot near the wall where I can watch without being watched. The girl with the braids is still playing—different game now, more running. The elderly couple has moved to the shade.

I eat the bread Mom packed. It's good. She makes good bread. When she remembers to make it. When she doesn't stand at the counter for ten minutes forgetting what she came in there to do.

All around me, people are living. Laughing. Talking. Being.

And I'm sitting here alone, eating bread that tastes like nothing, watching happiness I can't feel, thinking about my mother's shaking hands and the pill bottle on the counter and the empty pot she was stirring this morning.

I should tell someone.

The thought surfaces and I push it down immediately. Tell them what? That my mom is sad? That she takes too many pills? That I'm scared in a way I can't name?

They'd ask questions. They'd come to the house. They'd make everything worse.

Better to stay quiet. Better to pretend.

I finish my bread. The afternoon classes blur together—same desk, same windows, same view of children playing and couples being happy and life continuing like nothing is wrong.

By the time I get home, the sun is setting.

The pill bottle is still on the counter. Fuller than this morning.

She refilled it. When did she refill it?

"How was school?" Mom asks from the kitchen doorway.

"Fine."

She's smiling. That bright, wrong smile that doesn't reach her eyes. She's wearing a clean dress, her hair brushed, almost like the mother she used to be.

"I made dinner," she says. "Real dinner. The chicken you like."

The kitchen smells like cooking. Real cooking. There are plates on the table, food on the plates, everything arranged like a photograph of a family that has their life together.

"Mom, this is—"

"I wanted to apologize." She cuts me off, still smiling. "For yesterday. I was... I wasn't myself. But I'm better now. I took my medicine and I rested and I'm better."

She says it like she's reciting something she practiced. Like she rehearsed the words in the mirror until they sounded right.

The pill bottle isn't on the counter anymore. I check the trash while she's not looking. Two empty bottles. When did she go through *two*?

"Okay," I say.

"Okay." She nods, satisfied. "Good. Let's eat."

We eat. The chicken is good. She asks about school and I give her answers and she nods and smiles and it's all so normal, so perfectly ordinary, that I almost believe it.

Almost.

But I see her hands shake when she reaches for her glass. See the way her eyes drift to the window, then snap back like she caught herself doing something wrong. See the pill bottle on the counter, always in her peripheral vision, always within reach.

"I love you, Kitt," she says when dinner is over.

"I love you too."

"Promise me something."

"What?"

She opens her mouth. Closes it. Shakes her head.

"Never mind. It's nothing. Just... be good, okay? Be safe."

"I'm always safe."

"I know." She smiles again. Wrong again. "I know you are."

I help her clean up. We don't talk. The pill bottle stays on the counter.

That night, I lie in bed and stare at the ceiling and try not to think about the way she said "be safe" like it was goodbye.

Tomorrow will be normal.

Tomorrow everything will be fine.

I believe this because I have to.

# CRIMSON DREAMS

### CHAPTER III

A deep crimson coated the pine flooring as I rushed to him, tearing at his steel armor, the plating and straps, as fast as I could. The buckles wouldn't come free—my hands were shaking too badly to work the metal tongues loose—and my fingers fumbled with the leather straps, slick now and impossible to grip. The boat shook violently beneath the screams of the others outside, fighting off the onslaught.

The deck rolled under me, sending me sprawling across his body. I had to brace one hand against the wall to keep from sliding away from him. Everything was too loud, too red, too warm and cold at once—the sounds of pain and despair deafening.

I pressed my head to his cool chest, trying to force his entrails—collapsing in my hands like overripe fruit—back into the slit of his stomach. I could feel his ribs shifting under my hands—broken, crunching, all wrong. I wailed, my hands covered in his warm blood. When his dimming, bloodshot eyes found mine, I felt something inside my chest crack open.

My arms locked around him—if I just held tight enough, maybe he wouldn't break apart.

I gasped awake, sheets twisted in my fists, drenched in cold sweat.

My chest heaved like I'd been running for miles, heart pounding loud enough to drown out everything else. For a second, I swore I could still smell iron.

I lay still, processing. It felt too real. Too vivid to be false. My head pounded softly, still forcing me to hold everything I'd just witnessed.

I stared across the room, not moving. The morning sun caught the dust motes drifting through my window—tiny, directionless things. Outside, I could hear Krandor waking up: cart wheels on cobblestones, someone calling to their horse, the distant clatter of shop shutters opening.

A small movement caught my eye. A streetcat on the windowsill across the way. Orange tabby, maybe a year old. It looked soft. I watched it groom itself, letting the simple motion soothe something in me.

I blinked slowly. Waking up now. Really waking.

Another day. Still with Mom.

Today I was supposed to go to school. Mom thought I needed a proper education. I guess that's something normal people do. Go to school, learn things, pretend yesterday's nightmares don't follow you around.

A soft knock at my door. "Kitt? I made breakfast." Her voice lingered for a beat. "Kitt? Are you well?"

I hadn't realized I'd still been shaking. I glanced at my hands—trembling less now, but still caught somewhere between dream and waking. Still pale.

I pulled the purple blanket higher, tucking my chin underneath it. "I am well, Mom." The words came out smaller than I meant them to.

She stepped closer. I could feel her eyes studying me. Her hands trembled slightly as she adjusted the blanket around me—probably hasn't taken her pills yet.

"You look pale, sweetheart. Did you sleep all right?"

I closed my eyes, trying to block out the images. The boat. The screaming. His eyes locked onto mine.

I turned toward the window, pulling the blanket with me like armor.

"Kitt..."

"Really, Mom. I'm fine." But my voice cracked on *fine*, betraying me.

She was quiet for a long moment. I could hear her breathing. Could sense her hovering.

Finally: "Well, breakfast is on the table when

you're ready. Take your time."

Her footsteps retreated down the hall. Softer than usual. Slower.

I stood after she left, opening my dresser. Dresses, school uniform, pajamas. I stripped down to my undergarments, grabbed the white top and the plaid deep-sea blue skirt. Slid them on while drifting in and out.

The nightmare flickered through my mind. My hands started shaking again as I pulled on the skirt, trying to focus on the fabric rather than the images.

Downstairs, the faint clink of dishes. Mom, waiting. Breakfast, waiting.

Then the soft sound of a pill bottle opening.

Closing.

Silence.

Then the soft *clank* of a knife against a cutting board.

I finished dressing, adjusting the small tan leather belt Mom had insisted on—it didn't match, but she'd been so certain about it. I took deep breaths. Stared out the window at the merchant carriages passing on the road.

My stomach growled.

I moved toward the door. Down the wooden steps, the familiar creaking a comfort.

"Mom? Thank you for making breakfast!" I called

out cheerfully as I rounded the corner into the kitchen. The savory smell of eggs and bacon filled the air, making my mouth water.

But there was something else underneath it. Something metallic. Sharp.

"It smells wonderful, I—"

I stopped mid-sentence.

Mom is there.

# PILLS TO BLAME

◆

### CHAPTER IV

Mom is there, slumped against a floor-level cabinet. She's still looking at me. Her eyes find mine and hold—not fading. Not yet. Just... looking. The way you look at someone when you finally understand what they are.

I blink, tears filling my eyes involuntarily. I continue standing in front of her, though my knees are... are... shaking. "Mom?"

Her breathing is slow, wet-sounding, sickening to hear. I want to cover my ears, but something in me needs to hold her—needs to hug her as tight as possible. I try to take a step forward. My muscles don't respond.

I think I can hear something rattling where it shouldn't. Her blond hair is matted—I knew it would be. Her chest—

No.

Her chest is open. Deep cuts. The kind that take—

I don't finish the thought.

Deep crimson pools under her, spreading across the floor. Her apron isn't even set on right, too torn to hang properly.

Vomit wells up inside me, making my throat burn. I drop to my knees, watching her as she observes my reaction. She doesn't smile, she doesn't even cry. She looks like she wanted this from the start, like I wasn't enough reason to stay.

That's the story. That's what happened here.

My hands shake uncontrollably as I try to drag myself to her with stiff legs, trying to touch her fading warmth one more time. Her eyes follow me—every movement, every breath—asking something I won't answer.

"Mom..." I whisper shakily, trying to extend my hand to hers. "Mom... Please..." It sounds almost childishly small.

This can't be real... This isn't real... No...

I sob silently, tears streaming down my face as the blood reaches my own pants, as I hold her hand tightly, as she stops looking at me, even though her eyes are still open. Her pupils are tiny—smaller than they should be, even with the morning light streaming in. The pills. Still in her blood. Still doing their work even now. She slowly, barely, turns her head to face me. There's something in her eyes now—not pain. Recognition. And I get to watch it fade.

Net— No— *This isn't*— Not— *End*— No—

My eyes dart across the kitchen. The pills are where they should be—scattered, visible, the label facing up so anyone would see OXYCODONE in black letters. The tape I'd set aside. The crimson finding the grooves in the wood, following the grain toward the door.

I need... I NEED her to be alive. I NEED.

I reach for the medical tape, but it's soaked through with blood. My eyes blur with tears again as I debate giving up on saving her. She's alive... how much of her is left?

I slowly stand up with wobbly knees, moving to see what the pills really were. Soft green capsules are scattered everywhere, looking wrong somehow as I stare at them. My hands stain the cap with maroon as I read the label—**OXYCODONE ½ gr—one tablet every six hours**. The Kuruni apothecary's stamp is smeared—water damage, maybe from the day she picked it up.

I freeze, staring at the bottle. I can feel the blood drain from my face as Mom continues to dim. She looked so happy all the time. So... So... So... Relieved. So full of joy. And that was just THESE PILLS?

I WANT HER BACK.

I think I see her twitch, and my eyes light up in hope, just for it to be crushed when I see her eyes are empty, unfocused. She's alive. She's alive. My mind lingers on the false hope, before I take one last glance. She's...

Why would she do that to herself?

I look down at my hands. They're clean. When did I—

I wipe them on my skirt anyway. Habit.

I slowly get up from beside her, shaking still. My mind races—what did I miss, what did I forget, is there anything that—

No. *Stop.*

—if I'd just seen the signs, if I'd just been there—

I rush out of the house—not home anymore, can't be home after this, can't stay where they'll find her and ask questions I don't want to answer—sobbing as I run down the cobbled streets of Krandor, drawing the unwanted glares of passersby.

I run out of breath, leaning on a wall. Her body plagues my mind as I stare down at the floor, my vision going more and more blurry. *Why... Not... Not again...*

The noon sun beats down, the heat pressing against my face like something physical. I can barely breathe, barely move—

# ACCLIMATION

◆

## REFUGE
### CHAPTER V

I wake up, but I'm not sure if I'm really awake. The room spins slightly when I turn my head, and for a moment, I think I'm still in my bedroom, waiting for Mom to call me down for breakfast.

Then I remember.

The walls are wooden planks, not the soft green I'm used to. The floor looks dusty and dirty, though maybe everything looks wrong right now. There's only a lantern hanging from the top of the door frame, casting shadows that seem to move when I'm not looking directly at them.

My body feels disconnected, like I'm watching someone else try to sit up. Everything hurts in a distant way, like pain that belongs to someone else. When did I get here? How long have I been lying in this bed?

*Mom's eyes. Still watching me. Still—*

No. Don't think about that. Think about... about anything else.

The smell hits me then—alcohol and cooked mutton rising through the floorboards. A tavern. I'm in a tavern. But why? How did I...?

The blood. Running through the streets. People staring. Someone must have found me.

I try to piece together what happened after I left the house, but there are gaps. Big, empty spaces in my memory where time should be. I remember the cobblestones under my feet. I remember not being able to breathe. Then nothing until waking up here.

My stomach clenches—not with hunger, but with something worse. Everything feels fragile, like I might shatter if I move too quickly or think too hard about what I saw.

There's a sound at the door. It makes me freeze.

KNOCK, KNOCK.

The sound echoes in my chest, making my heart race. What if they know? What if they think I... what if they think I did something to her?

KNOCK, KNOCK.

A voice comes through the wood—gruff but somehow gentle: "Miss? Are you alright?"

I want to answer, but my throat feels raw. When did I last speak? When did I last do anything normal?

"Miss? Are you in there?"

I have to say something. I have to prove I'm... what? Innocent? Alive? Both?

"... I am alive, mister." The words come out

smaller than I meant them to, but they're true. Somehow, I'm still alive when Mom is not.

The door finally opens, and candlelight floods in along with the noise of the pub below.

I can finally see him—and he is not what I expected. I thought he was some sort of knight, but no, it's just a regular innkeeper. He's wearing a knee-length gray waistcoat over a white linen shirt and black worsted trousers, well-kept but shiny at the elbows.

Wait—why did I think about marriage? My mind feels scrambled, grabbing onto any story that makes this make sense. Knights rescue people. That's what they do in stories.

"Well, I am glad you are alive," he says in his gruff voice, "We found you with blood almost everywhere. Now, I will not force you to spit out what happened, but it's best to tell someone eventually. Food and drinks are on the house—just take a left in the hall and down the stairs."

I stare at him, processing what he just said. I stay silent.

After a while, he walks out the door and shuts it, muttering something about "injured schoolgirls."

The air in the room is thick and close, warm enough to make my borrowed clothes stick to my skin despite the chill outside. Sweat and old beer and something yeasty—the smell of too many bodies in too small a space—creeps under the door.

The hearth's smoke seeps through the floorboards. It's annoying. Makes me smell smoky. I focus on that—the annoyance—because it's easier than focusing on anything else.

I hear voices downstairs—the inn-man's gruff rumble and someone else. Official-sounding. My heart races until I catch fragments: "...just a tragedy... gone to stay with relatives in Celton..." The inn-man's voice is firm, protective. The official voice murmurs something I can't hear, then footsteps retreat. The door closes.

He lied for me. Why would he lie for me?

I sigh quietly after another minute of silence. The smoke is getting more annoying, and I am getting hungrier. My eyes drop down to my legs, still not wanting to move. The clothes I am wearing are not mine—they are clean and simple, clearly from the inn's supply. My hands and face feel scrubbed clean, too, though I have no memory of being washed. Someone took care of me while I was... wherever I was before waking up here.

I move the blanket to my side, pushing myself off the mattress

THUD!

I wasn't expecting the wood to be that hard. Well... I dust myself off, rearranging the clothes draped around me. I freeze. Tears well up before I can stop them. I don't know why—I don't let myself know why—and then I'm on the floor again, sobbing silently, curled into a tight ball.

My eyes glaze over with tears, making my vision go blurry. I shut my eyes for a moment, trying to wake from this nightmare.

The sunset hits the window differently from up on the second floor of this tavern. The pale windows reflect the yellowish-orange lighting across the cramped, wooden room. I've finally stopped crying, though I am still in the fetal position. I don't have the energy to get back up.

My stomach growls slightly, pleading to be fed. *How long has it been since I ate? Mom died today... or was it yesterday? Wait, how long has it been since her death?*

I am going to guess it was today, maybe a few hours ago, but I am starving and parched. I slowly push myself up, getting to my knees in more than a minute. Even that small movement exhausts me. After a few more minutes of trying, I make it to my feet, shaking. And then I fall over.

I stare at the closed door, as if the 'inn-man' (yes, that's what I am calling him, is it not cute?) would burst through the door and feed me. But he doesn't. Not at all. What would Dad do in this situation—alone, starving, and parched?

I hear footsteps in the hallway—heavier than mine, familiar now. The inn-man. He knocks gently before opening the door.

He opens the door slowly, and finds me on the floor, on my knees now. "Still on the floor, miss?" His voice is gentler than before, like he's talking to something wounded. "Come on then."

Before I can protest, he's helping me back onto the bed, pulling the blanket up to my chin like I'm a child. "Kanne will be up with soup in a moment."

Kanne must be his wife. I haven't met her yet, but I can hear her moving around downstairs sometimes, humming while she works.

He tucks me in, smoothing out the corners of the bed. A warm rush hits my head as I subconsciously snuggle into the blanket, curling into a ball. The inn-man doesn't say anything much, but he nods and walks off.

*Click.*

How much longer will I have to be here? It's already been a day from what I've seen.

The following weeks are a blur. Turns out, the inn-man's name is Kraft (I overheard it from Kanne). Kanne has been coming in and out of my room, bringing me snacks and proper meals. She's actually tried to show me how to knit, but it always devolves to us sitting around and talking about life, and her comforting me when I cry.

Kanne keeps telling me I should stay longer, that I'm not ready. She's probably right. But staying means thinking, and thinking means remembering, and I can't do that anymore.

I push the blanket off me, and I can hear the inn-man and his wife already moving downstairs. Kanne's light footsteps slowly ascend the stairs, and I can hear a soft knocking. "Kitt?"

"Yes, Kanne?"

"May I come in?"

I whisper "okay" (though I'm quite sure she can't hear it), and she opens the door slowly. She's holding a small basket of what she thinks is my favorite food, but I haven't had the heart to tell her it's not.

"Do you want some biscuits?"

I nod. She places the basket on the counter, and then sits on the bed with me. She pulls out a small brush and begins brushing my hair.

"Your hair is quite beautiful," Kanne murmurs while she brushes through some tangles. "Such a bright blonde, almost white in this light. And these little wisps? Oh, they frame your face oh so perfectly..." She pauses, studying my face. "You have such delicate features, like a little bird. How old did you say you were?"

I blush, mumbling "fifteen" under my breath.

"Fifteen," she repeats. "You look younger, maybe thirteen. Those big emerald eyes of yours, and you're so petite. Though, you're healthier than most girls I've seen come through here—you've got good color when you're not so pale from..." She trails off. "Everything."

She continues to tend to my hair in silence now. She reaches over to the basket and hands me a biscuit. I play with the biscuit in my hands as she continues brushing my hair. The biscuit looks good—berry filling, the outside is some sort of soft bread I haven't seen before.

Kanne eventually stops brushing, and hands me another biscuit.

I speak up, a small quiver in my voice. "Kanne?"

"Yes, dear?"

"Why are you still caring for me?"

She falls silent at my question, and I can see the subtle pain in her eyes. "I've met people like you, and I want to help everyone I can find."

*Quite a generic answer...* I don't push any more, simply resting my head on her shoulder. I suppose I'll take help wherever I can.

She's gentle. Patient. Her hands work through

the tangles without pulling, without hurting.

I don't understand why she does this.

Kraft and Kanne owe me nothing. I'm a stranger who collapsed in their street covered in someone else's blood. They should have called the guard. Should have asked questions. Should have wanted something in return for the food, the room, the care.

But they just... give it. Freely. Without expecting anything back.

"Why?" I ask before I can stop myself.

Kanne's hands pause. "Why what, dear?"

"Why are you helping me?"

She's quiet for a moment. "Because you needed help."

That's not an answer. That's not how people work. Everyone wants something. Everyone has motives. Kindness without expectation is either a trap or a weakness.

"Thank you," I say, because that's what you're supposed to say.

She smiles and keeps brushing.

Eventually, Kanne pats my head and I try to suppress a small giggle. "You should rest," she says after a while. I nod, complying by laying down on the bed. She pulls the blanket over my head, then back down to my chin, realizing her mistake.

I fall asleep in her hands.

CHAPTER V.I

I awake to moonlight flowing into the room, my vision blurry, my mind screaming one thing—ESCAPE. Visions of my mother tear through me as I try to get up. I fall to the floor, breathing heavily.

I stare at my hands, coated in blood that I can barely see in the dark. Tears flow down my face as my head hits the floor with a sickening thud. I drag myself up—knees, elbows, shaking.

I fall back to my knees, then force myself up to standing. I walk to the door with shaky feet, shaky breath, shaky everything. My index finger finds the long rectangle of the latch. My palm pivots on the circular plate.

I open it slowly. Warmth and drunk cheers rise from the pub below.

I take a step forward into the candlelight, shielding my eyes.

I take another step, looking down into the

hallway. Same wood walls. White trim. Smoke from the hearth below drifting up. There are a few doors to my left, and only one door to my right. Directly down the hall is a spiral staircase, which I assume leads down to the pub below.

A third step. My legs feel slightly more solid beneath me. I continue at a slow pace, moving toward the staircase. I look back. A trail of blood follows me. Catching up.

By the fourth step, I hear movement—someone running up the stairs. The wood creaks. The footsteps are closer than they should be—too fast.

Is that—?

# MILLY

### CHAPTER VI

My eyes travel up the suit of armor before me.

A paladin. That's what he must be—the formal stance, the quality steel, the way he holds himself like someone who's practiced standing in doorways. The candlelight from the hallway catches polished plates, but everything feels distant. Like I'm watching through water.

He speaks, and his voice sounds rehearsed. Careful. Like he's reading from something he memorized long ago: "Please pardon the intrusion, miss. Sir Lumber Mills, Paladin of Celton, at your service. I trust you'll forgive such an indelicate question, but would you happen to be the bloodied young woman that Kanne mentioned?"

*Bloodied young woman.*

The words hit like Father. That's me. That's what I am now—the girl who ran through streets covered in her mother's blood. The girl who might be a murderer, for all he knows.

I should say something. Should explain.

The words stick in my throat.

I just stare. The hallway feels smaller with his armored presence filling it. I can hear distant sounds from the tavern below—laughter, clinking glasses—but they're muffled. Unreal.

He waits.

Not demanding answers. Not grabbing me. Not looking at me like I'm a monster. Just... waiting. Discomfort crosses his face—slight, quickly smoothed away—but underneath it, something else. *When was the last time someone looked at me with concern?*

"Miss?" His voice is gentler now, though still formal. Still careful. "I am glad to have met you. Like I have said, I am Sir Lumber Mills, Paladin of Celton. If you wish, I can assist you in packing or unpacking, whatever you truly wish."

He's repeating himself. The same introduction, slightly varied. Like he only has one script and he's not sure what to do when it doesn't get a response.

*Paladin.*

The word feels safer than everything else. Safer than the kitchen floor. Safer than Mom's eyes going empty. I grab onto it like something solid in a collapsing room.

He extends his hand. Iron gauntlets creak softly.

A small smile appears on his face—effortful, not quite reaching his eyes, but trying. He's trying.

"Why?" The word escapes before I can stop it. "Why would you help me? You don't even know me."

He's quiet for a moment. Something shifts in his expression—not sadness, but something worn. Familiar. Like a groove in stone from water passing over it too many times.

"I am bound by sacred oath, miss. Any paladin of Celton who refuses aid to one who requests it forfeits both title and honor." A pause. His voice drops slightly. "Though I confess, even without the oath, I would struggle to turn away."

The words sound rehearsed too. But underneath them, something real. Something that costs him.

I take his hand. The leather of his gloves is surprisingly warm.

"Yes," I manage. My voice barely works. "Yes, I am... I am the bloodied girl. Kitt."

He nods. Clearly wanting to help. Clearly unsure how.

The silence stretches. He looks at me. Looks at the hallway. Looks back at me. His hand moves toward his belt pouch, stops, moves again.

"Are you hungry, miss?"

My stomach answers before I can. A loud, undignified growl.

He reaches into his pouch, pulls out a small piece

cf bread. Crusty. Golden-brown. One of the crunchy kinds.

He doesn't hand it to me directly. Just sets it on the counter beside me and steps back. Giving me space. Letting me choose.

He pulls off his gauntlets, sets them on the counter beside the bread. Flexes his fingers in the leather gloves underneath.

I stare at the bread. My hand twitches toward it. Stops. He's a paladin, so it should be safe, but what if—what if—

I grab it. Eat it in two bites.

The crunch is satisfying. Real. The first real thing I've felt in days.

Milly—I'm already thinking of him as Milly, though I don't know why—watches me eat. The faintest smile crosses his face. Genuine this time. Small, but genuine.

"Would you like some water, miss?"

Water.

The word hits wrong. Suddenly I'm back in the kitchen—throat dry, hands slick, Mom's eyes watching me from the floor—

I collapse.

Not dramatically. Just... my legs stop working. I'm on the floor before I realize I'm falling, and everything floods back. The helplessness. The red. The way she looked at me like she was asking a question.

Milly moves. Not rushing—deliberate, careful. He crouches beside me, close but not touching. Just present.

"I don't know what you've been through," he says quietly. "But I am here for you. I can take you to your bed, miss."

I nod. Barely a movement. He sees it anyway.

He picks me up—carefully, like I might break—and carries me back to my room. Sets me on the bed. Gentle. Careful.

I'm asleep before he reaches the door.

When I wake, Solis is at her peak.

Dad used to say Solis was like a scout for Astaris, running ahead to let people know when the real sun was coming. Right now, she's telling me it's midday.

Milly sits in a chair across the room, facing the door. His sword rests on the cabinet beside him—angled toward the entrance, away from me. Guarding. Even while I slept.

He sees me stir. "Water, miss?"

I nod.

He leaves. Returns with a glass, clear and full. Lifts it to my hands, holds it steady when my fingers shake.

The water is cool. Clean. I drink and feel something loosen in my chest.

He pulls the glass back after a few sips. Sets it within reach. Returns to his chair.

"Would you like to go downstairs?" he asks. "Perhaps socializing with others will help you out, miss."

"Perhaps later," I whisper.

He nods. Doesn't push.

We sit in silence. Him watching the door. Me watching him.

Hours pass like that. He brings food—small portions, nothing overwhelming. Checks if I'm comfortable. Asks if I need anything. Each time, the same careful formality. The same rehearsed courtesy. But underneath it, attention. Real attention. Like I'm a problem he's determined to solve correctly.

He cares, I think, watching him adjust his sword belt for the third time. A real paladin, and he cares about me.

The thought is warm. Dangerous.

By evening, the fog has lifted enough that I can think. Can want things beyond just surviving the next breath.

"Milly?" The nickname slips out. I don't take it back.

He looks up. Surprised. His mouth opens like he

might correct me, then closes.

"Would you mind if we went downstairs now?" I ask. "I think I'm ready."

"If you're certain, miss." He stands, movements precise. "The evening crowd can be quite lively."

"I want to try."

He nods once. Offers his hand to help me stand.

I take it.

# TAVERN

◆

### CHAPTER VII

He offers me his arm at the door.

I take it, and something shifts in his expression—a flicker of internal questioning, quickly suppressed. Like he's wondering why he's still here when he should be preparing for departure.

The tavern opens below us. Warm golden light, thick air heavy with ale and pipe smoke and too many bodies. The smell coats my throat—yeasty, dense, alive. Heat radiates from the crowd and the fire, making the temperature swing from the cool hallway almost dizzying.

Faces turn as we descend. Wooden tankards pause halfway to lips. Dice freeze mid-roll.

"Well, look who's finally joined us!" someone calls.

"Sir *Lumberrr* Mills!" Another patron raises his mug, rolling the R in that distinct Felidae way. I catch rounded ears, a tail swishing as he turns back to his companions. "Still playing guardian angel?"

Laughter. Good-natured, but with an edge. This isn't the first time he's helped someone like me.

The realization should make me feel ordinary. Instead, it makes him seem more noble. More like the knights in stories.

He guides me to a corner table, away from the crowd. "Water for the lady," he calls to the innkeeper. Signals for something stronger for himself.

I watch him settle into his chair. His eyes scan the room constantly—habit, probably. Professional awareness. But when his gaze returns to me, there's something almost gentle in it.

"You don't have to stay with me," I say. "I know you have important things to do."

"Do I?" The question seems to surprise him. He looks down at his armored hands. "Perhaps some things matter more than schedules."

Something warm blooms in my chest. Useful.

Our drinks arrive. He takes a measured sip of his ale. I wrap my hands around the water cup, not drinking. Just holding something solid.

Silence stretches. He's not good at filling it—I can see that now. He knows how to help people in crisis. Doesn't know what to do when the crisis pauses.

"Where are you traveling?" I ask. "If you don't mind me asking."

"The Vestperian border." He sets down his cup.

"There's been trouble. A small conflict—nothing too serious yet. I've been tasked with investigating."

"Vestperia." The word feels strange in my mouth. Foreign. "My father used to talk about it."

"Oh?"

I see it—the slight lean forward. The interest. He wants to ask about my father but doesn't know if he should. Doesn't want to push.

I could wait for him to ask. Let the silence do the work.

Instead, I give him something. A piece of bait.

"He died years ago. Border conflict." I keep my voice flat. Factual. "He used to say Vestperia's towers glowed brighter than the moons."

"He wasn't wrong." Milly's voice softens. "I've seen them. The towers do glow, though whether from magic or crystal formations, I cannot say."

"You've been there?"

"Once. Years ago." He pauses. Takes another sip. "It's not an easy journey. The borderlands are dangerous."

I nod. Look down at my water. Let the silence build again.

He breaks first. "Your mother?"

There it is. The question I was waiting for.

I don't answer immediately. Let my face do something complicated—grief, yes, but also something harder to name. Let him see me struggle with whether to speak.

"Recent," I finally say. "She... she's recent."

I don't elaborate. Don't need to. His expression shifts—understanding settling in. He thinks he knows what I mean. I think he understands the shape of my grief.

He doesn't. Not really. But he doesn't need to.

"I'm sorry," he says quietly. "That's a heavy burden for one so young."

"I don't have anywhere to go back to." The words come out smaller than I intend. That part, at least, is true. "The house isn't... I can't be there anymore. Everything reminds me of—"

I stop. Press my lips together like I'm holding something back.

He watches me. I can see him thinking. See him weighing.

"The journey to Vestperia is dangerous," he says slowly. "More dangerous than you can imagine. It's not some romantic adventure."

"I know that."

"Do you?" Not unkind. Just tired. "Because the road is long. The borderlands are unstable. There are things out there that—"

"I just need to go somewhere." I cut him off. Let desperation leak into my voice—not too much, just enough. "Anywhere. I can't stay in Krandor. I can't go back to that house. And Vestperia was their dream. My parents. Maybe if I could see it..."

I trail off. Let him fill in the rest.

He's quiet for a long moment. I watch him wrestle with it—duty warring with caution, compassion warring with practicality.

"You're grieving," he says finally. "Grief makes us seek meaning in places where there may be none."

"Then let me be wrong." I look up at him. Hold his gaze. "But let me be wrong somewhere that mattered to them."

The words land. I see them land.

He looks at me—really looks. I arrange my features into something between desperate and brave. The girl who's lost everything but still has hope. The girl who just needs someone to believe in her.

The girl Milly wants to save.

"If you were to accompany me," he says slowly, "it would be as far as the border settlements only. I cannot take responsibility for a civilian in active conflict zones."

"Yes." I nod quickly. "Yes, that would be—thank you. Thank you."

"And you would need to prove you can handle the journey. It's not a pleasure trip."

"I understand."

"I'm not certain you do." He studies my face. Something flickers in his expression—doubt, maybe. Or recognition of something he doesn't want to name. "But I suppose you'll learn."

He drains the rest of his ale. Sets the cup down with a quiet finality.

"We leave at dawn. Get rest tonight."

"I will." I'm already standing. "Thank you, Sir Mills. I won't be a burden. I promise."

"Milly," he says. Quietly. Almost to himself.

"What?"

"You called me Milly earlier. Before." He doesn't look at me. "That's... that's fine. If you prefer."

Something in my chest tightens. Guilt, maybe. Or something close to it.

I push it down.

"Goodnight, Milly."

"Goodnight, Kitt."

I climb the stairs to my room. Behind me, I hear him order another ale. Hear the weight in his sigh as he settles back into his chair.

He thinks he's saving me.

Maybe he is.

Or maybe I'm just using him to escape—his oath, his guilt, his need to protect. Maybe I'm no better than the chains I want to break.

I close the door. Lean against it.

*Tomorrow,* I think. *Tomorrow I leave Krandor. Tomorrow I start becoming someone else.*

The thought should scare me.

It doesn't.

# FAT MERCHANTS

◆

## CHAPTER VIII

I wake wrapped in warmth.

For a moment—one perfect, half-asleep moment—I think it's Mom. The steady presence beside me, the arm draped protectively, the smell of wool and iron underneath. Safe. Home.

"Morning, miss."

Not Mom.

I blink. The world resolves into unfamiliar shapes. Pink and orange sky above me. A bench beneath me. And Milly beside me, his arm around my shoulders, holding me against the cold morning air.

I must have fallen asleep against him. Must have stayed there all night.

"Morning," I manage. My voice is rough with sleep.

He doesn't move away immediately. Just watches me wake, his expression unreadable. When did he take off his gauntlet? His bare hand rests on my shoulder—warm, solid, real.

I want to stay here. Want to close my eyes and pretend this is something it's not.

"We've overstayed in Krandor," he says quietly. 'We should have left hours ago. The merchant's carriage was supposed to depart at dawn."

The words take a moment to register. Carriage. Dawn. We're late.

"How long did I—"

"A few hours." He withdraws his arm slowly, giving me time to adjust. "I didn't want to wake you."

He let me sleep. Sat here for hours in the cold, not moving, because I needed rest.

Something in my chest tightens.

I splash water on my face at a nearby fountain while Milly puts his armor back on. Each piece clicks into place with practiced efficiency—breastplate, pauldrons, gauntlets. The transformation is remarkable. One moment he's the man who held me while I slept. The next, he's steel and discipline and purpose.

"The carriage should be at the gates," he says. "If the merchant hasn't already left without us."

We walk through Krandor's pristine streets. Morning crews have already cleaned the cobblestones, trimmed the decorative hedges. Everything looks perfect. Picture-book perfect. The kind of place heroes leave behind.

Solis hangs overhead, small and bright. I used to think she was chasing Astaris. Dad said it was the other way around.

The gates loom ahead. Massive stone and iron, stretching higher than I can see. I crane my neck back, trying to find the top.

"Impressive, isn't it?" Milly's voice carries a hint of something. Amusement, maybe.

"It's very..." I search for the word. "Tall. Like you."

He pauses. Looks at me. "Was that a joke, miss?"

"An observation."

"Mm." He turns back to the gate. I can't tell if I've annoyed him or made him smile.

Then—

"YOU!"

A voice. Sharp. Furious.

A man storms toward us from a waiting carriage. He's broad and red-faced, sweat already darkening his collar despite the morning cool. His clothes are fine—merchant's clothes, expensive fabric—but they strain at every seam. He moves like someone used to being obeyed.

"Knight! You've kept me waiting six hours!" He jabs a finger at Milly. "Six hours! I have schedules. I have clients. I have—"

"My apologies." Milly's voice is level. Polite. "We were delayed."

"Delayed? DELAYED?!" The merchant's face

darkens further. "I run goods between here and Milldraugh twice monthly. You said you needed passage. You said you'd be ready at dawn. Dawn was six hours ago!"

"I understand your frustration—"

"Frustration? I'm canceling the arrangement. A six-hundred-Dōnis fine, or you can find another way to—"

He reaches for Milly.

I'm not sure what he intends. A shove, maybe. A grab at his arm. Some physical punctuation to his anger.

It doesn't matter.

Milly catches his wrist.

Not violently. Not with any apparent effort. Just... catches it. Mid-air. Holds it there.

The merchant stops talking.

Everyone stops.

The morning sounds fade—no more bird calls, no more distant conversations. Just Milly holding this man's wrist and looking at him with an expression I've never seen before.

His face hasn't changed. Not really. The same features, the same set of his jaw. But something behind his eyes has gone somewhere else. Somewhere cold and still and patient. The eyes of someone who has done things. Who could do them again.

"The journey is important," Milly says. His voice is

the same. Polite. Level. "More important than your schedule. More important than six hundred Dōnis."

The merchant's bluster drains out of him like water from a cracked vessel.

"Sir, I—"

"We will be taking the carriage now."

It's not a question. Not a request. Just a statement of what will happen.

Milly releases the man's wrist. Walks past him toward the carriage. Takes the reins like he owns them.

The merchant stands frozen. Opens his mouth. Closes it. Opens it again.

"I'll have you know," he tries, voice thin now, "I'm a respected trader. I have connections in the City of the Goddess. I could—"

Milly doesn't look back. Just settles onto the driver's bench, picks up the whip.

I hurry after him, climbing up beside him before I can think too hard about what just happened. About what I just saw.

"Milly," I whisper. "Are you going to—"

"He'll be compensated." Milly's voice is flat. "I'll send payment from the next town."

"But—"

The whip cracks. The horses leap forward. We're through the gates before the merchant can form another word.

Krandor shrinks behind us.

I don't look back.

But I keep stealing glances at Milly. At his profile against the morning sky. At the hands holding the reins—the same hands that held me while I slept, now commanding horses with quiet authority.

The gentle protector. The man with rehearsed courtesies and awkward silences.

And underneath, something else. Something that can catch a man's wrist and make him forget how to speak.

Both versions are real. Both versions are him.

I file this away. Add it to the picture I'm building.

The road opens ahead of us. Trees begin to close in on either side.

"Milly?"

"Yes, miss?"

"Thank you. For letting me sleep."

He doesn't answer. But his grip on the reins loosens slightly. The tension in his shoulders eases.

We ride in silence toward whatever comes next.

# HAPPY TIMES

## BUMPS & TALES
### CHAPTER IX

"One bump," I sing, trying to sound casual, slightly bored, "two bumps, three bumps, four bumps—Big bump!"

Milly glances over at me, not saying a word, but I can see amusement in his eyes, even if he doesn't want to show it.

The forest swallows us whole. Above, Solis reaches her peak with Astaris trailing. The canopy filters their light into moving patches, golden circles that slide across my hands, my lap, the wooden seat. I try to catch one with my palm but it slips away, reappears on my knee.

Every color here is different from Krandor. Richer. The greens aren't just green—they're a dozen shades I don't have names for. Deep moss on the north side of trunks (or is it south? I can never remember). Bright new leaves catching sunlight. Dark pine needles carpeting the ground in thick, springy layers that muffle sound.

Something dead on the road ahead. A rabbit—no, what's left of one. A hawk perches on a fence post nearby, beak red, watching us pass with yellow eyes.

I watch back.

The way it tore the rabbit open. Efficient. No wasted motion. Just beak and talons and patience, and now it has what it needs. In Krandor, I'd seen guardsmen work like that. Quick and efficient when they found a Felidae family hiding in the lower districts. I'd watched from my window. Mom pulled me away before I saw the end, but I heard it.

The hawk heard nothing when it killed the rabbit. No one to interrupt. No one to pull it away.

"Don't stare," Milly says. "Hawks don't like being watched while they eat."

I look away. But I think about it for the next half-kāl. The efficiency. The patience. The way no one stops nature from doing what nature does.

*Should I go back?* The thought sneaks in between watching the light. It looks like Milly doesn't even need me. Thoughts plague me, making my stomach twist—Mom, Dad, Milly, the inn-man. Everyone that was there. *Was.*

Stop thinking about home, Kitt. Adventure, adventure, not yearning for a cozy... warm... *home...*

But the forest is warm too. Not home-warm.

Different. The air smells like pine sap and earth and something sweet I can't identify. Flowers maybe? I crane my neck trying to find them but there are too many plants, too much green, everything layered on top of everything else.

I start to slowly nod off as I breathe it in, but another bump sneaks up and jolts me awake.

"The way Milly handled that merchant," I tell myself quietly, "that's exactly what a true knight would do. Decisive. Protective." I push away the memory of how cold his eyes went. That's not important.

Milly catches my words but doesn't reply.

"Six, seven bumps, eight bumps!" I say cheerfully despite my thoughts, trying to make the mood less awkward. Milly doesn't seem to get it.

The trees are getting taller. Not gradually—suddenly I look up and they're massive, trunks wider than the carriage, stretching up and up until their tops disappear into green shadow. Bark rough and plated like armor. Some of them have to be older than Krandor, older than anything I've ever seen. Ancient. That's the word. They feel ancient.

I sigh, leaning on Milly as he continues urging the horses forward with the reins, with the occasional WHIP! SNAP!

Sunlight hits the carriage from every angle, flowing through the leaves in shifting patterns. Each time the wind moves the branches, the light changes—bright, shadow, bright again. It's not like anything I've ever seen, since I've only ever been inside Krandor, only ever listened to Mom and Dad's dreams.

This should feel magical, I tell myself. This is what heroes see when they venture into the wild.

And maybe it is magical. The way moss glows almost green-gold where light touches it. The way spider webs stretched between branches catch the sun and turn into strings of diamonds. The way everything smells alive—not city-alive with people and food and waste, but forest-alive, growing and breathing and being without us.

Animal calls echo from deep in the woods—some musical, others sharp. A bird sings four notes, high and clear. Another answers from across the path, same four notes but lower. They're talking to each other. I wonder what they're saying.

Somewhere, I hear water running. Not close. Distant. The sound weaves through the trees like another layer of the forest's voice.

The path continues, dusty and light brown compared to the forest floor, which is dark with fallen needles and leaves and things decomposing into earth. Clearly, we are not the first to be here, nor the last. But right now, it feels like we might be the only ones. Like the forest has swallowed up everyone else who tried to pass through and we're next.

No. Not like that. Not scary.

Like the forest is so big we're just small things moving through it, no more important than the deer or birds or beetles I can hear clicking in the undergrowth.

It's exactly the kind of wilderness setting where epic quests begin. The kind of forest you see in paintings, all dramatic light and ancient trees and the promise of something waiting deeper in.

So why does part of me feel like it's a trap closing around us?

Milly's face tenses up slightly as we continue down the path. His eyes keep scanning—left, right, up into the branches. Not afraid. Just aware. Always aware.

Something moves in the undergrowth to our left.

Both horses' ears swivel toward the sound. Milly's hand drifts toward his sword, not gripping it, just... ready.

I hold my breath.

A deer steps out onto the path.

Not steps—emerges. Like it was always there and we're just now allowed to see it.

It's a doe. Young, maybe. Her coat is red-brown, darker along her spine, almost gold where the sunlight hits her shoulders. Dappled with white spots that look like someone flicked a paintbrush across her flanks. Her legs are so thin they look like they'd snap if she stumbled, but she moves with absolute certainty, each hoof finding exactly the right spot on the path.

Her ears are huge. They swivel independently, tracking sounds I can't hear—one toward us, one toward the forest behind her. Black-tipped, lined with white fur on the inside that catches light when she turns her head.

And her eyes.

So dark they're almost black, but when she looks directly at me, I see they're actually deep brown with flecks of gold. Liquid. Intelligent. She's not afraid of us. She's just... aware. Deciding if we matter.

Her nose twitches. Once, twice. Testing the air.

I don't move. Don't breathe. Don't want to break whatever this is.

She takes another step onto the path. Then another. Her white tail flicks once—not nervous, just swatting at something, maybe a fly. She's so close now I could reach out and touch her if I leaned over the carriage edge.

Close enough to see individual hairs in her coat, the way they lay flat and smooth except where they grow in little whorls around her shoulders. Close enough to see a small scar on her front leg, white against the brown. Close enough to count her eyelashes.

This is the most beautiful thing I've ever seen.

The thought comes sudden and complete, and I don't question it.

Then the wind shifts.

Her whole body tenses. Ears snap forward. She's looking past us, at something behind the carriage, something I can't see.

And she runs.

Not panicked. Graceful. Powerful. She leaps—impossibly high, clearing a fallen log I didn't even notice was there—and disappears into the forest. Gone like she was never there. Just the crash of undergrowth and the white flash of her tail marking where she went.

Milly's hand leaves his sword.

"What scared her?" I whisper.

He glances back down the path, frowning. "Don't know. Could be anything."

But his jaw is tight, and he doesn't relax.

We continue in silence. I keep looking back, trying to see what the deer saw, but there's nothing. Just trees and shadows and the path winding behind us until it curves out of sight.

The bump counting doesn't feel right anymore. The forest is too big for games.

A stone marker stands where the road forks. Knee-high, weathered, with a carved flame symbol—Fyūnoch, the Ember. Travelers' god. Someone's left a stub of candle in the hollow at its base, long since burned out.

But there's another marker beside it. Newer stone, different carving. Rounded ears. A curving tail.

Mīrrū.

In Krandor, that shrine would be rubble. The guardsmen made sport of finding them, smashing them, hunting whoever left offerings. "False goddess," they called her. "Beast-mother." The Felidae who prayed to her were "false people"—not protected by law, not counted in census, not really people at all.

Here, both shrines stand side by side. Unmolested. Someone even left fresh flowers at Mīrrū's feet.

Milly slows his horse. Dismounts. He doesn't kneel, but he bows his head briefly, touches Fyūnoch's stone, then—to my surprise—Mīrrū's as well.

"For safe passage," he says when he returns. "Old habit."

"You pray to Mīrrū?"

"I pray to all the Nine." He glances at me. "Is that strange to you?"

In Krandor, it would get you questioned. Maybe arrested. Definitely watched.

"No," I say. "Not strange at all."

I file the gesture away—the bow, the touch, the words. In case I need to perform it later. In case I need to look like someone who believes in things.

A merchant cart approaches from the opposite direction—and something in my chest tightens before I can name it.

The driver is Felidae. Fully Felidae—not half-blood like the girl at my school with her short tail and rounded-but-small ears. This one has fur edging his jaw, gray-streaked and visible. His ears are large, distinctly feline, swiveling openly as he scans the road. His tail—long, tabby-striped—curls around the seat behind him without any attempt to hide it.

In Krandor, half-bloods could pass. Could pretend. Could play in schoolyards if they kept quiet and didn't draw attention. But full Felidae? They hid in basements. They traveled at night, covered. They disappeared when the guardsmen came asking questions about "false people harboring."

This one is just... traveling. Alone. Unhidden. In daylight. Like it's nothing.

He raises a hand in greeting, ears swiveling toward us. "Road's clear to Byēnwick. Watch for mud past the stone bridge."

His voice is calm. Unafraid. No flinch when he sees Milly's Celtorian armor—if anything, his posture relaxes.

"Thank you," Milly calls back. "Anything else ahead?"

"Rain coming. Two days, maybe three." The merchant's ears flatten briefly—reading the sky, not fear. "And there's a patrol on the ridge road. Orenian colors. They don't cross into Drūn proper, but..." His tail flicks once. "Best to know."

"Noted. Safe travels."

The merchant moves on. I watch his tail sway with the cart's motion until he disappears around the bend.

"You're staring," Milly says.

"He's not hiding." The words come out flat. Observational. "In Krandor, even the half-bloods learn to tuck their tails. Keep their ears covered when they can. He's just... out."

"Different nation. Different laws." Milly pauses. "The Orenian view of Mīrrū isn't shared everywhere."

I think about the girl at school. The one with the braids and the short tail who laughed too loud and didn't seem to know she should be afraid. Maybe she didn't know. Maybe her parents never told her what happens to the ones who can't pass.

"How do you read their tails?" I ask. "The expressions. The ear movements."

"You learn. Ears forward means interest. Flat means fear. Swiveling means alert." He glances at me. "Why?"

"Just curious."

The merchant trusted us enough to warn us about the Orenian patrol. Trusted that we weren't a threat.

The trees thin slightly, and suddenly we're at a crossroad. Two signs, weathered and leaning:

KANNA'S RIDGE (50 DRŪMS AWAY)
RON'S MERCHANT DENT (87 DRŪMS AWAY)
*Drūms? Isn't that a musical instrument?* I peer over at Milly, and he seems to know what it means. He can see my confusion.

"Drūms. Trail measurements," he says, slightly blunt.

"I do not understand."

"Perhaps if you consider the context, miss..."

Heat flushes my cheeks. Of course, I should know—any real adventurer would understand basic distance measurements. I hop down from the carriage to examine the signs more closely, trying to look competent rather than lost.

The ground here is different. Rockier. The soil isn't the soft dark stuff from earlier—it's lighter, mixed with small stones that crunch under my boots. I crouch down, pick up a pebble. It's smooth on one side, rough on the other. Water-worn, maybe? But we're not near water. Or are we? I thought I heard water earlier.

"Milly, what's Kanna's Ridge?"

He stares at me as if I were a stupid fish, and then finally says, "It is a mountainous pass we must traverse, miss."

*Traverse...* The word sends a little thrill through me—that's adventure language, the kind of vocabulary heroes use. But it also makes me feel like a child, which I am, but that doesn't matter all that much. I'm on an adventure!

Rolling my eyes, I get back on the carriage. We depart in the direction of the ridge.

"About the ridge," he says again, "We have to cross it. It's a dangerous cliffside area," he adjusts his reins, "and it's the only way into Drūn from Orenia."

I fall silent. *Dangerous? Like... deadly type of dangerous? My stomach drops. But wait—dangerous cliffs. The only way through. Just like in the stories. The path that tests courage.* I take a breath, trying to sound annoyed rather than fearful, but there's still a shiver in my voice. "You could have mentioned that before, you... you great oaf!"

He doesn't respond. He simply whips the horses one last time before relaxing slightly as they hurtle us forward on the path. I think he says something—but I cannot quite catch it.

I pretend to ignore him, though my face flushes in anger and embarrassment. I stop leaning on him, now sitting upright. If this journey is truly dangerous, I need to prove I can handle it. That I'm not just some pampered city girl who needs constant protection.

The forest changes as we climb. The air gets thinner, cooler. The trees are different too—more pine now, less of the broad-leafed giants from before. These pines are twisted, growing at angles like they're leaning away from something. Wind, probably. Strong wind that blows constantly up here, bending them as they grow.

The path is steeper. I can feel it in how the carriage tilts, how the horses have to work harder. Their breathing gets louder, more labored.

We continue on our path for about two more hours, with Solis finally dipping under the horizon and Astaris following soon. My back aches from the constant jostling, and my stomach reminds me that the bread wasn't really sufficient. But discomfort is part of the adventure, isn't it? Heroes in stories never complain about being hungry or sore.

Though they probably should. This hurts.

I look over at Milly, studying him. "Are we going to stop for the night?"

"We have a half hour of sunlight left—we keep going until Astaris is almost at the horizon."

I nod, now disliking the constant bumps and roots we run over. My back feels like it's going through a massage of little blades throughout the whole ride, and someone punching me in the gut, over and over (though lightly). *Every bump in the road, every empty moment in my stomach—it's all proof that I'm finally living a real story.*

Before long, Milly forces the horses to stop.

"Do you know how to set up camp, miss?"

The question hits like cold water. In all my imagining of adventures, I somehow never considered the practical skills involved. "Not... not at all."

Milly hops over the seat frame, leaping to the back of the carriage in one clean move. Lands heavier than he should. A slight stumble before he catches himself. He gestures at a few crates draped with a gray cloth with the Orenian insignia—a shield being punctured by a spear—on the fabric. Milly points at a specific crate.

"Pick up that crate and drag it out."

I approach confidently, wrapping my hands around the wooden edges. How hard could it be? I'm young and healthy, and heroes in stories are always surprisingly strong when needed.

I lift.

Nothing happens.

*This isn't how it's supposed to go. Heroes don't fail at basic tasks. Heat floods my face as I drop the crate.*

Milly watches silently before sighing. "Miss, excuse me for being blunt, but are you weak, or do you simply lack knowledge of proper lifting technique?"

The question hits harder than any physical blow. I drop my grip on the crate and flee to the edge of the clearing, humiliation burning through me like fever.

I find a small rock to sit on and simply watch him, wanting to cry, but my ego won't let me.

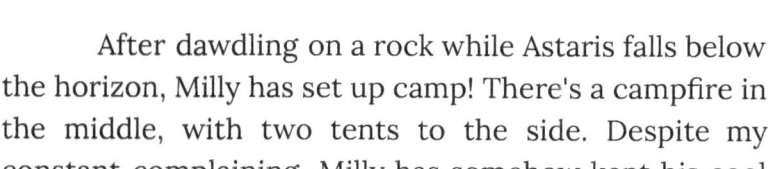

After dawdling on a rock while Astaris falls below the horizon, Milly has set up camp! There's a campfire in the middle, with two tents to the side. Despite my constant complaining, Milly has somehow kept his cool this whole time. But, alas, Astaris is down, and Mün is rising.

The fire catches, casting dancing shadows between the trees. The shadows look like the deer for a second—I can almost see her ears, her legs—then they shift and she's gone again.

Mün begins her rise, round and white and beautiful—just like in the old Celtorian stories Dad used to tell. Something about the Slayer and fragments of gods, though the details feel fuzzy now.

Her light is different from the suns'. Cooler. Gentler. She turns the forest silver-blue, makes everything look like it's underwater. The trees become dark shapes against her glow. The fire burns orange and warm in contrast.

I stare at my tent—a simple lavender tarp stretched over wooden stakes. Not the elegant pavilion I'd somehow expected, but practical shelter for the road. Milly's tent is larger, white with golden trim and an embroidered shield. Even his camping gear looks properly heroic.

I lie down in my cramped tent, staring at the campfire and Milly's tent through the gap in my tarp.

I can see Milly's feet sticking out as he sleeps, snoring quietly. He must have a stuffy nose, as no one snores that weirdly. His armor is hanging on a clothesline connecting both our tents, and I can count... one, two, five, eight different pieces of armor?! Who needs that much armor?

I stare up at the tarp above me, sighing reluctantly. "This is my life now for a few months, huh?" I mutter to myself.

I don't get a response from the world, but that's alright. I don't need a response to know I am doing something right, and a lot more wrong.

Through the gap in my tent, I can see Mün climbing higher. She's so bright tonight. So beautiful.

I can't sleep.

The tarp feels too close. The air underneath it too still. I push myself up, careful not to make noise, and crawl out into the clearing.

The grass is cold and damp against my bare feet. The fire has burned down to embers, just a faint orange glow. Milly's snoring continues, steady and strange.

I look up at Mün, meaning to just look at her for a moment.

And then I see the rest.

I stop breathing.

The sky is... I don't have words. I don't think there are words.

Stars. Not dozens, like in Krandor. Not hundreds. *Thousands.* So many they blur together in places, a river of light stretching from one horizon to the other, silver and white and colors I can't name, dusted across the black like someone spilled something precious and infinite.

I've never seen this before.

Krandor's glow ate everything. I thought the sky had maybe fifty stars, if you squinted. I thought Mün was the brightest thing up there.

She's not. She's not even close.

I sink down onto the grass without deciding to. My neck hurts from tilting back so far but I can't stop looking. The river of light has depth to it—layers, like clouds but made of stars, like looking into something instead of at it.

I'm so small.

The thought comes quietly. But it doesn't hurt the way it usually does. Not the smallness of you don't matter or just collateral or nobody will remember you.

This is different.

This is the smallness of being a single blade of grass in a field that stretches forever. Still part of the field. Still growing in the same soil, under the same sky, breathing the same air as everything else that ever looked up and wondered.

Mom and Dad saw this. Maybe not here, but somewhere. They looked up at the same river of light and dreamed about places beyond the horizon.

I'm under it now. Their sky. The same one.

My eyes sting. I don't wipe them.

I lie back in the wet grass and watch the stars wheel slowly overhead, and for the first time since the kitchen, I feel like I'm part of something that isn't broken.

Eventually, the cold wins. I crawl back into my tent, still looking up through the gap.

Tomorrow we reach Kanna's Ridge.

I fall asleep thinking about the deer's eyes, dark and gold and unafraid.

# EGGED ARMOR

### CHAPTER X

Dawn breaks, and I already hear Milly shuffling. I can hear the annoying sound of him sharpening his sword, the morning tweets of birds, and the lack of Krandor's busy sounds. Solis is in the sky, Astaris trailing behind like a dog chasing its master.

I glance at his sword—it's what my father called a 'greatsword'. Its hilt is wooden, wrapped in twine, with a metal handguard. The blade itself appears to be a little shorter than me, with the engraving 'DEATH TO ALL WHO OPPOSE' running down its center toward the handguard. The engraving is shallow, but I can still see it clearly from here.

I freeze, staring at the sword. My mind floods—Mom, and... STOP IT! I breathe loudly for a moment before shoving a finger in my mouth to shut myself up.

He catches my glance but doesn't pay much mind to it. He speaks up, "Do you want breakfast, miss?"

My stomach responds before I do, growling loudly. I nod, not trusting my voice yet.

Milly walks over to the campfire, setting a small metal pot on a metal grate. He pulls out what looks like an egg, but it's... dirty? Brown speckles cover the shell, and there's even a feather stuck to one side.

"That looks..." I stutter slightly, staring at the egg as if it's... I shouldn't be staring at it like *that*. "Different."

"These are fresh from wild birds, miss. They haven't been washed for market."

He cracks the dirty egg into the pot—no oil, no butter, just bare metal. His movements are careful, measured. Different from his usual efficiency. Like he's thinking through each step. I expected it to stick immediately, but somehow it doesn't. He slowly swishes it around with a long wooden spoon, and after a moment, popping and sizzling sounds emit from the pot.

"Shouldn't you use a pan? And oil?" I ask, desperately trying to sound fascinated despite my thoughts. "That's how they do it in the kitchens back home."

"This works fine for camping, miss. We make do with what we carry."

I walk over, trying to peer into the pot to see how he's managing to cook without proper equipment. I put my hands on the metal grate to lean closer. Milly smacks my hand lightly before I can touch it.

"Bad. That would have burned your fingers off, miss," he speaks directly after, his voice slightly cold.

I rub my hand. The subtle red mark makes me freeze. *Is that... red?* For a moment I'm somewhere else entirely—someone else's hand raised, someone else cowering—and then I'm back in the forest, walking away slowly. Instead of going to my tent, I sit on a nearby rock where I can still watch him cook. I rub my hand—making sure he sees—while trying to watch how he manages the egg without it sticking. After a few minutes of sulking and observing, Milly speaks up again.

"Miss, breakfast is ready."

My face arranges itself into what I hope looks like enthusiasm. "Finally!" I say with a relieved sigh. I practically run over, sticking my hands out toward him to serve me, trying to act normal.

*Sssssss-plop.*

The egg falls on the wooden plate. I stare at it—used to the clean clink of ceramic, not whatever that was. I slowly pick up the silver fork Milly left on the plate, piercing the egg.

I eat happily. Milly sits on a log near the fire, eating with his usual stoic face—though I can see his eyes soften. After eating the full egg, I peer up at him again.

"Was that it for breakfast?" I immediately regret it—sounding demanding rather than grateful.

"Yes, miss, that was it. Unless you want to hunt for more?"

"Net... No, never mind!"

We sit in what I decide to call comfortable silence. I organize the morning: blue sky (normal), green trees (normal), brown dirt (normal). Simple colors. Safe colors. Not red, definitely not red.

The forest still feels like a wall around us, but I push that thought away. We're going to Kanna's Ridge, then Milldraugh, then... the timeline stretches in my mind like a yawning mouth. Months. It will take months to reach Vestperia.

*That's fine. Normal traveling takes time. This is normal.*

But it's not fine, because Krandor is only half a day across, so why should anywhere else take longer? The math doesn't work, but I shove that worry down with all the others.

"Kitt?"

I hesitate for a moment, my mind hesitating too, making my eyes go blurry. I blink slightly before responding, "Yes?"

"Are you sure you want to continue the trek to Vestperia? It only gets harder from here, miss, and this is your last chance to head home."

I fall utterly silent, wanting to say a quick jab at him, yet I can't formulate anything.

*Home... Home. What home?* My mind goes completely blank. White noise fills the spaces where thoughts should be. *There isn't one left, at least not for me.*

When the static clears, I hear myself saying "Yes" in a voice that sounds far away—not because I want to continue, but because saying anything else would require thinking about what I'm running from.

Milly studies my face for a long moment, and I arrange my features into what I hope looks like determination. He nods slowly, not replying verbally. The silence stretches, giving me time to realize he's seen things like this before—this particular way to run away from home, the tone in my voice, everything. That's why he's so calm. He's seen this specific flavor of saying yes because no isn't survivable.

"We leave in an hour," he finally says, his voice slightly lower and gentler than before. "Rest while I pack."

I nod quietly, bright as morning sunshine, empty as a broken window.

Milly watches me for another moment, and I wonder if he can see through the brightness to whatever's underneath. His expression softens, just slightly—the look of someone who's held too many broken things and knows how carefully they need to be carried.

# KANNA'S RIDGE

◆

### CHAPTER XI

*Scrrrraaaaappppeeeeee...*

*Scrraaaapppee...*

I jolt awake to those hideous sounds—steel on steel. I spot Milly sharpening that huge sword of his. Why is he even bothering when he never uses the thing? I sit up in my sleeping bag in the 'tent' he had prepared for me yesterday, the cloth almost hitting my face as it draped on me.

He catches my scowl, puts down the sharpening stone, wets it, then returns to sharpening.

SCRREECHHH!

Is he purposefully doing it louder?!

"Milly! Stop being so loud!" I practically cover my ears as I yell at him from across the small camp.

*He doesn't stop-*

SCREEEECHHHH!!

I scoff loudly, getting up and walking over to him with heavy footsteps. "Milly! Stop!"

He finally glances up, slowly putting down the wet sharpening stone. He speaks in a measured tone, though there's something firmer beneath it: "This blade keeps us alive on dangerous roads, miss. If I had to bet, this steel has existed longer than you have. It's seen battles I hope you never witness."

He pauses, his eyes meeting mine. "This sharpened steel means we both return home safely. I suggest letting it do its work."

I fall silent, my mouth slightly agape in an 'o'. I cast a look down at the sword. He was right—it's sharpened now, really sharpened. I can see my own reflection in the blade. But I don't understand why he gave that speech if he was already finishing. I'm too shocked to speak.

He notices my reaction and simply deflects. "Breakfast, miss?"

The crackling of the fire stops a few minutes after I finish breakfast. Milly is already setting up the carriage again, feeding the horses and preparing supplies. Over breakfast, Milly explains: we need to stop at a town called Milldraugh soon—it's about half the journey to Vestperia. Today, we'll stop at a town about two hundred drūms—roughly eighty kāls—before

Milldraugh. A rest point. An actual inn.

We'd have to go through Kanna's Ridge, which Milly calls slightly dangerous, but we can handle it. It'll only be a short ride, and, plus, it's only going to last about a kāl before we reach the town.

The news excited me at first, until it dawned on me—Milldraugh is half of the journey, and this town is eighty kāls away from Milldraugh. This journey is going to take ages.

I finally glance up at Milly, deciding whether to assist him. *He's a strong knight... He can do it! But, what if he slips? What if he's really old and his bones are dust?*

I sigh, walking over to him. "Do you need help, Milly?"

"I suppose a bit of assistance would not hurt anyone. If you wish, miss, but only do so if you feel able."

I approach one of the horses, grabbing the wooden grooming brush Milly always uses. I brush its mane, watching its eyes droop and calm. Milly nods quietly, appearing to be proud of me, but knowing him, he's probably still having those weird cold thoughts in his eyes.

The horse does the little thing where they essentially pout, making me giggle.

"Kitt? Everything is prepared. We leave for Byēnwick in a few minutes. Take care of the necessities if you must, miss."

*Well-town. That's a funky name.* I shrug slightly, nodding at the same time. I go to the back of the carriage and lift myself into it. Milly follows suit, sitting at the driver's box. He whistles and grabs his whip, reaching to the back, which is where I'm sitting like a lost child.

SNAP! and off we go!

The morning passes slowly, a blur of rolling hills and winding paths parading endlessly before my eyes. I try counting the bumps again, but give up as soon as I forget the numbers and nod off to sleep for a few moments. And then another bump hits hard.

The landscape keeps changing, but gradually, and it no longer looks like the green fields around Krandor. It becomes rockier, drier, and I'm quite sure we're getting closer to the Shallow Desert. Though, I don't want to think about that for now.

Milly continues his stoic silence the farther we go, his eyes constantly scanning the horizon and occasionally "encouraging" the horses by whipping them.

"Milly, are we there yet?"

He remains silent.

"Milly, where are we even going?"

He remains silent.

"Milly, what are you searching for?"

He stays silent for a few moments. Slowly turning his head at me, I can see the disappointment in his eyes.

"We're searching for Kanna's Ridge. It's our only way to get to Byēnwick, miss."

"Oh." I pause for a moment, processing what he just said. "What's so special about Kanna's Ridge?"

Milly's grip tightens on the reins. "You'll see soon enough, miss."

And then...

Nothing on the horizon.

It's still the same old—

The path suddenly curves around a bend, ascending up a small mountain. The world utterly changes—towering walls of dark stone rise on both sides of us, but they're not normal walls—they're made of thousands of six-sided columns, all leaning inward like they're trying to touch each other above our heads. The columns create a natural roof over the road, but with gaps between them that let shafts of sunlight pierce through in golden beams.

Up close, the basalt isn't smooth—it's faceted, each six-sided column covered in fine ridges, like the surface has been scored by something ancient and precise. Where one column meets another, the seams are so tight I couldn't fit a fingernail between them.

*AHA! This is what adventuring feels like—what it looks like!*

I crane my neck back, trying to see where the columns end, but they simply don't—disappearing into the gray sky above us. The air is entirely different here—hollow, cooler, amplifying every sound like we're inside a cathedral.

Nothing moves. No birds. No insects. Just the columns, and the light, and us. The horses' hoofbeats change the moment we enter. The sound doesn't fade—it multiplies, bouncing off the columns, returning to us from directions I can't trace.

"It's *belu*," I say breathlessly, "absolutely gorgeous."

Milly's hand shoots up in a silencing gesture. "Quiet," he hisses. "Sound carries here. One wrong echo and—" He doesn't finish.

But I'm barely listening. This is exactly what I imagined when I dreamed about leaving Krandor—mysterious passages through ancient basalt, shafts of golden light, the feeling of being somewhere truly wild and untamed.

As the carriage rolls forward, the shafts of sunlight slide across us—across Milly's armor, across my lap, across the horses' flanks. The whole gorge is striped in gold and shadow, and we're moving through it like thread through a loom.

I lean over the side of the carriage, trying to see

past the edge of the path. The gorge drops away into shadow, basalt columns disappearing into darkness below. How far down does it go?

My weight shifts the carriage. The wheels grind against loose stone with a sharp, grating screech.

The sound echoes. Then echoes again. Amplifying.

I freeze.

Dust begins to rain down from above. Small at first, then larger pieces. The columns are shifting.

Milly's knuckles go white on the reins as he looks up. The whip cracks and we lurch forward. Rocks crash down behind us, shattering against the path where we'd been moments before. The rumbling grows louder, echoing off the stone walls.

I grab Milly's arm as the carriage bounces over rough stone. Dust fills my eyes, burns my throat. I can barely see the path ahead through the gray cloud.

"Milly! What's—"

"I told you to be silent, miss!" His voice cuts through the noise. "Rockfall. We should survive this." He pauses, jaw tight. "Hopefully."

A basalt pillar falls directly in front of us. Milly yanks the reins left just before we slam into it, and everything tilts. I let out a small cry of fear as Milly continues pressing forward through the deafening rockfall.

The falling persists, the dust continuing to fill my eyes and mouth. I catch the way Milly is affected too—his eyes are turning bloodshot due to all the dust. I lean out of the carriage, staring directly at where we're supposed to exit—but there's no way out. It's just a straight fall. Just gray sky and shadow.

Milly glances at me, then the "exit." A single bead of sweat drips down his forehead as he contemplates a way to escape. The ground disappears. We fall.

I scream as light blinds us and something explodes—

*Salt and pine. Salt and pine. Salt and pine. Salt and pine.* SALT AND PINE.

I gasp, looking at the view ahead of me, shrouded with pine at my peripherals. The Celtian Sea stands barely a drūm away from me, endless sea-blue, fish flickering through its calm waters.

Reality fades in and out, clouds covering the sky.

The waves lap against the shore soothingly. The birds chirp overhead. The sky is crystal blue, almost shining back at me. I peer over to my left and right.

"Mom? Dad?"

Both figures glance back at me, though their faces are covered in ash and shadow, flickering in and out of existence.

"Mom..? Dad..? Are you okay?" My voice rings out, an edge of fear in it. My words echo back after a solid lifetime of waiting.

Suddenly, a voice from the sky echoes: "Kitt! Wake up!"

It's Milly's voice. My eyes blink open rapidly as gray light floods my vision. Milly is holding my shoulder, shaking me.

I stare up at Milly's face—now with a noticeable streak of blood running diagonally across his forehead. He looks almost distraught as he stares at me before getting up.

"The carriage is wrecked," Milly says in a cold voice. "I'm sorry for taking us on this path, miss."

I slowly turn my head to look at the carriage, and lo and behold, it's a pile of wood now. Only one horse remains with us, the other must have bolted. The one that remains makes me look away quickly—split clean through by a pillar. All our supplies are scattered everywhere.

"Milly? Are we going to," my voice drops to a whisper. "Die?"

"No."

I try to get up, but everything hurts.

I scan the area we're in: essentially a cave with a ragged opening above. Though it's a bit high. At least...

very high. A massive basalt pillar lies across the cave floor—must have fallen with us. We're effectively trapped.

# IMPRISONMENT

◆

### CHAPTER XII

"Damn gorge!" Milly kicks a fragment of the basalt pillar that crushed one of our horses. The sound echoes through the cave, setting my ears ringing.

I've never heard him cuss before.

He runs his hand over his face, smearing blood across his forehead and temple. "We need to assess our situation." His voice is pragmatic now, controlled—not like the earlier outburst.

Following his orders, I check my arms, then my legs, then my torso. I lift my shirt up and catch sight of liquid reflecting the gray light of the cave. Blood.

"Milly, I'm bleeding."

It's not severe or anything, but his expression shifts immediately to concern. He rushes over, pulling out a bandage.

"It's not serious, Milly! Use it on your own head," I protest quickly as he tries to bandage me.

"Any injury is serious," he says firmly. "You could

get infected. Disease is a common way to-"

"You don't have to lecture me," I say quietly.

He nods, and begins to bandage me properly. After a moment, he speaks quietly: "That was the last of our bandages."

I slowly look up at him, his head still bleeding. "You can take mine-"

Before I can finish, he cuts me off with just a stare. I look down slightly, feeling what might be disappointment in his gaze.

"Kitt."

I lift my gaze to meet his eyes. "Yes?"

"I need you to take this seriously. This isn't a game anymore; your life matters, so act like it." His voice drops to something softer, "I've seen what happens to people when they ignore even the smallest of wounds."

I stay silent, processing his words as he begins searching around the cave. I follow his pacing with my eyes, occasionally drifting to the horse and the destroyed carriage. Thinking about the horse hurts.

My breathing quickens as I continue following Milly with my eyes. Watching his expression go from slightly hopeful to grim hurts me more than I expected.

Milly suddenly stops in front of the back half of the horse. I look away as I hear him stepping onto the horse. I'm too curious—I look back. Milly is now on the basalt pillar that split the horse in two. A trail of blood marks where he climbed.

"Miss, I have a possible solution to our dilemma. Get up here." His voice rings through the enclosed space. I can't ignore it.

I stare at the horse's carcass. From a distance, I'd thought it was a clean cut. Up close, I can see where the pillar crushed and tore through muscle and bone. The edges are ragged. Wrong.

My stomach lurches.

"Miss?"

I take a step forward. My boot touches the horse's hindquarters—still warm. The body shifts slightly under my weight and I freeze, bile rising in my throat.

*This is my fault. I caused this.*

"Kitt." Milly's voice is firm but not unkind. "Keep moving."

I force my other foot up, onto the horse's flank. The blood makes it slippery. I have to grip the torn hide to steady myself as I climb. My hands are shaking so badly I nearly lose my balance.

When I finally reach the top of the pillar, Milly extends his hand. His expression has softened, but there's something in his eyes—maybe recognition, maybe just sadness.

"Take it."

I grab his hand. With his other, he presses something into my palm—rope from the carriage rigging, coarse and still smelling of canvas, and a small hammer.

My breath catches as I realize his plan.

"You'll need to climb out first," he says quietly. "Tie the rope to something secure above. I'll follow."

I want to protest, but we both know he's right. Milly extends his hands down, palms up. I place my boot on his palms, gripping his shoulders for balance as he lifts.

I look up. The exit seems impossibly high, but light filters down through the opening—real sunlight, not the gray dimness of the cave. Escape.

"Before I lift you to the rocks," Milly says, his voice strained from holding my weight, "do you know how to tie a secure knot?"

I freeze. The truth sits heavy in my throat. I don't know. I've never learned. But admitting that now, after everything...

"Yes," I hear myself say. "I know how."

His eyes search my face for a moment—does he believe me?—then he nods once. "Good. Hold tight."

He launches me upward with surprising force, and suddenly I'm grabbing at rough stone, my fingers finding purchase on the edge of the opening.

Dust rains down into my eyes as I grip the first proper ledge. I look up—more rock face stretching above me. My feet dangle uselessly in air.

Deep breath. Find the next handhold. I reach up

with my left hand, then my right, pulling myself up in small increments. My arms burn with the effort. After what feels like forever, I manage to get one foot onto a narrow outcropping.

I glance down to check on Milly. The cave floor tilts and swims. My vision narrows, edges going dark. Too far. Too high. I'm too high and there's nothing beneath me and—

I force myself to look away, back up at the rock face. I reach for the next ledge. My fingers close on slick stone.

My right hand slips.

"Milly!" The scream tears out of me as my body swings sideways, all my weight suddenly on my left arm. Pain flares through my shoulder.

"Calm down, Kitt!" His voice echoes up from below, steady and firm. "Find your grip. Deep breaths—in and out. You're doing fine."

I'm not doing fine. I'm hanging by one hand and I can't breathe and everything hurts.

"In and out, miss. Slowly."

I force air into my lungs. Out. In. Out. My right hand finds a new hold—testing it carefully this time before trusting my weight to it.

In. And out.

The exit looks closer now that I've caught my breath. The sky pierces through the gray, somber clouds. *It's so close... So, so close.*

"Kitt, tie the rope on the rock directly to your left."

My heart pauses for a solid beat—*tie a knot?*

I maneuver my hand toward the rock that juts out. I toss the rope over it, making an upside-down 'u'. My breath catches as I try to remember what was the way to tie a knot—which I can't remember.

"Milly..."

"Kitt?"

"Help," I whisper.

Milly falls silent, and I don't dare look down. He speaks up eventually: "I thought you said you knew how." He pauses. When he speaks again, his voice is flat. "Loop it twice around the base, then thread the end back through."

I oblige, completing the knot.

"Done!"

"Now, climb all the way up."

I look up at the remaining distance and my arms already ache. It's so close that it's cruel. The sunlight filters through, reflecting off the rocks into my eyes, blinding me.

*This is getting harder...*

I lunge upward, grabbing a new rock. My other foot finds a hold, and I keep climbing.

Each step, each grab gets harder and harder as my breath becomes more labored and ragged.

Finally—*finally*—my hand closes on grass instead of stone. I haul myself over the edge and collapse on solid ground, gasping.

I crawl back to the opening and look down. Milly has the rope in hand now, testing its hold. He glances up, sees me watching, and begins to climb.

I flop onto the ground, giggling uncontrollably as I finally feel the softness of the grass. Imagine rabbits... cute, little rabbit fur. That's how it feels.

After what feels like forever, Milly gets to the top, panting lightly. He opens his mouth. When he speaks, his tone is cold:

"We need to talk."

# CONSEQUENCES

### CHAPTER XIII

"We need to talk."

The words ring out in my head for a moment before I fall out of my trance. I speak cautiously, an edge of fear in my voice: "About?"

"What just happened." His voice is cold. Flat. His eyes are soft yet hollow, fixed on me until I look away.

"What about it?"

"Kitt," he says firmly. "You didn't follow my warnings. You almost got us killed. And then you lied to me about knowing how to tie a knot."

I fall silent, still lying down on the ground. I stare up at the blue sky, scattered with gray clouds. Milly remains quiet as he watches me.

"It's going to rain soon," I say softly.

"Sit up and look at me," he cuts in sharply. "We're discussing this now, miss. Not the status of the weather."

I stay down, but Milly's stare doesn't waver.

"But we survived."

"Up."

I slowly sit up, not standing. His gaze is sharp and concerned. He doesn't speak for a moment, simply staring at me.

It feels like torture. "Milly?"

"Kitt. What you did was reckless, and I am, frankly, disappointed."

Despite the words being simple, they cut deep. I focus my attention on his face, studying him.

"You're still bleeding, Milly-"

"That doesn't matter. We have to push toward Byēnwick on foot. We'll be there by nightfall."

I don't argue. *What's the point?*

"On your feet. Now."

I stand reluctantly, legs still shaking from the climb. Milly doesn't wait for me to fully steady myself—he's already moving, heading away from the gorge toward a gap in the trees.

I follow, stumbling slightly on uneven ground. After a few minutes of walking through underbrush, we find it: a narrow trail, barely visible—just compressed earth winding between trees. No signs. No markers. Just Milly walking ahead with the confidence of someone who knows exactly where he's going.

"Milly..."

"Yes?"

"Can you carry me?"

He stays silent, continuing to walk. I guess that means no.

My legs start to throb as I push forward, seeing no end of the path in sight. My eyes constantly look down to see if there are any roots in the path, and then back up to see Milly already two paces ahead of me. He stays at the same pace, not even breaking a sweat, while I struggle to keep up.

The first kāl passes in a blur of pain. My feet feel like they're on fire, each step sending sharp jolts up my calves. The bandage on my stomach pulls with every movement, a constant reminder of my stupidity.

"Milly? Do you have water?"

"No."

I stay silent from that point, letting the landscape fill my head instead. The gray clouds are still splattered across the sky, but not as much as when we were right next to Kanna's Ridge. The grass is lush and green, contrasting with the dirt brown path and the brown bark of the trees. The light occasionally filters yellow through the leaves, but the grayness holds.

*Step. Step. Step. Breathe. Pause. Step. Step. Step. Breathe. Pause.*

The rhythm becomes everything. I stop looking up. Just feet, path, roots, feet, path, roots.

My tongue feels thick in my mouth. When did I last drink water? This morning? Yesterday? The timeline blurs.

I stumble over a root I didn't see. My knee hits the ground hard, sending a shock of pain through my leg. I stay there for a moment, hands pressed against the dirt, breathing hard.

Milly's footsteps stop ahead of me. He doesn't turn around.

"Up," he says quietly.

I push myself to my feet, legs shaking. He starts walking again before I'm fully standing.

The trees thin slightly, and I can see the path winding ahead for at least another half-kāl. My heart sinks. The muscles in my thighs are burning now, not just aching. Each step feels like I'm dragging weights.

"Milly, please—"

"Keep walking, miss."

Not cold. Not angry. Just... firm. Final.

I try to count my steps again. One, two, three, four... I lose track around thirty-seven. Start over. One, two, three...

Sweat runs down my back, making the borrowed clothes stick to my skin. The bandage on my stomach feels wet—sweat or blood, I can't tell. I don't want to look.

The light changes. Astaris is moving lower now, casting longer shadows through the trees. How long have we been walking? It feels like days.

A drop of water hits my face. Then another. Light rain begins to fall, barely more than mist, but enough to make the path slippery. My borrowed clothes start to feel heavier, clinging to my skin.

Milly doesn't acknowledge it. Doesn't slow down. Doesn't look back.

I watch the way his shoulders move with each step, steady and mechanical. The blood on his head has dried into a dark streak, but he doesn't seem to care. He just keeps walking.

My left boot is rubbing wrong. I can feel a blister forming on my heel, the skin hot and tender. Each step makes it worse. I try shifting my weight, walking on the outside of my foot, but that just makes my ankle hurt.

"Milly?"

He slows slightly. Not stopping, but... listening.

"I'm sorry." My voice cracks. "I know I messed up. I know I almost—"

"Do you?" He still doesn't turn around, but his pace slows just a fraction more. "Do you truly understand what could have happened?"

I open my mouth, but nothing comes out.

"That rockfall could have killed us both." His voice is measured, but there's something underneath it. Something that sounds almost like... fear? "The lie about the knot could have killed me. Your recklessness in that gorge—" He stops walking. Finally turns to face me.

His expression isn't angry. It's exhausted.

"You wouldn't be the first person I've lost to carelessness, miss." He looks at me for a long moment. "And I cannot... I will not let you be another name I carry."

The words hang in the air between us. Another name. How many has he carried?

"I don't want to die," I whisper.

"Then prove it." He adjusts his belt, his hand brushing the hilt of his sword. "Actions, Kitt. Not words. When I tell you to be quiet, you be quiet. When I ask if you know something, you tell me the truth. Your life depends on it. Our lives depend on it."

He starts walking again, but slower this time. Just barely slower.

I follow, my legs screaming in protest. But I don't complain. Don't ask to be carried. Don't ask for water.

The rain continues, light and persistent. It runs down my face, mixing with sweat and probably tears, though I'm too tired to tell anymore. At least it's cool. At least it keeps my throat from feeling quite so dry.

After what feels like another eternity, Milly speaks again. His voice is quieter now, almost thoughtful.

"There was a squire. Years ago. Reminded me of you, in some ways." He pauses, navigating around a fallen branch. "Eager. Brave. Too brave, really. Thought he was invincible."

I wait, but he doesn't continue right away. Just walks, the rain pattering against his armor with soft metallic taps.

"What happened to him?" I finally ask.

"He died." Milly's voice is flat. "Took a risk he shouldn't have. Thought he knew better than his commander. By the time I reached him..." He trails off. "He was fifteen."

My age.

The words settle in my chest like stones. Fifteen. The same age as me. Did he have blonde hair too? Did he make stupid jokes? Did he think he was special, chosen, meant for great things?

"I'm not going to let that happen again," Milly says, more to himself than to me. "Not if I can help it."

We walk in silence after that. My feet have gone numb in some places, which is almost a blessing, though the blister on my heel still burns with each step. I focus on his back, on the steady rhythm of his steps. Matching them when I can.

The trees start to thin more noticeably now. Through gaps in the canopy, I can see the sky changing—less gray, more orange and pink as Astaris continues her descent. The path widens slightly, roots becoming less frequent.

My breath comes in ragged gasps. In through my nose, out through my mouth. In. Out. In. Out. It's all I can focus on besides the steps.

The path starts to slope downward slightly. Through the trees ahead, I think I can see... buildings? Walls? Or am I imagining it because I want to see it so badly?

"We're close," Milly says, as if reading my thoughts. "Byēnwick. A major city in Drūn, though Celtor acts like Drūn doesn't exist." He glances back at me for the first time in what feels like hours. His expression softens, just barely. "Another quarter-kāl. Can you make it?"

I nod, not trusting my voice.

"Good." He doesn't smile, but something in his eyes changes. "You did better than I expected, miss. Most people would have collapsed by now."

It's not quite praise. But it's not disappointment either.

The words give me something to hold onto. Most people would have collapsed. But I haven't. My legs find strength I didn't know they had left, pushing through the burning pain.

The buildings grow clearer through the trees. Not imagination—real structures, real walls. Byēnwick. The path becomes more defined, the dirt more packed. We must be on a proper road now, one that actually leads somewhere.

I can see the wooden palisade walls clearly now, and beyond them, stone buildings. The outer structures are simpler—wooden homes and what looks like a stable. Smoke rises from chimneys, carrying the smell of cooking fires.

My feet hit something different. I look down—cobblestones. Actual cobblestones instead of dirt. The shift is jarring after so long on the forest path, harder under my aching feet but somehow more real.

The rain has stopped, though I didn't notice when. My clothes are still damp, clinging uncomfortably, but the evening air is warm enough that I'm not cold.

The checkpoint at Byēnwick's outer gates is thorough—guards in red and gold examining every traveler, checking papers, asking questions in flat, official voices. The merchant ahead of us has to unpack three crates before they're satisfied. It takes twenty minutes.

When we finally clear the gate, I feel lighter. Like I can breathe fully for the first time.

"You don't miss it?" I ask Milly.

"The security?" He glances back at the walls. "There's a difference between safety and control. Orenia has control. Whether that makes it safe..." He doesn't finish.

We pass the first outlying building—a wooden structure with a thatched roof. An old woman sits on the porch, mending something in her lap. She glances up at us, her eyes lingering on Milly's armor and the dried blood on his face, but she doesn't speak.

More buildings appear. A blacksmith's forge, the fire still glowing inside. A small shop with closed shutters. The street widens as we approach the main gates.

Byēnwick's walls loom ahead, tall wooden posts sharpened at the top. Guards stand at the gate, but they barely glance at us as we approach. Just another traveler and his charge, nothing remarkable.

Through the gates, I can see the town proper. The air changes as we enter—less salt than Krandor, more earth and dust and the particular smell of inland settlements: horse manure, wood smoke, grain stores going slightly musty. It's warmer here too, the coastal breeze blocked by the walls, heat trapped between stone and timber buildings. The dust we kick up hangs in the still air, catching in my throat.

Stone buildings cluster around a central square. At the center, a stone stronghold rises above everything else, three towers forming a triangle at its corners.

"We're here," I rasp, my voice barely above a whisper.

Milly stops walking and turns to face me fully. He studies my face for a moment—taking in the exhaustion, the dried tear tracks, the determination that kept me moving.

"I'll find us lodging," he says, his voice gentler

now than it's been all afternoon. "You need to purchase supplies—bandages, rations, water. Can you handle that?"

The question sounds like a test. After everything, after the walk, after his disappointment—is he trusting me with this?

I nod, though my legs feel like they might give out any second. "Yes."

"Meet me at the main gate when you're done." He reaches into a pouch at his belt and pulls out a small leather purse, placing it in my hand. The coins inside clink softly. "Don't wander off. Don't talk to strangers more than necessary. Purchase what we need and come straight back. Understood?"

"Yes, sir..." I mumble, my fingers closing around the purse.

He watches me for another moment, as if debating whether to say something else. Finally, he just nods and turns toward the town center, his armor catching the last rays of Astaris's light.

I stand there for a moment, legs trembling, watching him walk away. Then I force myself to move, stumbling toward what looks like a general goods shop near the gates.

One foot in front of the other. Just like the walk here.

# BYĒNWICK

---◆---

### CHAPTER XIV

The coin purse feels heavy in my hand. Heavier than it should for just leather and metal.

I stand outside the general goods shop, watching people pass by on the cobblestone street. They move with purpose—a woman carrying a basket of bread, a blacksmith's apprentice hauling iron rods, children darting between adults in some game I don't understand.

Everyone is speaking Unital—not just scattered words like in Krandor, but full sentences, the formal merchant dialect. The children chatter in it like it's nothing, their words flowing faster than I can follow.

My stomach twists. This place is different. Foreign.

Ahead, there's an intersection. Through my blurry vision, I spot a sign: MĒRON KĀLT'S KĒMOR. *Kēmor... buy... shop.* That's it. That's where Milly sent me.

I approach slowly, my hand trembling as it reaches for the door handle.

The door is heavier than expected. I push with my shoulder, and a bell chimes overhead—sharp and sudden.

I flinch.

"Just a bell," I whisper. "Just a bell."

Inside, shelves crowd every wall. The smell hits hard: wood smoke, lavender, something musty.

"*Mēron Kālt, ijū dī Bēris Kālt, merchant dī Byēnwick*, at your service."

I jump. A man behind the counter—graying hair, dusty apron. His formal Unital is perfect. Name, parentage, occupation, town.

"Um." My voice cracks. "Kitt."

He waits. Patient. Expectant.

"Just Kitt," I whisper, cheeks burning.

His expression shifts—understanding, not judgment. He switches to Common. "You need supplies?"

Relief floods through me. "Bandages. Rations. Water skins."

He's efficient. Bandages, salve, bread, meat, oats, fruit, water skins—everything piles onto the counter while he explains each item quickly. My hands shake as I count out seven Dōnis.

He packs everything into a canvas bag. "This should serve you well."

"Gratid," I mumble.

"Safe travels."

The bell chimes as I leave.

A small cart leans against the wall just outside—an old woman selling odds and ends. Wooden spoons, leather pouches, a few children's toys carved from pale wood.

My eyes catch on one: a horse. No bigger than my palm. Gray wood, four legs frozen mid-stride, mane carved in simple grooves.

I'm counting coins before I realize I've moved. Two Dōnis. The woman takes them without a word, wraps the horse in a scrap of cloth, presses it into my hand.

Stupid. Impractical. Milly asked for bandages, not toys.

I tuck it into the bag anyway.

Outside, evening has deepened. Astaris paints everything orange-gold. The streets are busier—people heading home, to taverns, living normal lives while I—

The bag digs into my shoulder. Heavy. Real. I did it.

Keep walking. Just get back to Milly.

A group of men laugh outside a tavern. I cross to the other side of the street, head down.

My boots sound too loud on the cobblestones. *Step. Step. Step.*

Then—

A woman's voice, warm and gentle: "—and that's why you must always check your stitching, love. See?"

I glance up without thinking.

A woman stands near a fabric merchant's stall, holding up embroidery to show a young girl beside her. The girl—maybe ten—has blonde hair catching the evening light. She laughs at something her mother says, bright and carefree.

The woman tucks a strand of hair behind the girl's ear with such casual tenderness that—

*Mom's hand, tucking my hair back. "My curious Kitt-y."*

The cobblestones beneath my feet shimmer. Ripple.

No. Not rippling. *Liquid.*

The street is gone. I'm standing in an ocean of blood—warm and thick, rising past my ankles, my knees. The evening sky above me bleeds into it, orange and red mixing until I can't tell where horizon ends and water begins.

I try to move but my legs won't respond. The blood is up to my waist now, pulling at my clothes, dragging me down. I'm swimming—no, *drowning*—in it.

*Mom's eyes. Empty. Watching from beneath the surface.*

I reach for her but my hands close on nothing. Just more blood, endless blood, filling my mouth when I try to scream—

"Miss? Are you alright?"

The woman's voice breaks through. She's looking at me. Concerned. The girl has stopped laughing.

I'm still on the street. Dry cobblestones. No ocean. But I can still feel it—the warmth, the weight, the taste of iron in my mouth.

I can't move. Can't breathe. The blood is still there, invisible but real, rising around me.

"Miss, you look pale. Do you need—"

I run.

The bag slams against my hip with each step. Boots skidding on stone, nearly tripping, lungs burning. Every footfall splashes through phantom crimson.

I don't know where I'm going. Just *away*.

Buildings blur past. Voices call out but I don't stop.

My chest hurts. Everything hurts. I can't get enough air and my vision keeps going dark at the edges and—

The main gate. I see it through the haze. Milly's silhouette in armor. Milly's adjusting the bandage on his forehead when I return, fingers careful around the edges. The white cloth has a rust-colored spot seeping through.

I make it to the wall beside the gate and collapse against it, gasping. The stone is cool against my back.

Real. Solid.

*In. Out. In. Can't. Out. Can't breathe. In. Too fast. Out. Too—*

"Kitt?"

Milly's voice cuts through the panic. His boots appear in my downward vision, then he's crouching in front of me.

"Look at me, miss. Eyes here."

I try. My gaze keeps sliding away.

"Breathe with me. In." He demonstrates, slow and exaggerated. "Out."

*In. Out. In. Out.*

It takes forever, but gradually the world stops tilting. The phantom ocean recedes. My boots are dry.

"Better?" His voice is quiet.

I nod, not trusting my voice.

He takes the supply bag from where it fell beside me, checks the contents methodically. Everything intact despite my running.

"You got everything I asked for." It's not a question, but there's something approving in his tone. "Well done."

The praise feels distant.

"What happened?" he asks.

I shake my head. Can't explain. Don't have words for *I drowned in my mother's blood on a dry street.*

He studies my face for a long moment, then seems to decide not to push. "Can you walk?"

"Yes." My voice sounds hollow.

He stands, offers his hand. I take it, letting him pull me upright. My legs feel weak but hold.

"The inn isn't far." He keeps my hand for a moment longer than necessary, making sure I'm steady. "Come."

We walk through Byēnwick's streets together. He matches my slow pace, staying close. The supply bag over his shoulder, his presence solid and real beside me.

The inn appears ahead—two stories, timber and whitewashed plaster. A sign: THE CROSSROADS.

Inside smells like bread and ale. Warm. Safe. Nobody looks at us.

"Two rooms," Milly tells the innkeeper. "One night. Meals included."

Two iron keys. He hands me one. "Get cleaned up if you want. We'll eat, then rest. We leave at dawn."

I clutch the key. Cold metal. Real.

"Milly?"

"Yes?"

"Thank you." The words stick in my throat. "For... for not asking."

He's quiet. Then: "You did well today, miss. Getting the supplies. That's what matters." A pause. "The rest... you'll tell me when you're ready. Or you won't. Either way."

It's not comfort, exactly. But it's permission.

Permission to break without having to explain all the pieces.

I climb the stairs. Each creak of wood feels loud in my ears, but normal. Safe.

The room is small. Bed, washbasin, window. Mine for tonight.

I should wash. Should eat.

Instead I collapse onto the bed, boots still on. The mattress is thin, the pillow lumpy.

My hands are still shaking. I can still feel it—the blood rising, warm and thick. I press my palms against my eyes until I see spots.

Not *real. It wasn't real. The street was dry. It was dry.*

But I can still taste iron.

My eyes close.

Nightmares come—blonde hair and empty eyes and oceans that pull me under—but my body is too exhausted to fight them.

I sleep anyway.

# SLEEPLESS

◆

### CHAPTER XV

*I sleep anyway.*

What a lie. I've been tossing and turning in this bed for the past hour. It's midnight, with Mün high in the dark sky. I've tried everything.

I move the pillow to the side, staring straight up at the wooden ceiling. I glance left and right without turning my head. Nothing's changed.

I look to my left and right again. Nothing's changed.

I stare up at the ceiling again, then the walls, then the ceiling.

My arms automatically move to do something, anything. I lift the sheets off of me, and then sigh quietly.

Yet, in the stillness, I see it again. Mom's face. The woman in the street. The blond girl laughing.

*She ended it all. In front of me. And I didn't have the guts to say anything. I've never said anything about it.*

My stomach lurches and tightens at the same time. The thought sits in my mind like a weighted blanket.

I've been carrying all of this since... the kitchen. Through the inn. Through the ridge. Through the walk. Through the sea of the dead. Just... carrying it.

I can't anymore.

I can't.

I can't.

I can't anymore.

It doesn't feel like relief.

It feels like I'm drowning.

Drowning in my own blood. My own spit. My own thoughts.

I need to tell someone.

I need to tell *him*.

I push my legs over the side of the bed before I can even hear myself think; talk myself out of it. The floorboards are smooth and cold against my bare feet. I didn't even put my boots back on after collapsing earlier.

The lanterns in the hallway are snuffed out. Dark enough that I see shapes that aren't there. Silent. My hand finds the wall, using it to guide me.

My eyes land on Milly's door. I stand barely a step away from it. My fingers, my toes, everything compels me to open it. My fist hovers just above the wood.

*What if he's angry? What if he sends me back? What if–*

I knock.

I knock.

I knock.

Silence.

I hear footsteps from inside the room, then the door slowly opens.

"Kitt?" Milly's voice is thick with sleep. He's in a plain shirt and sleeping pants—I've never seen him without armor. His eyes are half-closed, not really focusing on me yet.

I open my mouth. Nothing comes out. Just a choked sound that doesn't sound like Common or Unital.

His eyes sharpen. He's awake now, truly seeing me. "What happened? Are you hurt?"

I shake my head. I nod. I shake my head. I nod. I shake my head, finally.

*How do I even say it?*

"Come in." He steps back, holding the door open. "You're trembling."

I am? I look down at my hands. I'm shaking.

The room is tiny, almost claustrophobic. Not much different from mine. His armor rests in the corner, sword propped beside it. The bed is unmade, sheets pushed up and away in an almost frantic tangle.

I stand just inside the doorway. Unable to move, unable to speak, unable to think.

He waits. He stays silent. He watches me calmly.

"Mom..." I whisper, sounding hoarse.

He stays silent.

"She didn't..." My throat closes. I try again. "It wasn't an accident or a murder."

The words hang in the air between us.

"My mother killed herself." It comes out flat. Empty. Like script on paper. "I found her in the kitchen. Blood—" I choke on the word. "Blood everywhere."

"Her eyes were so small. The pupils. Tiny, even in the dim light. She was still on the pills, even at the end. She was never taking just one—I knew that. I just didn't... I thought it made her happy. She always looked so relieved after she took them."

"She... She cut herself open. And I just stood there. I couldn't move. Couldn't walk. Couldn't run. Couldn't help. I just..." I trail off.

Milly's expression doesn't change as he processes the words. He doesn't look shocked or horrified. Just... sad. Almost understanding.

"That's why you ran," he says quietly. Not a question. A statement.

I nod. "I couldn't stay there. In that house. In Krandor. Everything reminded me of..." My voice breaks. "And then I met you and I thought... I thought if I could get to Vestperia, if I could see what they dreamed about, maybe it would make sense. Maybe it could all click. Maybe I could understand why she'd..."

I can't finish.

"Maybe you could forgive her," Milly finishes softly.

The words find something I didn't know was there. Tears spill over, hot on my cold cheeks.

"I'm so angry at her," I choke out. "She left me. She just... left. And I don't know if I'll ever stop being angry."

"That's permitted," he replies in a softer tone than usual.

Silence stretches across the room. I sob loudly, almost uncontrollably. Unable to stop. Unable to be brave.

"Sit," he says, gesturing to the bed. Not a command, just... a choice. An offer.

I sit, the mattress dips barely under my weight. He pulls the blanket from where it's tangled and drapes it over my shoulders. The gesture isn't exactly comforting, but it helps anyway.

He sits beside me, maintaining a subtle, careful distance. Not touching. Not speaking, just... present.

"I've been carrying it alone," I whisper brokenly. "Since that morning. And I thought if I just... if I just kept moving, kept going forward, maybe it wouldn't hurt so much."

"Does it?" he asks quietly.

"What?"

"Hurt less. From the moving."

I think about the gorge. The blood ocean in the street. The nightmares. "No. It just... stays, and follows me."

He nods slowly, like this confirms everything he suspected. "Grief does that. It doesn't like staying where you left it."

There's weight in those words. Personal weights.

"The squire you mentioned," I say. "The one who died. Is that why you..."

"Why I took you with me?" He's quiet for a long moment. "Partially. I swore I would not watch another brother... child walk into danger they weren't prepared for." A pause. "But I didn't know you were running from something else. Something you weren't prepared for, either."

"I'm sorry I lied. About the knots. About... everything."

"I know." He doesn't expand on it.

The silence sits between us, like a physical object. He doesn't try to touch me or comfort me physically. I glance up at the ceiling, unsure what to say.

"Can I stay with you tonight? I don't want to be alone." My voice is barely there.

He's quiet for a long moment. "I understand. But that wouldn't be appropriate, miss." His voice is gentle but firm. "What I can do is leave my door open. You can sleep in your room with your door open as well. If you need anything—nightmares, fear—you call out and I'll hear you. I won't be far."

It's not what I asked for, but... it's something. Knowing he's listening. Knowing I'm not completely alone.

"Okay," I whisper.

"Can you make it back to your room?"

I nod, standing slowly. The blanket slips from my shoulders.

"Kitt," he says as I reach the door. "What you told me tonight—that took courage. Real courage. More than charging into battle ever requires."

The words settle something in my chest. Not peace, but... acknowledgment.

"Goodnight..." he pauses. "Kitt."

"Goodnight, Milly."

# STEADY HANDS

◆

## DAWN
### CHAPTER XVI

The morning light casts long shadows across my small room, illuminating the dust in the air. I blink slowly, staring at the ceiling as golden light floods my vision. I turn to my side, facing away from the window.

A slow, steady three-beat knock. "Kitt?"

Milly's voice. I stand wearily and open the door. He's back in his armor, sword at his hip, holding a small cloth bag with steam rising from it.

"I brought you breakfast." He sets the bag on the bedside counter. His eyes meet mine for a moment—not pity, just... awareness. He knows now. "Fresh bread. Still warm. Don't let it get cold."

"Thank you," I mumble.

He nods. "We leave in an hour for Milldraugh. Eat first. I'll check your wounds after, then we'll repack." He moves toward the door. "I need to arrange transport—a carriage if I can find one, horses at minimum."

He glances over his shoulder—a new expression

on his face, something soft, indescribable—before leaving. "Take your time, Kitt."

The door shuts with a soft *click*.

I sit in silence, looking at the bag. My hands reach for it, caressing the surface as I lean over to smell the bread. *Wonderful.* I reach in and pick up the still-warm bread.

It's about the size of my hand, if not a bit longer. It's perfectly brown. Perfectly baked. When I bite into it, it's crunchy. A small smile appears on my face. He remembered. *Even after everything, he noticed something that small about me.*

After finishing the small loaf, more knocks sound at the door.

"Kitt?"

"Come in."

Milly enters with a small canvas bag marked MEDICAL in rough lettering. "We should check that wound. Make sure it's healing properly." He pauses. "Are you comfortable with that?"

I nod, moving to lie on the bed.

He sets the bag on the bedside table, pulling out supplies—a bottle of alcohol, clean gauze, and a roll of brown tape. "This might sting," he says, more warning than apology.

I lift my shirt just enough to expose my stomach. The bandage from yesterday is still there, spotted with old blood. His hands are careful as he peels it away, examining the wound beneath.

"No infection," he says after a moment. "Healing well, considering. You were lucky."

The alcohol stings when he cleans around the edges. I hiss through my teeth.

"Almost done." His movements are efficient, professional. New gauze, tape securing it. "There. That should hold until we reach Milldraugh. We'll change it again tonight."

I pull my shirt down as he packs the supplies away.

"Thank you," I say quietly.

He nods. "Gather what you need. We leave shortly."

Milly stands up, extending his hand to me. I grab it for a brief moment, pulling myself up, then promptly letting go.

I walk over to the wall, grabbing my traveling bag as Milly goes back downstairs to ready the new horses. I peer into the bag. Basic supplies, and now a book about tying knots.

I sling the bag over my shoulder and head downstairs.

The common room is mostly empty—just a few early risers nursing morning ale. Milly stands near the door, settling accounts with the innkeeper.

Outside, two horses wait, already saddled. No

carriage—just the mounts and our supplies tied behind the saddles.

"Couldn't find a carriage on short notice," Milly says, noticing my look. "Can you ride?"

I hesitate. "I've... ridden before. In Krandor. Just around the city."

"That'll do. We'll take it slow until you find your seat." He helps me mount the smaller of the two horses—a dappled gray mare with patient eyes.

The saddle feels foreign, too high, the reins awkward in my hands. But the mare doesn't seem to mind my inexperience.

Milly swings onto his horse with practiced ease. "Milldraugh is three days' ride. We'll stop at midday, camp tonight." He glances at me. "Stay close. If you need to stop, say so."

I nod, adjusting my grip.

We ride out of Byēnwick as the sun climbs higher. The town gates pass behind us, and the road opens ahead—packed earth winding through farmland toward distant forests.

# WASH AWAY

### CHAPTER XVII

*Ploof. Ploof. Plok.*

The steps are steady across the uneven terrain, yet I can't seem to find the rhythm. Each step jars through my spine. My hands grip the reins too tight. My shoulders rise to my ears without meaning to. The saddle feels wrong—too high, too hard. It's almost as if I'm sitting on a wooden plank that's trying to hurl me off.

Milly rides just a bit ahead. His whole posture is relaxed, like he's been doing this for his whole life. His horse—some big dark beast that probably costs more than a house in Krandor—moves with him, not against him. They look like one thing, not two.

I look down at the mare beneath me. She's gray with white dapples across her hindquarters, and her ears flick back occasionally like she's listening to me struggle. And enjoying it.

"You're fighting her."

Milly's voice cuts through my thoughts. He's slowed his horse to ride beside me, watching with that assessing gaze of his.

"I'm not-"

"You are." He gestures at my hands. "Loosen your grip. She knows where to go. You're just making both of you miserable."

I try to relax my fingers, but they don't listen. Everything in me wants to hold on as tight as possible—to control, to keep myself from falling.

"Breathe," he says, not unkindly. "Move with her stride, not against it."

I focus on breathing. In. Out. The mare keeps walking, patient despite my best efforts. Gradually—so gradually I don't even notice—the jarring lessens. My body starts to remember it's supposed to move, not stay rigid.

"Better," Milly says after a while. He nudges his horse forward again, back to leading.

The morning stretches on. Farmland on both sides. Wheat fields, a distant farmhouse, scattered trees marking lines. Solis climbs higher, Astaris trailing. The sky stays clear, crystal blue and endless. My thighs start burning. Then my lower back. Then my shoulders scream from the effort of staying upright. I don't complain. Milly glances back occasionally, but doesn't comment on whatever he sees in my face.

By the time he finally stops, the sun is low and orange. My legs are shaking when I try to dismount, and I have to grab the saddle to keep from falling.

"First day's always the hardest," Milly says, unsaddling his horse. "Your body will adapt."

I want to sit down. Lie down. Never move again.

"Come here."

I force my legs to work, stumbling over to where he's pulled a brush from his saddlebag.

"She carried you all day. The least you can do is care for her properly." He demonstrates on his own horse—long strokes down the neck, checking the legs, picking debris from hooves with a curved metal tool. "Your turn."

I take the brush. The mare stands patiently while I mimic his movements. The brushing is soothing, repetitive. Her coat is soft under the bristles, and she makes a low sound in her throat that might be contentment.

"I should name you," I mumble under my breath. She flicks her ear toward me. "Horsey?"

She doesn't respond.

"Horsey it is, then."

When I glance over at Milly, he's setting up the tents, not watching me.

"Kitt," he says after a bit. "When you're done, there's dried meat in the left saddlebag. Eat, then sleep. Long day tomorrow."

I finish brushing Horsey, my arms aching with the effort. The campfire Milly built crackles softly, orange lighting dancing across the small clearing.

He hands me a piece of jerky without ceremony, and we eat in silence.

The ground is hard under my bedroll, and every muscle in my body screams. But when I close my eyes, I don't see blood oceans or empty stares.

Just the road ahead, the steady rhythm of hoofbeats I'm starting to understand, and somewhere distant, the towers of Vestperia waiting.

The sky changes while we ride. Gray clouds roll in from the west, low and heavy. Thunder rumbles. Lightning flickers distantly. Horsey's ears flick back and forth, more alert than yesterday.

"Rain coming," Milly says without looking back. "An hour, maybe less."

I glance up at the darkening sky. He's right—I can smell it in the air now, that particular edge in the air, metal and smoke.

The first drops hit twenty minutes later. Light at first, just specks on my borrowed clothes. Then heavier. Then constant.

The road turns dark, then muddy. Horsey's gait changes—more careful, picking her way through the slick patches. My instinct is to tighten my grip, control her, but I remember yesterday. *Loosen up. Let her do the work.*

I relax my hands. She finds her own path through the worst of it.

The rain soaks through my clothes, plastering my hair to my face. Milly's bandage is soaked too, the white cloth gone gray. When he adjusts it, I see him wince. Everything is gray and wet and cold. But Horsey keeps moving steadily, and I stay with her rhythm. Not fighting. Just moving.

By evening, we're both dripping. Milly dismounts in a clearing with decent tree cover and immediately starts unpacking.

"Tent stakes," he says, tossing me a canvas bag.

I catch it, fumbling slightly. My hands are numb from the cold and wet. He's already got the first tent frame up, working quickly despite the rain.

I kneel in the mud, trying to remember how the stakes go. The first one slips, won't catch in the soft ground. I angle it differently, push harder. It holds.

"Good," Milly says, moving to the next corner.

We work in silence, rain drumming on half-erected canvas. Milly pauses halfway through hammering a stake, closes his eyes briefly. Then continues. I get two stakes wrong, have to redo them.

But by the time we're done, both tents stand. Not pretty, but functional.

The jerky tastes like wet leather. We eat it anyway, huddled under the larger tent's overhang while rain pours around us.

"You did well today," Milly says quietly. "Didn't panic."

I nod, too cold and tired to feel proud. But something warm flickers anyway.

When I crawl into my tent, everything is damp. My bedroll, my clothes, my hair. But I'm asleep before I can care.

Outside, I can hear the rain continuing to fall, steady and relentless. Somewhere in the downpour, Milly's tent rustles as he settles in for the night. The horses shift and snort under their shelter.

Two days down. One more to Milldraugh.

# DISTANCE

### CHAPTER XVIII

The third morning breaks clearer—the storm having passed overnight. My body still aches, but differently now—a dull soreness instead of sharp pain. I can mount Horsey without Milly's help, settle into the saddle without thinking about every movement.

The rain brings things out of the earth. Slugs crossing the path, pale and glistening. Frogs calling from somewhere in the wet grass—small ones, green and brown, leaping away from the horses' hooves. Earthworms surfacing, pink and segmented, crawling blind across the mud.

Horsey's hooves find them without trying. Soft sounds I shouldn't be able to hear over the light rain, but I hear them anyway. Small wet crunches. Tiny endings.

I count them for a while. Twelve. Thirteen. Fourteen.

Milly doesn't notice. Or doesn't care. It's just

nature. Just the small deaths that happen constantly, everywhere, without anyone meaning them to. Without anyone being blamed.

I stop counting eventually. But I keep listening.

We ride in comfortable silence. The farmland has changed, becoming sparser, more tired-looking. Fields of stubble instead of wheat. Fences in disrepair. The road widens, packed harder from more traffic.

"Milldraugh ahead," Milly says around midday. "You'll smell it before you see it."

He's right. The air shifts—smoke, animals, something sour underneath. Not the clean scents of farmland or forest, but the concentrated smell of too many people living too close together.

Then I see it on the horizon. Not towers or grand walls, just a sprawl of buildings clustered together like they're holding each other up. Wood and thatch, some stone. Smoke rises from dozens of chimneys, creating a haze over everything.

The road becomes more crowded. A farmer herding goats. A merchant's wagon loaded with barrels. People on foot, most carrying bundles or pulling carts. Nobody looks at us with much interest—just another traveler and his charge.

"Stay close," Milly says, his voice taking on that edge it gets when he's assessing threats. "Milldraugh is... practical. Keep your coin purse inside your shirt, not on your belt."

I nod, tucking the nearly-empty purse he gave me in Byēnwick deeper into my clothes.

The buildings close in around us as we enter the town proper. No gates, no guards—just the road becoming a street, dirt becoming packed earth mixed with refuse. Structures lean at odd angles, built close enough that neighbors could reach through windows and touch hands.

We pass through a smaller square first. A pillory stands at its center—heavy wooden frame, three holes. Two of them are occupied.

A human woman on the left, head and hands locked in place. Her sign reads THIEF in crude paint. Someone's thrown rotten vegetables at her. The mess drips down her face, into her hair. She's not moving. Might be unconscious. Might be dead.

A Felidae man on the right. Younger, maybe twenty. His ears are pinned back as far as they'll go, tail hanging limp through a gap in the wood. His sign just says VAGRANT. Nothing thrown at him—he's too new, the wood around his neck still clean.

His eyes track us as we pass. Pleading.

I open my mouth. Milly's hand touches my arm—not restraining, just... warning.

"We can't," he says quietly.

"But—"

"We can't."

A few people mill around the square, barely glancing at the pillory. Normal. Just part of the scenery.

We keep moving.

The streets narrow as we go deeper. Buildings press closer, creating shadows even at midday. Laundry hangs overhead, dripping onto the cobblestones. Children dart between adults, playing some game involving a ball and a lot of shrieking.

Two streets over, I notice the wall.

Someone painted something there. Not just painted—carved first, then filled with red paint so it couldn't be scrubbed away easily. The letters are deep, angry, urgent:

THEY BLEED LIKE US

Below it, in smaller letters, fresher paint:

WHEN DO WE STOP BLEEDING FOR THEM

And below that, newest of all, still wet enough to gleam:

RISE. DRŪN STANDS FREE!

Someone tried to scrub it. The stone around the words is lighter, scraped raw. But the carved letters remain, filled with red that looks too much like blood.

Milly sees me looking. His jaw tightens. "Don't stare," he says quietly. "Not here."

But I can't look away. There's more—I notice it now that I'm really looking. On the building across the street, someone's painted a simple symbol in white: a broken chain. And another, on a door we pass: three horizontal lines with a slash through them. Code, maybe. Messages for people who know how to read them.

"Milly, what does—"

"Not here," he repeats, firmer. His hand finds my elbow, guiding me forward.

We turn onto a wider street. More people here, more activity. Merchant stalls line the edges—vegetables, cloth, tools. The smell of cooking food mixes with less pleasant odors.

Near a fountain, two merchants are arguing, their voices carrying over the crowd:

"—I'm just saying, if they're calling it 'naval exercises' we should take the land route—"

"It's *posturing*. Both sides do this twice a year. Nothing ever—"

"Three warships is not posturing, that's—"

His companion cuts him off with a sharp look, glancing around to see who might be listening. When his eyes pass over us, he lowers his voice. "—positioning. Just positioning."

They move away, still talking in tones too low to hear.

The street opens into a larger square—merchant stalls, the smell of roasting meat and fresh bread, the normal chaos of commerce. People bartering, children running, someone calling out prices for fish.

Then the crowd goes quiet.

Not all at once. It ripples outward from the center, voices dropping, people stepping back, creating a circle of empty space.

I crane my neck to see what's happening.

A Felidae man is on his knees in the center, hands bound behind his back. He's begging in that rolling, purring Unital that carries even over the crowd—words I can't quite understand but the desperation is clear. His ears are flat against his skull—complete submission, terror. His tail is tucked so tight against his body I almost don't see it.

A guard stands over him. Red and gold uniform. Orenian colors. The same uniform I saw every day in Krandor.

We're not in Orenia anymore. We haven't been for days. But the guard doesn't care about borders.

Some in the crowd look uncomfortable—Felidae especially, their ears back, tails low. Others don't seem to care at all. A few look... satisfied. Like this is justice being done.

"Milly, what's—"

His hand finds my shoulder, firm. "Don't watch."

But I'm already watching. The guard's hand moves to his sword.

The Felidae man screams something—a name, maybe. A plea. The word rolls and breaks in his throat, half-human speech, half-feline keen. It's the most terrible sound I've ever heard.

The blade comes down.

How... *easy.*

I don't see it clearly—Milly's already turning his horse, putting himself between me and the square. But I hear the sound. Wet. Final. Then a different sound—something heavy hitting the cobblestones.

Then silence.

When I look back, the crowd is already moving again. A woman steps carefully around something dark spreading across the stones. A merchant continues calling his prices, voice slightly louder now, drowning out the quiet. A child asks his mother something, gets shushed.

Life continuing.

"What—why did no one—" My voice won't work right.

"The guard can do what they want here," Milly says quietly. "This isn't Krandor. This isn't even really Drūn anymore. There's no trial. No questions. Just authority."

"But that's—"

"I know." He keeps his horse moving, navigating us away from the square. "That's why we don't draw attention."

My hands are shaking on Horsey's reins. I can still hear that scream. That terrible, broken sound.

"The graffiti," I whisper. "The messages on the

walls. That's why?"

"That's why," he confirms. "And that's why people who write them disappear."

We ride in silence after that. The streets continue—children still playing, merchants still selling, people going about their day. But I can't unsee it. Can't unhear it.

Every Felidae we pass, I wonder: Do *they* know? *Did they see? Are they next?*

Every person in Orenian colors, I wonder: How many? How many have they—

"There," Milly says, pointing. "The inn."

It's a two-story building, timber and whitewashed plaster. A sign hangs above the door: THE GRINDING WHEEL. Not welcoming, exactly, but functional.

We approach slowly. Milly dismounts first, helps me down. My legs are shaking—not from riding, but from everything else.

That's when I see him.

A man sits slumped in the doorway next to the inn. Not blocking it, just... there. Against the wall. His breathing rattles—wet, labored, loud enough to hear from several pās away.

Even from here I can see the wound on his leg. The fabric of his pants is torn, stained dark. The skin around the wound has gone gray-green, spreading up toward his knee. The smell hits me—sweet and rotten at the same time.

He lifts his hand weakly as we pass. "Please... coin... Kurune... apothecary..."

I start to reach for my purse. Milly's hand on my wrist stops me.

"We can't," he says quietly.

"He's dying—"

"I know." Something pained crosses his face. "But if we stop, others will see. Will see we have coins. Will see we're soft."

"But—"

"Kitt." His voice is gentle but firm. "We can't help everyone."

The man's hand drops. His chest still moves, barely. Each breath a struggle.

I look at Milly. Really look at him. There's pain in his eyes—real pain. This isn't easy for him either.

"By tomorrow?" I whisper.

"By tomorrow," he confirms. "Maybe tonight."

And no one will care. Just another body. Just another person who couldn't survive in Milldraugh.

Milly ties the horses to a post outside the inn, then guides me inside with a hand on my shoulder. The common room is dim after the bright street, my eyes struggling to adjust. The innkeeper looks up—a tired woman with gray hair, wiping down the bar.

"Two rooms," Milly says. "One night. Meals

included."

She quotes a price. He pays without haggling.

Two iron keys. He hands me one. "Get cleaned up if you want. We'll eat, then rest. Tomorrow we'll figure out how long we're staying."

I clutch the key. Cold metal. Real.

"Milly?"

"Yes?"

"Thank you." The words stick in my throat. "For... for not asking."

He's quiet. Then: "You did well today, miss. Getting through all that. That's what matters."

It doesn't feel like I did well. It feels like I witnessed three different kinds of horror and did nothing about any of them.

But I nod anyway.

I climb the stairs. Each creak of wood feels loud in my ears, but normal. Real.

The room is small. Bed, washbasin, window. Mine for tonight.

I should wash. Should eat.

Instead I collapse onto the bed, boots still on. The mattress is thin, the pillow lumpy.

My hands are still shaking. I can still hear that scream. Still see the man's gray-green leg. Still see the Felidae in the pillory, ears flat with fear.

Still see the words carved into stone: WHEN DO

WE STOP BLEEDING FOR THEM

I close my eyes.

Sleep doesn't come. Just the images, over and over. The wet sound. The spreading darkness on cobblestones. The man's rattling breath.

Eventually, there's a knock. Milly, saying food is ready.

I force myself up. Down to the common room. Eat bread and cheese that tastes like ash. Answer his questions with single words. Fine. Tired. Tomorrow.

Back to the room.

Lie in bed, staring at the ceiling.

This is Milldraugh. This is what the world looks like when authority breaks down, when one nation occupies another, when people are too scared or too tired to fight back.

This is what I wanted when I left Krandor. Adventure. The real world.

I got it.

Through the thin wall, I hear Milly moving in the next room. The scrape of a chair. The scratch of a quill on parchment—he must be writing something. A letter, maybe.

I close my eyes and try not to see red.

Try not to hear that scream.

Try not to think about the man outside, still breathing. Still dying.

Still there when morning comes, or gone, and which would be worse?

Sleep finally comes, but it's not rest.

Just darkness, and the sound of a blade falling, over and over and over.

TO DR. ARRONAX VERNE,
*Vestperian Institute of Mind and Healing*

I write to request your services on behalf of a young woman who is currently in my care. Her name is Kitt—no family name, or perhaps none she wishes to claim anymore. Fifteen years of age. Blond hair, eyes of emerald, small for her years. She witnessed her mother's death approximately two weeks past.

The mother used a blade. Kitt found her in the kitchen. From what I understand, the mother had been using oxycodone—perhaps for the pain, perhaps for something else. The dependency went unnoticed until it was too late.

The girl exhibits symptoms I imagine you would recognize: dissociative episodes, intrusive memories, difficulty sleeping. In Byēnwick, she experienced what I believed was a flashback—stood frozen on a street, unresponsive as if drowning in something only she could see. She described it later as "an ocean of blood."

She also displays periods of apparent normalcy—laughter, curiosity, even contentment. These shifts are rapid, sometimes within the same hour. I do not know if this is typical for traumatic stress in the young, or if it indicates something more severe.

I am bringing her to Vestperia, Kurune. The journey will take months, but I have given my word to see her there safely. When we arrive, she will need someone qualified to help her process what she has experienced. You helped me once. I am hoping you will help her.

I must confess: I am writing this as much for my own clarity as for hers.

You know about Sawyer Mills. You know what happened at the border—how I led my own brother into an ambush I should have anticipated, how he died while I lived, how his blood soaked into sand I can still feel under my boots when I close my eyes. You know what happened after Ryn. I cannot watch another girl drown while I stand breathing.

And yet, here I am. Responsible for Kitt.

She reminds me of him—not in appearance, but in that same desperate need to prove herself, to matter, to be more than what the world has told her she is. She manipulated me into taking her with me. I am aware of this. She told me a story about honoring her parents' dreams, about needing to see Vestperia to understand them. It was a calculated appeal, and it worked because I am weak where grief is concerned.

But knowing she manipulated me does not change the fact that I cannot abandon her. My oath binds me—any paladin who refuses aid forfeits title and honor—but even without the oath, I would struggle to turn away. You warned me about this. About trying to save Sawyer through others. About repeating the pattern.

I am repeating the pattern.

She is learning to ride. I am teaching her basic survival skills—how to care for a horse, read weather, set up camp. Small things. Practical things. She is competent when she chooses to be, though grief makes her scattered. I find myself watching her the way I used to watch Sawyer—assessing threats, calculating risks, trying to anticipate what might go wrong before it does.

I am terrified I will fail her the way I failed him.

This fear is not useful. It makes me hesitate when I should be decisive, makes me protective when I should be preparing her for reality. You have told me many times that guilt is not the same as responsibility, that I cannot control every outcome, that some deaths are not my fault.

I do not believe you. But I am trying to.

When we reach Kurune, please see her. Help her process her mother's death in ways I cannot. Teach her that survival is not the same as living, that carrying trauma does not mean being defined by it.

And if you have time—if you believe it would help—I would not object to continuing our own correspondence. It has been two years since my last letter. I thought I was managing well enough alone.

I am not managing as well as I thought.

We should arrive within three months, weather and roads permitting. I will send word when we reach the outer settlements.

Thank you for your time and expertise. For Kitt's sake, and perhaps for mine.

May the Goddess forgive what I cannot.

*Sir Lumber Mills*
*Paladin of Celton*
WRITTEN ON THE ROAD TO MILLDRAUGH, THIRD DAY
OUT FROM BYĒNWICK.

# MILLDRAUGH

◆

### CHAPTER XIX

*Dull.*

*Sharp.*

*Dull.*

The headache wakes me up before the morning light can.

*Dull. Sharp. Dull.* Sharp again, the kind that sits behind my eyes and makes the dim lights from the window feel wrong. I press my palm against my lower abdomen. The familiar ache is there—the monthly one. But when I shift under the blanket to check... nothing. Just the ache without the blood.

I stare at the ceiling. Wooden beams, darker than the ones in Byēnwick. The inn here is older, more worn. I can hear someone moving downstairs, in a room below—footsteps, then the scrape of a chair.

My body feels heavy. Not the sharp pain from the first days of riding, but something deeper. Like I'm carrying stones in my skin.

The window glows a gray yet golden pre-dawn light. Solis has barely risen, Astaris just appearing on the horizon. I should get up. I should do something. But the bed is so soft. Softer than anything I've slept on since Krandor, and moving feels impossible.

The headache pulses again. I shut my eyes briefly.

*Mom is standing overhead, tucking a piece of hair behind my ear.*

*The door suddenly bursts open, blood spewing out across my room as Mom shatters into hundreds of pieces. Her eyes fade as she watches me, falling apart.*

I open my eyes. My breathing is ragged. Wooden beams. Gray-golden light. The sound of someone coughing in another room.

*Not there. Here. Milldraugh.*

I force myself to sit up slowly. The room tilts and sways, then steadies. My traveling bag sits in the corner where I left it last night. Milly will ask about breakfast—he always does.

The days are blurring together.

I swing my legs over the side of the bed. The floor is cold under my bare feet. Real. Solid.

Breathe. In. Out.

The headache doesn't leave, but it becomes something I can crawl around. I reach for my clothes. My fingers fumble with the buttons on my shirt. Once, twice—I get them wrong, I have to start over. The fabric feels strange, like it belongs to someone else. By the time I finish, my hands are shaking slightly.

I don't look in the small mirror on the wall.

The hallway is quiet when I step out. Most people are sleeping, or maybe already gone to work—I don't know what time it is anymore. Just that it's early. A bit too early, but staying in that room felt worse.

Downstairs, the common room is nearly empty. A few early risers sit at the tables with bowls of something steaming. The smell hits me first—porridge, maybe, and something sweeter underneath. Bread baking somewhere in the back.

I blink slowly, finding Milly's figure sitting at a corner table, already armored despite the hour. His sword leans against the wall beside him, and he's studying a piece of parchment—a map, maybe, or a letter. He looks up when I approach, his expression shifting from focus to something softer.

"Kitt."

I sit across from him without asking. The chair scrapes against the floor, too loud in the quiet room.

"How did you sleep?" he asks, though his eyes suggest he already knows the answer.

"Fine," I lie.

He doesn't call me out on it. Just nods once and folds the parchment away. "Breakfast?"

I'm not hungry. The headache makes the thought

of food feel wrong. But I nod anyway, because saying no means questions I don't want to answer.

He signals the innkeeper, and a few minutes later, there's a wooden bowl in front of me—porridge with honey drizzled on top, and a chunk of bread still warm enough that steam rises when I tear it open.

The bread is crunchy. A small smile appears on my face.

I take a bite, and just for a moment—just one small moment—something eases. The bread is fresh, the honey sweet, and it tastes like something other than travel rations and exhaustion.

"Good?" Milly asks, watching me calmly.

I nod, taking another bite. The headache is still there, the ache in my stomach still present, but the bread is real and warm and *good*.

"The baker here is skilled," Milly says, matter-of-fact. "Kanne, back in Krandor, mentioned you prefer the crunchy kind."

He remembered.

I eat slowly, letting the warmth settle. Outside the window, Milldraugh has already woken up, though still sleepy. Carts roll past, someone shouts about fish, sounds of hammers on metal reverberate from a nearby forge.

"We're staying another few days," Milly says after a while. "Rest. Resupply properly. The next leg to Vestperia is longer—we'll need to be prepared."

Not looking at me when he says it. Like he's deciding something he doesn't want to admit.

I nod again, not trusting my voice yet.

"Take your time today," he continues. "Explore if you want. Stay here if you need to. Just—" He pauses, choosing his words carefully. "Don't push yourself."

The soft kindness in his voice makes my throat tighten. I focus on the bread instead, tearing off another piece.

By the time I finish eating, the common room is filled with people. The noise rises—conversations in Unital I can't quite follow, laughter, the clatter of dishes. It's overwhelming, yet grounding at the same time.

"I think I'll go see Horsey," I say quietly.

Milly nods. "The stable is two streets over. I'll be here if you need me."

The stable smells of hay, leather, and something earthy I can't name. It's warm inside despite the morning chill, and the sound of horses shifting in their stalls creates a gentle rhythm that almost drowns out the headache still pulsing behind my eyes.

Horsey lifts her head when she sees me, ears perking forward. She nickers softly—a greeting, I think.

Recognition.

"Hey, girl," I murmur, running my hand down her neck. Her coat is soft, gray dapples catching the light from the stable's high windows. She leans into my touch, patient as always.

I grab a brush from the hook on the wall and start working through her mane. The repetitive motion is soothing. Stroke, stroke, stroke. Her ear flicks back, listening to me breathe.

There are other horses here. Five, maybe six in the stalls around us. A stablehand is working at the far end, pitching fresh hay. Normal sounds. Normal sights.

I glance over at the other horses. Three of them are tied to posts near the entrance—waiting to be saddled, probably. Their reins loop around the wood, keeping them in place.

My hand stills on Horsey's neck.

Three horses. Tied. Ropes pulling taut when they shift.

*Six horses. Six ropes. My wrists. My ankles. My neck. My—*

*They slap the horses. All at once. The ropes snap tight—pulling—each direction—my shoulders dislocating with wet pops, tendons screaming, skin splitting where the rope cuts through—*

*The horses pull harder. I feel my left arm tearing—not breaking, TEARING—muscle separating from bone, sinew snapping like wet rope, the socket giving way*

*with a sound like ripping fabric—*
*Blood everywhere. So much blood. Pouring from*
*where my limbs used to—*
*The horses keep pulling and I'm still ALIVE, still*
*feeling every—*
"Miss?"

I blink. The stablehand is standing a few pās away, holding a pitchfork, looking concerned. "You alright? You went pale."

I'm gripping Horsey's mane so hard my knuckles are white. She's shifted uncomfortably, sensing my tension.

"I'm fine," I manage, my voice thin. I force my fingers to release, one by one. "Just... tired."

He doesn't look convinced but nods anyway. "Let me know if you need anything."

I wait until he's gone before I let out the breath I was holding. My hands are shaking again. I press them against Horsey's warm side, trying to ground myself.

*Not real. Didn't happen. Just horses tied to posts.*
*Normal. Safe.*

My heart is still racing, and the image won't leave—ropes pulling, limbs tearing, the awful sound of—

"Stop," I whisper to myself. "Stop it."

Horsey turns her head, looking at me with one dark eye. Calm. Steady. Real.

I finish brushing her in silence, forcing my hands

to move, forcing myself to stay present. By the time I'm done, the shaking has mostly stopped, but the exhaustion has doubled.

When I step back outside, the sunlight feels too bright. I squint against it, trying to orient myself.

Two streets over. Back to the inn. Milly said he'd be there.

I walk slowly, keeping my eyes on the cobblestones. One foot in front of the other.

When I make it back to the inn, Milly is still at the corner table. The parchment is gone now, replaced by a half-empty mug. He looks up when I enter, and something in his expression shifts.

"Kitt."

I don't want to talk. Don't want to explain. I just shake my head slightly and move toward the stairs.

"Are you hurt?" His voice follows me, concerned but not demanding.

"No." The word comes out flat. "Just tired."

I don't wait for his response. The stairs creak under my feet as I climb to the second floor.

I'm passing Milly's door when I hear it—Milly's voice, muffled through his door. Talking to himself?

I pause.

*Flip. Flip.* Pages turning. Quick, impatient.

"—nineteen. The oath felt like..." A pause. More pages. "No, that's not right."

*Flip.*

"It felt like I'd found what I was supposed to do. Like everything before that moment had been..."

Pause.

"Ryn, Nessa, help..."

*Flip. Flip.*

Silence. Longer this time.

"Leading to it." His voice is flatter now. Frustrated. "That's stupid. She won't care about—"

*Thud.* Something closing. The book, probably.

A long exhale.

I keep walking before he hears me listening.

My room is exactly as I left it—unmade bed, traveling bag in the corner, small window showing Milldraugh's rooftops.

I close the door and sink onto the bed.

The image won't leave. Every time I close my eyes, I see the ropes. Feel the pulling. Hear the—

I open my eyes. Stare at the ceiling beams.

My stomach growls, reminding me I only had porridge and bread hours ago. But the thought of going back downstairs, sitting in that crowded common room, pretending I'm fine...

I stay in the room.

The light through the window shifts as the day passes. Morning becomes afternoon. The sounds of Milldraugh filter up—cart wheels, voices, hammering from some nearby smith. Normal sounds that feel distant, like they're happening to someone else.

At some point, I must have dozed off, because when I open my eyes again, the light is orange-gold. Late afternoon, almost evening. My mouth is dry, and the headache from this morning has returned, duller but persistent.

A knock at the door. Three beats, measured.

"Kitt?"

Milly's voice. I sit up slowly, my body stiff from lying in one position too long.

"Come in."

The door opens. He's removed his armor—just the padded underclothes now, which makes him look less like a paladin and more like... a person. Tired lines around his eyes. The scar on his forehead from the gorge more visible without his helmet.

He takes in the room—me on the bed, still in the same clothes from this morning, the untouched water pitcher on the table.

"You didn't come down for lunch," he says quietly.

"Wasn't hungry."

He doesn't argue. Just steps inside and closes the door behind him, leaning against the wall. "Something happened at the stable."

It's not a question.

I look away, focusing on the window. "I'm fine."

"Kitt."

The way he says my name—gentle but

firm—makes my throat tighten. I shake my head.

"I just... saw something. In my head. It wasn't real."

Silence. Then: "What did you see?"

I don't want to say it. Don't want to make it more real by speaking it aloud. But he's waiting, patient, and something about the quiet concern in his voice makes the words come anyway.

"Horses. Tied to posts. And my brain just... decided to show me what it would be like if I was tied to them. If they pulled."

The words sound clinical. Distant. Like I'm describing someone else's nightmare.

Milly is quiet for a long moment. When he speaks, his voice is lower. "Intrusive thoughts. Your mind is trying to process fear through... graphic imagery."

"You've had them too?"

"Yes."

Just that. No elaboration. But the weight in that single word tells me enough.

I pull my knees up to my chest, wrapping my arms around them. "Does it get better?"

"Sometimes." He pauses. "Sometimes it gets quieter. Less frequent. Sometimes it just... becomes something you learn to live with."

Not the reassurance I wanted, but honest.

He pushes off from the wall. "You should eat something. Even if it's just bread."

"I will."

He moves toward the door, then stops, and turns back. "Kitt, I think a walk might do you good. Tomorrow, meet me here."

Not a command. An offer.

I nod slowly. "Okay."

He leaves, the door closing softly behind him.

I sit in the darkening room for a few more minutes, then force myself to stand. Downstairs, the common room is busy with the dinner crowd, but I manage to get bread and cheese from the innkeeper without having to talk to anyone.

I eat in my room, watching the last of the daylight fade through the window.

Tomorrow. A walk. Fresh air.

# WARM LIGHTS

◆

### CHAPTER XX

I stare down at my choice—a simple plaid gray skirt and a black shirt. My gaze shifts to the small mirror, finally looking. Ready. A faint smile appears on my face as I smooth out a crease on my skirt.

Stepping out of the room, I make my way down the hallway. The inn's stairs creak softly under my feet as I descend, searching for Milly's figure below.

He's waiting near the door, no armor again—just the padded underclothes and a simple cloak draped over his shoulders. His sword is absent too, left upstairs probably. He looks... smaller without all the steel. More human.

"Kitt," he says when he sees me, something approving in his expression. "Ready?"

I nod.

The warm night air greets us when we step outside—not hot, just pleasantly warm, carrying the smell of cooking fires and bread from nearby homes.

---

But there's something else underneath: the particular sweetness of evening flowers opening, the dusty-dry smell of sun-baked stone releasing its heat, a hint of livestock from the stables. The air feels softer at night, less harsh than the daytime dust, almost gentle against my skin.

Milldraugh at dusk is different from Milldraugh in daylight—softer somehow, the harsh edges smoothed by shadow and lamplight.

Lanterns are being lit along the main street. A lamplighter moves from post to post with his long pole, touching flame to wick, leaving warm pools of light in his wake. The market stalls are closing—merchants packing away unsold goods, pulling canvas over their wares, calling goodbyes to neighbors.

We walk without a destination, just moving through the maze of streets. Milly keeps an easy pace beside me, hands clasped behind his back. Not watching for threats the way he usually does. Just... walking.

"Better today?" he asks after a while.

"A bit." It's true. The headache is gone. Though the exhaustion is still there, it's manageable. "Slept more."

He nods. "Sleep helps."

We pass a group of children playing some game with a ball and chalk marks on the cobblestones. Five of them, maybe six—mostly human, but I spot two with the rounded ears and swishing tails that mark them as

Felidae. One of the cat-children, a girl with brown-striped fur on her tail, is arguing passionately about the rules in Unital, her ears flicking back in frustration when the others don't listen.

Milly moves to the side to let them pass, then pauses, one hand against the wall.

"Just crowded," he says before I can ask.

Their laughter echoes off the close-packed buildings, completely unbothered by whether someone has a tail or not. One of the human boys nearly crashes into Milly, squeaks an apology, and darts away giggling. The Felidae girl chases after him, her tail streaming behind her like a banner.

The corner of Milly's mouth twitches. Almost a smile.

"You don't see many in Krandor," I say, watching them play.

"Felidae?" He glances at the children. "More common the closer you get to Celtor. Milldraugh's on the border—you'll see a few families here. Nothing like Celton, though. There they're everywhere."

We fall silent for a moment, watching them.

"Did you ever...?" I start, then stop. "Were you even a kid?"

"Once." He's quiet for a moment. "Sawyer and I used to play a game like that. With a ball made of rags and string. I always let him win."

"Sawyer?"

"My brother."

It's the first time he's mentioned his brother's name to me directly. I glance at him, but his expression hasn't changed—just watching the children play, something distant in his eyes.

"He was good at games," Milly continues softly. "Good at making people laugh. I was always too serious."

"You're still too serious," I say before I can stop myself.

He looks at me, eyebrows raised slightly. Then something shifts in his face—amusement, maybe. "Fair."

We keep walking. The streets narrow as we move away from the main market area. Smaller shops here, homes with laundry still hanging from windows. A cat watches us from a doorstep, amber eyes reflecting lamplight.

The smell of roasting meat grows stronger. We round a corner and find the source—a street vendor with a small cart, selling skewers of spiced lamb over a charcoal brazier. The vendor himself is human, but his assistant—a teenage Felidae boy with orange-and-white markings on his ears—is busy turning skewers, his tail swishing in rhythm with his work.

The boy's ears perk forward when he sees customers approaching, and he calls out in accented Common: "Fresh lamb! Still hot!"

Milly stops. "Hungry?"

He buys two skewers, hands me one. The meat is hot, almost too hot to hold, but I manage. The first bite is salty, spiced with something I can't name but tastes good. Really good.

We eat standing there, watching people pass. A couple arguing quietly in Unital—the woman's tail lashing in irritation, marking her as Felidae even in the dim light. An old woman carrying a basket of vegetables. A young man leading a donkey loaded with firewood.

"Thank you," I say quietly.

"For the food?"

"For this." I gesture vaguely at the street, the lanterns, everything. "For not... making me explain."

He chews thoughtfully, quiet for a moment. Then: "You don't owe me explanations, Kitt. You don't owe anyone your pain."

The words settle something in my chest. Not healing, exactly. Just... acknowledged.

We finish eating and keep walking. The streets loop back toward the inn eventually, but we take the long way. Past a small fountain where water trickles over stone. Past a tavern where music spills out—someone playing a fiddle, badly but enthusiastically. Past darkened shop windows reflecting our shapes as we pass.

Mün rises, round and white above the rooftops. Her light adds to the lanterns, making everything glow soft silver-gold.

"It's pretty," I say, surprising myself. When was the last time I called something pretty and meant it?

"It is," Milly agrees.

We walk in comfortable silence after that. My feet are tired by the time the inn comes into view, but it's the good kind of tired. The kind from doing something instead of just surviving.

At the door, Milly pauses. "Tomorrow?"

"Tomorrow what?"

"Another walk. If you want."

I think about it. The warm air, the lanterns, the taste of spiced lamb, the sound of children laughing. Small things. Normal things.

"Yes," I say. "I'd like that."

He pauses at my door, reaches into his pack. Pulls out a small book, leather-bound, well-worn.

"Here." He hands it to me. "For practicing. You won't always have me to ask."

I take it. The cover reads The Traveler's Guide to Essential Knots in faded lettering. When I flip it open, detailed diagrams fill every page—loops and crosses and step-by-step instructions.

"Thank you," I say quietly.

As he tucks his pack closed, I catch a glimpse of another book underneath—thicker, with gilt edges. The title is partially visible: A Guardian's Duty: Counsel and—

He shifts the pack, and it disappears from view.

He nods once, satisfied. "Good. Sleep well, Kitt."

"You too."

I climb the stairs to my room. The bed is still unmade from this morning, my traveling bag still in the corner. Everything the same as when I left.

But something feels lighter.

I get ready for bed, pulling on my sleeping clothes, and climb under the blanket. The window shows Mün hanging in the sky, stars appearing around her one by one.

Tomorrow. Another walk. Another attempt at normal.

But before sleep comes, my hand finds my bag. Pulls out the small carved horse—the one I bought in Byēnwick. I turn it over in my fingers, feeling the smooth wood, the carved mane. Rock it gently, hoof to hoof, like it's walking across the blanket. The repetition is soothing. Mindless. Safe.

I close my eyes.

For the first time in weeks, I fall asleep without seeing blood.

# CORRUPTED WELLS

◆

CHAPTER XXI

The warmth from last night's walk should have carried into today.

It doesn't.

I'm taking the alley shortcut to the stable when I hear it. A whisper. Faint. Barely there. Coming from somewhere low, somewhere dark.

An old stone well sits half-hidden behind stacked crates and overgrown weeds. No bucket, no rope. Just a crumbling rim and a wooden cover rotting from age.

The whisper comes again. Words I can't quite make out.

My heart picks up. Not again. Please not again.

But I step closer anyway. Lean over the rim. The darkness below is complete.

"Hello?"

Silence.

Then: "*Liberatem... liberatem...*"

A voice. Real. Definitely real.

I run.

"There's someone in the well," I say, bursting into the inn's common room.

Milly looks up from his maps. "What?"

"The old well. By the stable. Someone's down there."

His expression shifts—gentle but skeptical. The look he gave me after the stable incident. "Kitt, sometimes our minds—"

"I know what I heard."

He studies my face. Then folds the map.

"Show me."

The well looks worse in the afternoon light. Milly approaches it cautiously, one hand near his sword.

"You heard a voice from down there?"

"Yes."

He leans over the rim. "Hello? Anyone down there?"

Silence.

I grab my lantern—the one Milly insists I carry now—and hold it over the opening.

A shriek erupts from the depths. Raw. Panicked.

"THE LIGHT! THE BURNING LIGHT!" The voice cracks with pain. "Remove it, I beseech thee! REMOVE IT!"

I yank the lantern back. Milly's hand goes to his hip, grasping for the absent sword.

"Who are you?" he calls down.

The voice comes again, quavering but clearer. "I know not mine own name. 'Tis lost to me. The folk above call me the Corrupted Well." A pause. A wet, rattling breath. "I have dwelt here... so very long."

Milly and I exchange glances.

"How long?" he calls.

"The moons have turned many seasons. I cannot reckon how many. Time moves strangely in endless dark."

"Can you climb out?"

"Nay. I have not the strength. I am... much diminished."

Milly straightens. Runs a hand over his face.

"We need rope," he says.

It takes twenty minutes to find rope thick enough. Milly ties one end to a post, tests it with his weight, lowers it down.

"Can you reach it?"

"Aye... aye, I have it..."

The rope goes taut. Milly braces and pulls, hand over hand. I grab behind him, adding what strength I can.

Slowly, something rises from the darkness.

Hands first—pale, skeletal, gripping the rope. Then arms. Then a head.

The elf that emerges barely looks like a person.

His skin is corpse-white, almost translucent. His hair hangs in matted ropes past his shoulders. His clothes are rags. But his eyes are worst—huge, completely black, pupils dilated beyond the iris. They water constantly in the daylight, flinching from even indirect sun.

Milly hauls him over the rim. The elf collapses, gasping, trembling.

"Blessed light," he wheezes. "Blessed air... though it burns..."

"Who are you?" Milly asks. "How did you get down there?"

"I fell." He says it simply, like it's obvious. "I was fleeing... something. The memory is but fragments. I fell, and could not climb hence."

"An elf should be able to climb seven pās."

"An elf with strength. With will." The creature laughs—bitter, broken. "I had none of these. Only darkness. Water. Stone."

He pulls himself into a sitting position, trembling with effort. His black eyes find mine. Then Milly's.

"But I remember things," he says. His voice shifts—stronger, fevered. "From before. From the Old World."

"The Old World?"

"Before thy kingdoms. Before thy gods took their present forms." He leans forward. "I remember the Dread Colossus."

Milly goes very still. "The Slayer."

"Aye. Thy people's name for it." The elf's ruined face twists into something like reverence. "I have seen it. Not in legend. With mine own eyes. Before I fell."

"That's impossible. The Colossus hasn't been seen in—"

"Centuries? Longer?" The elf shakes his head. "It walks still. As it always has. Steel and sorrow, they called it. A fragment of Death itself."

I shouldn't interrupt. But I can't help it. "A fragment of Death?"

The elf's black eyes fix on me. "Aye, child. Sundered from the whole and cast down. Punished."

"Punished for what?"

"For mercy." His voice drops. "Or for cruelty

prolonged when swift end was commanded. The tales differ. But the punishment was most severe."

He's quiet for a moment. Gathering strength. Or gathering memory.

"I saw it on the battlefield. The silence it brings—not through magic, but through presence alone. The grinding of metal upon stone. Each footstep echoing in thy chest, thy very bones." His hands shake as he speaks. "It moves slowly. So slowly. And that slowness is mercy, giving its foes time to flee."

"But?" Milly prompts.

"But the sound." The elf shudders. "The sound of its blade scraping earth... that sound froze warriors where they stood. Those who did not flee..." He trails off.

"What happened to them?"

"The blade. One edge sharp, one edge jagged. And fire somehow bound to steel." He stares at nothing. "I saw the light of it against the night sky."

Silence. The afternoon sun feels too bright. Too warm.

"You said it appeared during the Founding Times," Milly says carefully.

"Aye. It guarded Queen Kitt Reelseda whilst she established her rule."

My breath catches.

Kitt Reelseda.

My name. My actual name.

"Some worship her as divine for this," the elf continues, not noticing my reaction. "If a fragment of Death itself served her, surely she was blessed? But the Colossus serves no one truly. It simply... appears. Where the helpless gather. Where the innocent suffer."

His voice takes on a strange cadence now—reciting, almost chanting.

"The Colossus kneels to nothing. It holds no vows, swears no oaths—that is its nature. Unbound. Unchained." He laughs, hollow and wet. "No chain could hold it. No prison could contain it. It bows to no throne, no god, no mortal power."

"Kitt?" Milly's voice. He's noticed me staring.

"That's my name," I say. My voice sounds far away. "Kitt. Same as the queen."

The elf blinks his black eyes. Studies me with new interest.

"A common name in Celtor," Milly says. "Probably just—"

"Is it?" The elf tilts his ruined head. "I wonder."

He doesn't elaborate. Just reaches into his tattered clothes, pulling something from an inner pocket.

A book. Or what was a book. The pages are swollen with water, the leather cover cracked.

"A grimoire. Ancient text." He offers it with shaking hands. "Spells and knowledge from the Old

World. Though I fear the water has rendered it useless."

Milly takes it carefully. The pages are stuck together. What little text is visible is in a script I don't recognize.

"Can I carry it?" I ask.

Milly looks at me, then shrugs. "It's ruined anyway."

I tuck it into my bag. It's heavier than it looks.

"Thank you," Milly says to the elf. "For the information. For the book."

"I have given thee all I possess." The elf's black eyes drift toward the well. "Knowledge and ruin."

He starts crawling back toward the rim.

"Wait—" I start.

"Nay." His voice is gentle. Final. "The world above is not for me. I have been below too long. The light burns. The air burns." He peers into the darkness. "The well is mine home now. Prison and sanctuary both."

Then he pauses. His black eyes find mine again.

"Child. Thou art traveling west, yes? Toward Celtor?"

I glance at Milly. He nods slightly.

"Yes," I say.

"Then heed me." The elf's voice drops—not reverent now, but warning. "If thy path takes thee through the Gut... be wary."

"The Gut?"

"A tunnel. Through the hills. The locals call it by cruder names—the Throat, the Innards." He shudders. "The stone there looks like flesh. 'Tis only mineral and light, but the eye sees what it fears."

Milly's hand moves toward his sword. "What's in the tunnel?"

"Something that is not the Colossus." The elf's black eyes are distant now, seeing something we can't. "Something older in a different way. Something that did kneel. Something that swore a vow... and broke it."

"What do you mean?"

"I told thee—the Colossus cannot kneel. It holds no oaths to break." His voice drops to barely a whisper. "But there are others who did. Who made promises to powers beyond mortal ken. And when those promises shattered..."

He trails off. His skeletal fingers grip the well's rim.

"The Kneeling Statue," he breathes. "Chained to its podium for five centuries. Condemned to kneel forever for its betrayal. They say it was an artpiece once—a symbol. But symbols have power, child. And that tunnel has drunk deep of death since the statue was placed within."

"What kind of death?"

"The kind that moves." His laugh is brittle, broken. "The kind that waits. The Celtorian lords blame bandits. Rockfalls. Beasts." He shakes his head. "But the bodies they find... when they find bodies at all... they are not killed by bandits."

Milly and I exchange glances.

"Why are you telling us this?" Milly asks.

The elf looks at me—really looks, those black eyes somehow piercing despite their ruin.

"Because she carries a queen's name," he says softly. "And queens should know what kneels in darkness. What broke its vows. What waits."

Before either of us can respond, he lowers himself back down. The darkness swallows him.

For a moment, we just stand there.

Then I start laughing.

I can't help it. It bubbles up from somewhere deep—not humor exactly, but something that needs release. The absurdity of it. An ancient elf who knows legends about gods and queens, who gives us a waterlogged book we can't read, warns us about flesh-tunnels and kneeling statues, and then just... climbs back into the well.

"He just—" I gasp. "He just went back down."

Milly's mouth twitches. Then he's laughing too—quiet, restrained, but real.

"A thousand years," I manage. "In a well. And we pull him out and he's like 'actually, I prefer the well.'"

We stand beside the Corrupted Well, laughing until my sides hurt. Until the absurdity releases its grip.

When we finally calm down, Milly's expression sobers slightly.

"The tunnel," he says. "The Gut. That's on our route."

"I know."

"We could go around. Add a few days."

I think about it. The elf's warning. The Kneeling Statue. Something that broke its vows.

But I also think about the Colossus—unbound, unchained, kneeling to nothing. And about a queen who shared my name.

"Let's decide tomorrow," I say.

He nods. Tucks the grimoire into his pack.

"Well," he says. "That was educational."

"Very educational. I learned that elves are idiots."

"Apparently."

We walk back toward the inn. The sun is warm. I can still hear the elf's voice in my head—*Queen Kitt Reelseda*—but I push it aside for now.

Tonight, another walk. Tomorrow, maybe we start thinking about leaving Milldraugh.

But right now, I'm smiling.

That feels like enough.

# PREPARATIONS

◆

### CHAPTER XXII

The name sits in my mind like a stone I can't swallow.

*Queen Kitt Reelseda.*

I wake on the fifth morning in Milldraugh with those words echoing. The elf's voice, rasping and ancient: *First Queen of Kurune. The Dread Colossus was her guardian during the Founding Wars.*

My name. The same name.

I try to remember what I learned about her in school. Not much—Krandor's teachers focused on Orenian history, not Celtorian legends. She was just a name in a list of foreign rulers. Founded the nation during some ancient war. Protected by... something.

Did my parents know? Did they name me after her deliberately, hoping I'd live up to some impossible standard? Or was it just a name they liked?

Dad used to talk about Kurune like it was a dream. Did he ever mention the founding queen? Did he ever think about the connection?

I'll never know now.

The thought sits heavy. I push it away, swing my legs out of bed. The floor is cold under my bare feet. Real. Solid.

Whatever the name means, I can't change it. I'm just Kitt. Not a queen. Not a legend. Just a girl barely holding herself together.

Downstairs, Milly is at his usual corner table, supplies laid out in neat rows. Rope, rations, bandages, oil for his sword.

"We should leave in two days," he says without preamble. "The journey to the coast is long."

Two days. Relief mixed with something else. Reluctance, maybe. Milldraugh has been good.

"Okay," I say quietly.

He returns to his inventory. Every movement practiced, certain. There's comfort in watching him work.

"Milly?"

"Yes?"

"Thank you. For letting me rest here."

Something softens in his expression. "You needed it, Kitt. We both did."

◆ ◆

The next day, we move through Milldraugh's market together.

It's busier than usual—market day. Vegetables in wooden crates, dried fish on lines, bolts of cloth in blues and greens. The noise hits first—vendors calling prices, customers haggling, children laughing somewhere in the chaos.

I navigate the streets with confidence now. I know which alley leads to the stable. Which vendor has the best bread. Where the fountain is.

Milly notices. "You've learned the city well."

"It's not that big," I say, but there's pride in my voice.

We stop at stalls. Dried meat, hard cheese, oats for the horses. At an oil merchant's, Milly haggles in formal Unital until the merchant throws up his hands.

"Fine, fine. Three Dōnis. But you're robbing me, sir knight."

While Milly finishes, I wander to a woman selling carved figures. I pick up a tiny horse—gray wood, smooth under my thumb.

"Pretty, yes?" she says in broken Common. "Seven Dōnis."

I hand over the coins, tuck the carving into my

pocket. Horsey might like a friend.

When I rejoin Milly, he raises an eyebrow at the bulge in my pocket but doesn't ask.

At the stable, the stablehand looks up from mucking stalls.

"The pale girl," he says. Not unkindly. "Come to say goodbye?"

"How did you—"

"Word travels." He leans on his pitchfork. "You look better than when you first came. Less haunted."

The word hits harder than it should.

"Everyone's haunted by something, miss. You just wore it louder."

I move to Horsey's stall. She lifts her head, ears perking forward. That familiar nicker.

I brush her coat, check her hooves. The motion is automatic now. When I show her the carved horse, she sniffs it once, unimpressed.

"It's supposed to be you," I tell her.

She snorts.

I glance toward the entrance. The posts where horses are tied. This is where the worst intrusive thought hit me—the ropes, the pulling, the tearing.

Nothing. No flash of violence. No image forcing

itself into my mind.

Just posts. Just horses. Just a stable.

I let out a long breath.

"You okay?" the stablehand calls.

"Yeah," I say. And I mean it. "I'm okay."

◆　◆

That evening, we walk again.

It's become routine—expected, comfortable. The same streets, the same lanterns being lit. But it feels different knowing it's the last time.

We stop at the same food vendor. He recognizes us, grins.

"The usual?"

Two skewers of spiced lamb, still hot. We eat standing there, watching Milldraugh's evening life. A woman singing to her baby. Two old men arguing over dice. The lamplighter making his rounds.

"I'll miss this," I say quietly.

Milly glances at me. "The food?"

"The walking. The quiet."

He's silent for a moment. Then: "We can walk other places."

"It won't be the same."

"No," he agrees. "It won't."

I want to say more. Want to tell him these walks have been the first good thing since Mom died. Want to thank him for not making me explain every breakdown. Want to tell him I'm scared to leave because what if I fall apart again?

The words stick. Instead, I just keep walking beside him.

Mün rises above the rooftops, full and bright. Her light mixes with the lanterns, turning everything silver-gold.

I try to memorize it. The wet cobblestones. The smell of bread and smoke. Milly's steady breathing beside me.

Tomorrow we leave. Tonight, we walk.

When we return to the inn, Milly pauses at my door.

"Get rest. Long day tomorrow."

"You too."

He turns toward his room. I watch him go.

"Milly?"

He stops.

I want to say thank you. Want to say this mattered. Want to say I'm scared and grateful and don't know how to be either properly.

"Sleep well," I say instead.

Something crosses his face—understanding, maybe. "You too, Kitt."

I close the door and lean against it. My packed bag sits in the corner. Everything I own in one canvas sack.

This room watched me break down and put myself back together. These walls heard me cry. Saw me sleep without nightmares.

I walk to the window. Milldraugh one last time—the rooftops, the distant market, the lanterns still glowing. This place wasn't supposed to mean anything. Just a stop on the way to somewhere else.

But it gave me something. Time. Space. Warm lights to walk through when everything felt dark.

I climb into bed. The mattress dips in the middle the way it always does.

Tomorrow I leave. Tomorrow the road opens again. Tomorrow I have to be brave.

But tonight, I'm here. Resting.

I close my eyes.

For the first time since Krandor, I fall asleep without fear.

# ORDER BRINGS CHAOS, CHAOS BRINGS ORDER

◆

## LEAVING, AGAIN

### CHAPTER XXIII

Morning comes too quickly.

I wake before dawn, the room still dark except for the faint gray glow at the window. For a moment, I just lie there, listening to Milldraugh waking up below—footsteps on the street, a cart rattling past, someone calling out a greeting in Unital.

Last time I'll hear these sounds.

I dress slowly, running my hands over the simple clothes—the plaid gray skirt, the black shirt. The same ones I wore for our walks. They feel familiar now, comfortable. Mine.

I check the room one last time. Nothing left behind. Just the bed I slept in, rumpled blanket still warm from my body heat. The window that showed me Milldraugh's rooftops every morning. The small mirror I finally started looking into again, seeing a girl who looked a little less broken each day.

I touch the windowsill briefly—goodbye, I think,

though I don't say it aloud.

Downstairs, the innkeeper is already awake, sweeping the common room floor. He looks up when I descend, nodding once.

"Early riser," he says in accented Common. "The paladin is outside with the horses."

I nod back, then pause. "Thank you. For... everything."

His expression softens slightly. "You are welcome here anytime, miss. Should you return."

I won't return. We both know it. But the kindness in the offer makes my throat tight anyway.

Milly is settling the bill when I step outside. The morning air is cool, carrying the smell of bread from a nearby bakery and smoke from morning fires. The streets are mostly empty—just a few early workers heading to their shops, a woman drawing water from the fountain.

"For the hospitality," Milly says, adding extra coins to what the innkeeper asks for.

The innkeeper counts them, then looks up at Milly. "Safe roads, sir knight." His gaze shifts to me. "And you, miss. May the Goddess watch over you both."

The blessing catches me off guard. I mumble something that might be thanks.

Outside, the horses are already saddled and waiting. Horsey nickers when she sees me—that familiar greeting that means finally, you're here. I run my hand down her neck one last time before mounting, feeling the smooth warmth of her coat, the solidness of her.

"Ready?" Milly asks, already settled on his horse with that easy confidence he always has.

I look back one more time.

The inn, with its weathered sign swinging slightly in the morning breeze. The lantern posts lining the street, dark now but soon to be lit again for other travelers, other people walking through warm light. The fountain in the distance, water trickling over stone. The rooftops I watched from my window, turning gold in evening sun.

Milldraugh gave me something I didn't know I needed. Time. Space. A place to remember what normal felt like.

"Yes," I say, turning Horsey toward the road. "I'm ready."

We ride out through the unmarked edges of town—no gates, no guards, no ceremony. Just the road widening beneath us and the buildings thinning until we're in open country again. I don't look back a second time.

The road ahead is packed dirt, hard from years of

travel and weather. It winds between rocky hills, following the natural contours of the land. On either side, farmland stretches—neat rows of crops, stone walls marking property lines, the occasional farmhouse with smoke rising from its chimney.

But as the morning wears on, the farmland gives way. The fields become smaller, more scattered. The walls crumble into piles of loose stone. Scrub brush replaces cultivated crops—tough, wiry plants that don't need tending. Boulders dot the landscape, some as tall as houses, casting long shadows in the morning sun.

The road becomes rougher too. More stones, more ruts from cart wheels. Fewer people maintaining it this far from town.

Horsey's gait is steady beneath me, her rhythm familiar after weeks of riding. My body has adapted—the soreness from those first days is gone, replaced by a kind of easy competence. I barely think about the reins anymore, about my posture, about moving with her stride. It just happens.

Milly rides slightly ahead, as always. Not far—just enough that he's leading, watching the road, assessing. His hand rests near his sword hilt, casual but ready.

We see fewer travelers now. Just the occasional merchant cart heading toward Milldraugh, loaded with goods. A farmer leading a donkey carrying firewood. They nod as we pass, some calling out greetings, others just watching us with that careful wariness people have for armed strangers.

The sun climbs higher. The air warms, though not uncomfortably. A breeze picks up, carrying the smell of dry grass and dust and something sharper—pine, maybe, from distant forests.

My stomach growls around midmorning. Milly must hear it because he glances back, the corner of his mouth twitching.

"We'll stop soon," he says.

We find a spot off the road—a flat rock big enough for both of us to sit, shaded by a scraggly tree. I dismount, legs slightly stiff, and stretch while Milly unpacks dried meat and cheese.

We eat in silence, watching the road. A bird circles overhead—some kind of hawk, maybe. Its cry is sharp and lonely.

"How far to the tunnel?" I ask.

"Few more hours. We'll reach it by late afternoon."

I chew slowly, thinking about the old man's warning from the day before. Things in that tunnel. Old things.

"What do you think we'll find in the tunnel?" I ask.

Milly takes a drink from his water skin before answering. "Could be anything. Bandits. Wild animals. Structural problems." He pauses. "Or nothing. People tell stories about dark places. Makes them feel less afraid if they can name what's lurking."

"But you don't think it's nothing."

He looks at me, his expression serious. "I think we should be careful. But we've been careful this whole journey, Kitt. The tunnel is just another obstacle. We go through, we come out the other side, we keep moving."

Simple. Practical. The way Milly sees everything.

But my stomach still twists with unease.

We finish eating and mount again. The road stretches ahead, winding through increasingly wild terrain. The trees here are different—twisted, stunted things clinging to rocky soil. The grass is yellower, drier. Fewer signs of human presence.

The landscape feels older here. Untouched. Like we're riding backwards through time, away from civilization and toward something more primitive.

I try to distract myself by thinking about other things. About Milldraugh. About the evening walks. About the carved wooden horse in my saddlebag that I bought for Horsey.

About Queen Kitt Reelseda.

The name still sits heavy in my mind. I wonder if the real queen felt this lost when she was fifteen. If she knew she was going to found a nation, or if it just... happened. If destiny chose her or if she chose it.

I'm not choosing anything. I'm just following

Milly because I don't know what else to do.

The sun continues its arc. My shadow shortens, then begins to lengthen again as afternoon wears on.

We make camp early that evening.

Not because we're tired. Not because the light is failing. But because we round a hill and find them, and Milly stops his horse without explanation.

Three figures. Stone. Larger than life.

They stand at the crest of the next rise, silhouetted against the sky. Even from a distance, I can see they're facing east—toward where Astaris will rise in the morning.

"Who are they?" I ask.

"Heroes," Milly says simply. "From the Founding Wars."

We ride closer. The figures resolve into detail.

The center one is human—a woman, I think, though the stone is weathered enough to make it hard to tell. She wears armor, not the squared-off style of Orenia's soldiers, but something older, simpler. Her hand rests on a sword hilt. Her face looks... tired. Not the proud, noble expression you'd expect. Just tired. Like she's been standing watch for a very long time.

To her right, an elf. Taller, more slender, pointed ears just visible beneath a carved hood. One hand raised, palm out—a gesture of blessing or maybe farewell.

To her left, a dwarf. Stockier, beard carved in

intricate braids. Holding an axe loosely, like he's set it down mid-swing and never picked it back up.

All three face the sunrise. Waiting for something that happened centuries ago.

The base is covered in offerings. Not fresh—these are old. Flowers dried to brittle brown, coins turned green with age, small carved tokens scattered in the grass. Someone tends this place, but not recently.

Milly dismounts. I follow.

Up close, the stone is beautiful. Not perfect—there are cracks, places where weather has worn the details soft—but beautiful. Someone carved this with love. With grief, maybe. With something that needed to be remembered.

"Who were they?" I ask again.

Milly's quiet for a moment, studying the human figure's face. "The Watcher. That's what the stories call her. She held a pass during the Founding Wars—kept Orenian forces from pushing into what would become Celtor. Her companions stayed with her even when retreat was called. All three died on the third day."

"They lost?"

"They held." He touches the stone—just briefly, fingers against the warrior's boot. "Long enough for reinforcements to arrive. Long enough for the war to turn. They lost their lives. But they held."

The elf's carved face is serene. The dwarf's is

fierce. The woman's is just... present. Not smiling, not scowling. Just there.

"Why face the sunrise?" I ask.

"Orenian forces came from the east." Milly steps back, looking at all three. "They're still watching. Still holding the line."

Something about that makes my throat tight. They've been standing here for centuries. Stone doesn't get tired. Doesn't falter. Doesn't quit.

The flowers at their feet are old, but someone placed them. Someone remembered. Someone cared enough to climb this hill and leave an offering for people who died before their grandparents were born.

Milly and I set up camp in their shadow. As the sun sets behind us, I watch the last light catch on the stone—the woman's sword, the elf's raised palm, the dwarf's axe. For just a moment, they almost look alive. Like they might lower their hands, turn their heads, speak.

Then the light fades, and they're stone again. Just stone.

But I can't stop looking at them.

"Milly?" I say into the darkness.

"Mm?"

"Do you think they knew? That they'd be remembered like this?"

He's quiet for a long time. "I don't think they had time to think about it. When you're holding the line, you're just... holding."

I fall asleep watching their silhouettes against the stars. Three figures. Still watching. Still holding.

In the morning, before we leave, I pick a handful of wildflowers from the grass—small purple things, nothing special. I add them to the offerings at the base.

The stone doesn't react. Doesn't acknowledge. Doesn't care.

But I feel better anyway.

We ride on. The statue fades behind us. But I keep thinking about it. About three people who decided something mattered more than living. Who stood and held and died and somehow that was enough.

Enough to be remembered. Enough to be honored. Enough to watch the sunrise for a thousand years.

By late afternoon, we encounter the old man.

He's leading a mule loaded with sacks—grain, maybe, or flour. His clothes are dusty, his face weathered and creased with age. When he sees us approaching, he stops, waiting in the middle of the road.

"Heading toward Gut Tunnel?" he asks in Common, his accent thick and rural.

Milly nods. "We are."

The old man's expression sours immediately, his mouth pulling into a deep frown that carves new lines around his lips. "Don't go through at night. And stay on the path." He leans forward slightly, lowering his voice like he's sharing a secret. "There's... things in that tunnel. Old things. Things that don't like light, don't like noise. Things that have been there since before my grandfather's grandfather."

His eyes are rheumy but intense, boring into us with the weight of someone who's seen something he can't unsee.

"What kind of things?" I ask before I can stop myself.

He shakes his head slowly. "Don't rightly know. Never went in myself. But I've heard the stories. Travelers who went through at dusk and never came out the other side. Screams echoing in the dark. Shadows that move wrong." He spits into the dust. "Old magic, maybe. Or old curses. Either way, not natural."

Milly's jaw tightens slightly. "We'll be careful."

The old man looks at us both—taking in Milly's armor, his sword, then me. His gaze lingers on my face, and something like pity crosses his expression.

"Careful don't always help, sir knight. But I'll pray to the Goddess for you both anyway." He tugs on his mule's lead. "Safe roads. Or as safe as they can be."

He walks past us, continuing toward Milldraugh, muttering something under his breath that sounds like a prayer.

I glance at Milly. "Things?"

"Probably just stories," he says. But his hand rests

on his sword hilt, and he doesn't sound convinced.
We ride on in heavier silence.

By late afternoon, we see it.

The Gut Tunnel.

It appears on the horizon first as just a dark smudge against the hillside. As we get closer, it resolves into shape—an enormous opening carved into living rock, easily thirty pās high and just as wide. The entrance is framed by worked stone, ancient beyond measure, the edges worn smooth by countless centuries of wind and rain.

Markings cover the archway. Not writing exactly—or if it is writing, it's in no language I've ever seen. Spirals and geometric patterns, lines that intersect at strange angles, symbols that hurt to look at too long. Some of them are so weathered they're barely visible. Others seem fresher, like they've been re-carved over and over through the ages.

The tunnel itself cuts straight through the hillside, a dark mouth swallowing the road whole. I can't see the other end—just darkness, absolute and complete, like staring into a void.

Even from a distance, it feels wrong.

The air around it is too still. No birds sing near the entrance. No insects buzz. The scrub brush grows right up to the edge of the worked stone and then stops abruptly, like even the plants know better than to get closer.

The silence is oppressive. Not peaceful—empty. Like sound itself is afraid to exist here.

My skin prickles. Every instinct I have screams turn around, go back, don't go in there.

Horsey feels it too. She slows without me asking, her ears flicking back nervously. She doesn't want to approach.

"We're not going through tonight," Milly says, pulling his horse to a stop about a hundred pās from the entrance. His voice is tight, controlled. "We'll camp here, go through at first light."

Relief washes over me so strongly I feel lightheaded. I hadn't realized how tense I'd become, how hard I'd been gripping Horsey's reins.

"Why not now?" I ask, though I don't want to go in now either. "There's still a few hours of daylight."

"Because," Milly says, his eyes fixed on the tunnel entrance, "I don't want to be caught inside when the sun sets."

The way he says it—matter-of-fact but final—sends a chill down my spine.

We make camp in a small clearing off the road, within sight of the tunnel entrance but not too close.

Maybe fifty pās away. Close enough to watch it. Far enough to feel... slightly safer.

Milly sets up both tents with quick efficiency, his movements practiced and sure. But I notice he positions them so the openings face away from the tunnel. So we don't have to look at it while we sleep.

I tend to the horses, brushing them down, checking their legs and hooves. Horsey keeps glancing toward the tunnel, ears swiveling nervously. I don't blame her.

"I know," I murmur, running my hand down her neck. "I don't like it either."

The evening passes in tense quiet. We eat dried rations—the same meat and cheese from lunch, some hard bread. Milly builds no fire.

"Why no fire?" I ask.

He's silent for a moment, staring at the tunnel entrance in the fading light. "Because I don't know what's in there. And I'd rather not advertise our presence if something comes out."

Something comes out.

The words settle in my stomach like stones.

The sky darkens gradually, the sun sinking behind the hills to our west. The tunnel entrance becomes a pool of absolute blackness, darker than the surrounding dusk. Somehow, looking at it feels like looking at nothing—a hole in the world.

Stars appear one by one overhead. Mün begins her rise, round and pale.

I sit near my tent, knees pulled to my chest, unable to stop staring at the tunnel. From here, it's just a void. No light penetrates that darkness. Not even moonlight seems willing to touch it.

"Something wrong?" Milly asks from his own tent.

"It feels wrong," I say. "The tunnel."

"I know." He's checking his sword again—the third time since we made camp. Running the whetstone along the blade with slow, deliberate strokes. The sound is rhythmic, almost meditative. *Scrape. Scrape. Scrape.* "We'll be through it by midday tomorrow. Then it's just open road to the coast."

He's trying to sound reassuring. It doesn't work.

"What if the old man was right?" I ask quietly.

"Then we'll deal with it." He tests the blade's edge with his thumb, nodding in satisfaction. "We've dealt with everything else so far."

"We almost died in Kanna's Ridge."

"Almost." He slides the sword back into its sheath. "But we didn't."

I nod, but I can't shake the feeling sitting heavy in my chest. The weight of dread that's been building since we first saw the tunnel on the horizon.

That night, I lie in my tent staring at the canvas above me. Sleep doesn't come easily.

Every time I close my eyes, I see that dark entrance. Waiting. Patient. Inevitable.

# GUT TUNNEL

◆

### CHAPTER XXIV

I wake to gray dawn light and the weight of dread in my chest.

Milly has already risen and begun packing the tents with swift, silent efficiency. He doesn't speak. Doesn't need to. We both know what today means.

I force myself through the motions—rolling my bedding, checking Horsey's saddle, eating a few bites of dried meat that tastes like ash in my mouth. The tunnel looms in my peripheral vision, that dark mouth waiting. Patient.

"Ready?" Milly asks when everything is packed.

I'm not. Yet I nod anyway.

We mount. Horsey shifts nervously beneath me, ears swiveling toward the tunnel entrance and then away, like she can't decide whether to look or not. I don't blame her.

The morning is cold. Quiet. No birds sing. No insects buzz. Just our horses' hooves on packed dirt as we approach the entrance, and even those sounds feel too loud, too intrusive.

The tunnel swallows us whole.

One moment, gray morning light. The next, darkness so complete it feels solid, pressing against my eyes.

Milly's lantern flares to life with a sharp click, casting a weak circle of yellow light that barely pushes back the black. The flame gutters, struggling, like even fire doesn't want to exist here.

"Stay close," he says, his voice flat and controlled. "Don't wander. Don't touch anything."

I nod, though I'm not sure he can see me. Horsey presses close to his horse's flank, seeking comfort in proximity. Smart girl.

The entrance disappears behind us within seconds—just gone, swallowed by the dark. When I glance back, there's nothing. No light. No opening. Just void.

The road continues beneath us, packed dirt worn smooth by centuries of traffic. But everything else is stone. Carved stone, ancient beyond measure. the walls rising thirty pās on either side before disappearing into shadow above.

Our hoofbeats echo strangely. Not the clean echo of empty space, but something muffled and wet, like the sound is being absorbed by something soft.

The markings from the entrance continue along the walls here—those spiraling symbols that hurt to look at, geometric patterns that suggest meaning without revealing it. Some glow faintly in the lantern light, a sickly phosphorescent green that makes my stomach turn.

"What are those?" I whisper.

"Don't know. Don't care." Milly's hand rests on his sword hilt. "Just keep moving."

The air is wrong. Too thick, too moist, clinging to my skin like invisible film. It tastes like salt and copper and something underneath I can't name—something old and organic and rotten. Every breath feels heavy, like inhaling through wet cloth.

We ride in silence, the only sounds our horses' hooves and our breathing. Even those seem too loud, intrusive, like we're disturbing something that should be left undisturbed.

The tunnel doesn't curve. Doesn't branch. Just continues straight, endless, swallowing us deeper.

And then the walls begin to change.

At first, I think it's just the stone changing texture. The carved surface becomes rougher, more uneven. Less like worked stone and more like... something else.

Then the color shifts.

The gray stone fades to a pale pink. Not painted—the stone itself is pink, banded with streaks of white running through it like-

Like fat.

Like the marbling through raw meat.

My breath catches.

"Milly," I whisper.

"I see it." His voice is tight. "Keep moving."

But I can't look away. The pink deepens in places, becoming fleshy and organic. Dark red veins branch through it—actual veins, translucent when the lantern light hits them, glowing faintly like they're still carrying something wet and alive.

This isn't stone. Or it is, but it looks exactly like the inside of a body.

The white streaks. The pink tissue. The red veins branching and splitting like capillaries.

I've seen this before.

*Mom's kitchen. Her stomach opened. The wet pink of her insides spilling—*

I press my hand over my mouth, swallowing hard against the bile rising in my throat.

"Kitt." Milly's voice cuts through. Sharp. "Eyes forward. Breathe."

I force myself to look at the road instead. At Horsey's ears. At Milly's back. Anywhere but the walls.

But I can still see them in my peripheral vision. Still smell the salt and copper and decay. Still feel the wrongness of being surrounded by something that looks so much like flesh.

The texture changes too. The surface isn't smooth anymore—it's fibrous, striated, with ridges running vertically along the walls like ribs. Like we're inside something's chest cavity.

Gut Tunnel.

We're inside something. Something massive. Something that died or was killed or is sleeping, and we're walking through its preserved remains.

Salt crystals coat everything now, white and crystalline, crusting over the pink stone like preservative. Like someone—something—wanted to keep this from rotting. Wanted to keep it exactly as it was.

The air is so thick I can barely breathe. Every inhale tastes like brine and old blood.

Horsey's breathing is labored too, her sides heaving. She wants out. We all want out.

"How much longer?" My voice shakes.

"Not far now." But Milly sounds uncertain. Like he's never been through here before. Like he's guessing.

The walls close in slightly. Not much—just enough to feel claustrophobic. Like the tunnel is tightening. Like something is squeezing.

And then, ahead in the darkness beyond our lantern's reach, I see light.

Not sunlight. Something else. A faint glow, greenish and wrong.

"Do you see that?" I whisper.

Milly raises the lantern higher. The glow becomes clearer—phosphorescent, emanating from the walls themselves where those spiral symbols are carved deeper, more intricate.

We're approaching something. The center of the tunnel. The deepest part.

The glow illuminates a widening in the path ahead—a chamber carved into the flesh-stone, circular and vast. And in the center—

A statue.

Kneeling.

Chained.

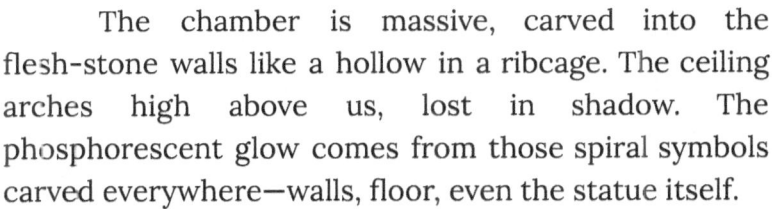

The chamber is massive, carved into the flesh-stone walls like a hollow in a ribcage. The ceiling arches high above us, lost in shadow. The phosphorescent glow comes from those spiral symbols carved everywhere—walls, floor, even the statue itself.

And the statue.

It kneels in the center of the chamber on a raised stone podium, head bowed, arms hanging at its sides. Eight pās tall, even kneeling. Made of two different stones—dark andesite for the body, white marble veining through it like scars or cracks in armor.

The detail is incredible. Every piece of armor is rendered perfectly—breastplate, pauldrons, gauntlets, greaves. Squared-off, old-fashioned design, the kind you'd see in history books about wars from generations past. The helmet covers the face completely, blank and expressionless.

At its hip, there's a sling for a sword. Empty.

Heavy chains wrap around it—thick iron links crusted with rust and salt. They bind its arms to its sides, loop across its chest, anchor it to the podium beneath. The chains are old, ancient, the metal pitted and corroded.

"What is this?" I whisper.

Milly dismounts slowly, one hand on his sword. "Art. A monument. I don't know." His voice is tight. "And I don't care. We're leaving. Now."

But I can't look away.

There's something about it. The way it kneels—not in defeat, but in waiting. Patient. Like it's been here for centuries and will wait centuries more.

"Why is it chained?" I ask, sliding off Horsey's back.

"Kitt. Get back on your horse."

I step closer, drawn despite myself. The statue doesn't move, doesn't react. Just kneels, silent and still.

"It's just art," I say, more to myself than him. "Why would you chain art? It should be free. That's the whole point, isn't it?"

"Kitt." Milly's voice cuts like steel. "Do *not* touch anything. We go straight through this chamber and out the other side. Do you understand me?"

But I'm already reaching for the chains.

They're cold under my fingers. The rust flakes off, reddish-brown dust coating my skin. The metal is corroded, weakened by age and salt and whatever else has been eating at it for who knows how long.

"The chains are wrong," I say. "Art shouldn't be imprisoned—"

"KITT. NO."

But my hands are already working at the first link, finding where it's weakest, where the corrosion has eaten through most of the iron. It's not hard. Just a little pressure, a little twisting, and—

SNAP.

The chain breaks.

Then another. And another.

They fall away, clattering against the stone floor with sharp metallic echoes that ring through the chamber.

"What have you—" Milly starts, his voice raw with anger and fear.

The statue's head turns.

Slowly. Deliberately. The blank helmet facing us now instead of the floor.

And then it stands.

# GUTTURAL SCREAMS

### CHAPTER XXV

The statue stands.

Not quickly. Not violently. Just... rises. Eight pās of stone and ancient armor unfolding from its kneeling position with the slow inevitability of a nightmare.

The sound is wrong. Stone grinding against stone, but wet somehow. Organic. Like joints cracking after centuries of stillness.

Its head stays fixed on us. That blank helmet, empty and patient.

Then it takes a step.

One foot forward. Slow. Deliberate. The podium cracks under its weight.

"Run." Milly's voice is tight. "Kitt, RUN—"

I try. My legs don't respond right. They're heavy, too heavy, like I'm moving through water. My lungs burn with each breath, the air thick and chemical-sharp, coating my throat.

"I can't—" My voice comes out strangled. "Milly, I

can't move—"

This isn't how I wanted it.

The thought cuts through the panic, sharp and unwelcome. I've thought about dying. Dreamed about it. The quiet end, the release, the *choosing* of it.

This isn't that. This is stone fingers reaching for my chest. This is a thing that doesn't care what I want.

I don't want THIS.

He's struggling too. His hand reaches for his sword, movements sluggish and wrong.

The statue takes another step. Closer. Patient.

The air around it shimmers slightly, like heat haze. And that smell—copper and salt and something acrid that makes my eyes water. Chemical. The corrosion. It's coming off the statue in invisible waves, paralyzing us.

My hand closes on Milly's sword hilt before he can draw it. The weight is enormous, far heavier than I expected, but I yank it free anyway with clumsy, numb fingers.

"Kitt, NO—"

I hurl it at the statue with everything I have.

The blade spins through the air, catches lantern light, and—

Passes straight through.

The statue doesn't even react. The sword just goes through its chest like the stone is made of smoke and clatters on the ground between us—maybe six pās ahead, right in the statue's path.

The statue keeps walking.

Now we have no weapon. And it wouldn't matter anyway.

"You—" Milly's voice cracks. "It's not solid. It's not—" He can't finish. Can't breathe right.

I try to back away. My legs barely respond. One step. Two. So slow. Too slow.

The statue is faster. Not running. Just walking. But we're paralyzed and it's not, and the distance closes anyway.

Ten pās.

Eight.

Six.

I can see the detail now. The way the marble veins through the andesite like cracks. The empty sword sling at its hip. The helmet's blank surface, smooth and featureless.

"Milly—" My voice is barely a whisper.

He grabs my arm, tries to pull me back, but his grip is weak. We're both moving like we're drowning, limbs useless and heavy.

The statue reaches for us.

Its hand—massive, stone gauntlet—extends toward Milly's chest. And as it moves, the stone becomes translucent. Ghostly. I can see through its fingers to the chamber wall behind.

It's dematerializing.

It's going to walk into him.

"No—NO—" I try to scream but my throat won't work right.

Milly raises the lantern.

Not deliberately. Not with understanding. Just pure instinct—holding light between himself and the threat, trying to see it better, trying to—

The lantern's beam hits the statue's reaching hand.

The translucent fingers solidify instantly. Become stone again. Real. Solid.

But only the hand.

The rest of the arm, the shoulder, the body—still ghostly. Still moving.

The solidified hand drops like dead weight, heavy and useless. The statue's other arm—still translucent—reaches across its own chest, ghostly fingers closing around its frozen wrist.

And it drags the solid hand forward.

"Goddess—" Milly's voice breaks. "It's still coming—"

The statue advances. Slower now, uneven, hauling its own petrified limb like a broken wing. But still coming. Still patient. The sound is horrible—stone scraping against stone as the solid hand drags across the floor.

"The light doesn't stop it," I gasp. "It just slows

it—"

"Back—BACK—" Milly shuffles backward, the lantern shaking in his grip. "Kitt, the sword—grab the sword—"

The greatsword. Between us and the advancing statue.

I force myself forward those few agonizing steps, every movement a battle. My numb fingers close on the hilt. Too heavy. I can barely lift it, just drag it backward across the stone.

The statue takes another lurching step, closer. Four pās now.

I stumble back, the sword scraping behind me. Milly takes it with his free hand, nearly dropping the lantern in the process.

"Keep the light on it—different parts—" His voice is raw. "Slow it down—"

He swings the lantern beam lower. The light catches the statue's advancing leg.

The leg solidifies mid-step. Becomes immovable stone.

The statue's momentum carries forward but the frozen leg doesn't. It pitches slightly, off-balance. The other leg—still ghostly—has to compensate, dragging the petrified limb.

But it doesn't fall. Doesn't stop. Just adjusts. Adapts.

Uses its translucent arm to brace against the frozen one. Uses its free leg to haul the solid one forward.

*Scrape. Drag. Scrape.*

Three pās away now.

"It's learning—" I choke out. "Milly, it's—"

"MOVE—"

We back away faster, but the paralysis is getting worse, not better. The chemical smell is overwhelming. My vision swims.

Milly keeps the light moving—hitting the statue's chest, its arm, its head. Each part that solidifies becomes dead weight. But each time, it just... works around it. Drags its frozen parts with its ghostly ones.

Slower. But never stopping.

Two pās.

Its free hand reaches out—still translucent, unaffected by the light beam. Those ghostly fingers extend toward my face.

"KITT—"

Milly yanks me backward so hard I nearly fall. The lantern swings wild. For just an instant, the beam leaves the statue completely.

The statue moves.

Not the slow drag of hauling petrified limbs. Just—closer. Five pās forward in the space between heartbeats, like it skipped the distance.

All its limbs translucent again. Free.

The beam snaps back. Catches its torso.

The chest solidifies. The statue's advance stops dead, its ghostly arms suddenly supporting a stone torso that weighs hundreds of pounds.

"Keep moving—don't let the light drop—" Milly gasps.

We're at the chamber's edge now. The horses shift nervously in the darkness beyond the lantern's reach. Horsey's eyes roll white, foam forming at her mouth.

Five steps back.

Ten.

The statue drags itself forward. One translucent arm pulling, then the other. The solid torso scraping across stone with a sound like grinding teeth. Relentless.

"The horses—" I can barely speak. "We have to—"

"I know—"

Milly backs into his horse, never letting the light leave the statue. He loops his reins around one arm, sword in the other hand, lantern gripped white-knuckled.

"When I mount," he says, voice hoarse, "keep talking. I need to know where it is."

"What—"

"DO IT—"

He swings up one-handed, the lantern dipping

for just a second.

The statue lurches forward. Six pās. Eight.

"IT'S COMING—" I scream.

The light snaps back up. Catches its helmet.

The head solidifies. The whole top-heavy weight of it becomes stone, and the ghostly neck can barely support it. The statue's movements turn jerky, uncoordinated, its head lolling like something broken.

But it still comes.

"MOUNT—NOW—" Milly shouts.

Milly's horse is already moving. He's ahead of me. If I don't mount fast enough—

He'll wait for me. He's that kind of person. He'll wait and the statue will catch him and it will be my fault.

Or I could scream for him to go. Tell him to leave me. And he'd hesitate, and I could use that hesitation to—

No. Mount. NOW.

I grab Horsey's reins. Try to pull myself up. Can't. My arms won't work. Legs won't lift.

The statue is ten pās away. Nine.

"KITT—"

I try again. Get one foot in the stirrup. Haul with everything I have left. Nearly fall. Try again.

Eight pās.

I'm up. Barely. Slumped in the saddle, gasping.

"GO—" Milly spurs his horse.

The lantern swings wildly as he rides. The beam

leaves the statue.

I see it in that instant—all its parts translucent again, free, moving with sudden terrible speed.

Then we're galloping.

Hooves pounding stone. The chamber falls away behind us. The flesh-stone tunnel walls blur past in a nightmare of pink and red and white.

Behind us, I hear it.

*Scrape. Scrape. Scrape.*

Heavy footsteps. Not the dragging anymore. Just walking. Fast as a horse can trot.

"IT'S FOLLOWING—"

"DON'T LOOK BACK—"

But I do. Can't help it.

The darkness behind us. The glow from those spiral symbols. And in that faint phosphorescent light—

A silhouette. Eight pās tall. Arms swinging. Walking with mechanical precision.

Getting closer.

"MILLY—"

"I SEE IT—"

He raises the lantern behind us, twisting in his saddle. The beam lances back down the tunnel.

I see the statue freeze mid-step—its leading leg solidifying, throwing it off balance. It stumbles. Catches itself with ghostly hands.

"Keep riding—" Milly's voice cracks. "Just keep—"

The beam swings forward again as his horse jolts over rough ground. We plunge back into darkness.

Behind us, the footsteps resume.

Faster now.

The tunnel seems endless. The flesh-stone walls press close, ribbed and organic and wrong. My lungs burn with the thick air.

Then—light. Real light. Gray and distant but real.

"THE EXIT—" I sob.

"ALMOST—"

Fifty pās. The daylight grows brighter. The walls transition from pink flesh-stone back to gray carved stone. The air changes.

Thirty pās.

The footsteps behind us stop.

Complete silence except for our horses' labored breathing and pounding hooves.

"Why—" I gasp.

"DON'T QUESTION—JUST GO—"

Twenty pās.

Ten.

The circle of daylight expands. Sky. Grass. Clean air.

We burst through.

Morning sun hits like salvation. I gasp, filling my lungs with air that doesn't taste like death. Horsey doesn't stop running until we're a hundred pās from the entrance.

Then she finally slows, sides heaving, legs shaking.

I nearly fall off. My whole body is trembling. When I dismount, my legs give out completely. I collapse onto the grass.

Milly slides down more controlled but just as desperate. He turns immediately, sword raised, lantern still gripped in his other hand.

The tunnel entrance is empty. Just dark stone. Just a hole in the hillside.

Nothing emerges.

We wait, gasping, shaking.

Nothing.

"It stopped," I whisper. "Why did it—"

"The stories," Milly says, voice hoarse. "It returns to its podium. After everyone escapes or dies."

I stare at the dark entrance. Imagining that thing walking back through the tunnel. Through the flesh-stone. Back to its chamber. Kneeling on its podium.

Waiting.

For the next person stupid enough to unchain it.

My fault.

The words burn in my throat.

"I'm sorry," I whisper. "Milly, I'm so—"

"Not now." His voice is flat. Dead.

"But—"

"I said NOT NOW."

I nod. Close my mouth.

The apology sits wrong in my throat anyway. Not because I don't mean it—I do, I think—but because part of me is still calculating. Still thinking: *if he'd fallen behind, would I have stopped?*

I know the answer.

I don't like knowing it. But I know.

He won't look at me. Won't even turn in my direction. Just stares at the tunnel entrance, sword still raised, like he's waiting for it to come through anyway.

After a long moment, he lowers the blade. Sheaths it. His hands are shaking.

"We need to move," he says. Voice empty. "Put distance between us and this place."

He mounts his horse again. Movements stiff, mechanical.

I watch him start riding away from the tunnel.

Then I force myself back onto Horsey. Every muscle screaming.

We ride in silence.

The weight of what I've done sits in my chest like a stone I can't swallow.

Behind us, the Gut Tunnel waits.

Patient.

Ready for the next traveler.

# CANNOT MAKE YOU

### CHAPTER XXVI

Astaris is setting, Solis already gone beneath the horizon. Our horses walk slowly, hooves falling in a rhythmic pattern. Horsey is clearly affected, too, by what we've seen together.

Milly remains about three horse-lengths in front of me, dead silent. Every time I try to move Horsey closer so I can talk to Milly, her ears flatten in something akin to fear.

The landscape rolls past—rocky hills giving way to flatter terrain, scrub brush becoming sparse grass. Signs we're leaving Drūn behind, entering Celtor proper. I don't really see any of it.

All I see is the statue's blank helmet turning toward us. The chains falling. Milly's voice: "KITT, NO—"

My fault. Again.

The gorge was my fault—I yelled when he said be quiet. The statue was my fault—I unchained it when he said don't touch.

I keep doing this. Keep ignoring him. Keep almost getting us killed.

Why can't I just *listen*?

Milly's back is rigid. His shoulders tight, his hand resting near his sword hilt even now. Always ready. Always careful.

Everything I'm not.

My throat is dry. I reach down to Horsey's side, grabbing the water skin from the pouch. The leather is warm from the sun, the water inside barely refreshing when I drink. It tastes like dust and old leather and guilt.

I want to say something. Anything. *I'm sorry. I didn't mean to. I'll do better.*

But the words stick. What's the point? I've already proven I won't do better. The gorge should have taught me. It didn't.

Hours pass like this. Astaris disappears completely, leaving only Mün's pale light and the first stars. The air cools. My legs ache from riding, my back stiff, but I don't complain.

Complaining feels like asking for something I don't deserve.

Finally, as full darkness settles, Milly pulls off the road into a small clearing. Trees on three sides, open space for the horses. He dismounts without a word.

"Make camp," he says.

Those are the first words he's spoken since we left the tunnel. His voice is flat. Empty. Like I'm a stranger he's obligated to travel with, not someone he's spent weeks protecting.

I slide off Horsey, my legs nearly buckling. Everything hurts—muscles, bones, the weight in my chest that won't go away.

Milly moves with mechanical efficiency. Unsaddling his horse, checking its legs, brushing it down. Every movement practiced, controlled. He doesn't look at me.

I tend to Horsey with shaking hands. The routine helps—brush, check hooves, make sure she's okay. She nuzzles my shoulder once, gently, and I have to swallow hard against the tightness in my throat.

At least she doesn't hate me.

Milly sets up his tent. Then mine. I try to help with the second one but he's already done before I can move. He's moving on autopilot—practiced motions that don't require thought. Good, because he doesn't seem to have any to spare. He builds a small fire—just enough for light and warmth, nothing extravagant.

We eat in silence. Dried meat, hard cheese, stale bread. I can barely taste any of it. Every bite feels like swallowing stones.

The fire crackles between us. Milly sits on the opposite side, staring into the flames. His face is shadowed, unreadable.

I can't take it anymore.

"Milly—"

"Not now, Kitt."

"Please. I need to—I have to say—"

"I know what you're going to say." His voice is quiet. Too quiet. "You're sorry. You didn't mean for it to happen. You didn't think—"

"I didn't," I whisper. "I just thought it was wrong. Art shouldn't be chained, and I—"

"And you didn't listen." He finally looks at me. His eyes catch the firelight, and I see something in them I haven't seen before. Not anger. Exhaustion. "I told you not to touch anything. Explicitly. Clearly. And you did it anyway."

"I'm sorry—"

"I know you are." He picks up a stick, pokes at the fire. Sparks drift up into the dark. "That's not the issue."

I wait, throat tight.

"The gorge," he says slowly. "I warned you. Stay quiet. And you didn't. We nearly died."

"I know—"

"The statue. I warned you. Don't touch it. And you didn't listen. We nearly died."

He sets the stick down. His hands are steady, but I can see the tension in his shoulders, the way his jaw works.

"I can teach you to ride," he continues, voice still that same terrible calm. "I can teach you to set up camp, to tie knots, to survive on the road. I can warn you of danger. I can put myself between you and threats. I can do everything in my power to keep you safe."

He pauses. Looks directly at me.

"But I cannot make you choose safety, Kitt. I cannot make you listen when it matters. I cannot force you to value your own life enough to follow simple instructions that might save it."

The words land like stones in my chest.

"You want to be saved," he says quietly. "But you keep sabotaging the saving. And I don't know how to help someone who won't be helped."

"I'm trying—"

"Are you?" Not cruel. Just tired. "Because from where I'm sitting, you keep making the same choice. Impulse over caution. Curiosity over safety. Your judgment over mine, even when you don't know what you're doing."

I open my mouth. Close it. No words come.

"I'm not angry," Milly says, and somehow that's worse than if he were shouting. "I'm disappointed. And I'm afraid. Because next time—and there will be a next time, Kitt—I might not be able to pull you back. The light might not work. The escape might not be there. And I will have to watch you die because you wouldn't listen."

He stands, brushing dirt from his pants.

"I've lost someone like you before," he says

quietly. "Someone who thought they knew better. Someone who was reckless and brave and didn't listen when it mattered." His voice catches, just slightly. "I can't do it again. I won't survive it again."

He looks at me one more time.

"We leave at dawn. Get some rest."

Then he walks to his tent and disappears inside.

I sit by the fire alone, his words echoing.

*I cannot make you choose safety.*

*I cannot make you listen.*

*I cannot make you.*

The fire burns down to embers. I don't move. Just sit there with the weight of what I've broken, what I keep breaking, settling into my bones.

Eventually, I crawl into my tent. Lie on my bedroll. Stare at the canvas above.

Sleep doesn't come.

Just the endless loop of his voice, calm and tired and final:

*I cannot make you.*

# ACCUMULATION

◆

### CHAPTER XXVII

Morning comes gray and cold.

I wake before Milly, which almost never happens. I lie in my tent listening to his steady breathing from across the camp, trying to work up the courage to face another day of silence.

When I finally emerge, he's already packing his tent with mechanical efficiency. He glances at me once—brief, assessing—then returns to work.

"Good morning," I try. My voice comes out small.

"Morning." Flat. Not unkind, just... empty.

I move to pack my own tent. My hands shake as I fold the canvas. Is this the right way? I can't remember. I redo it. Then redo it again. The third time, it looks... maybe right?

I check the ties. Double-check. Are they secure enough? Too tight? I loosen one, then tighten it again.

"Kitt?" Milly's voice. "We need to leave soon."

"Right. Yes. Sorry." I fumble faster, making it

worse. The canvas slips. I have to start over.

When I finally finish, Milly's already loaded everything onto his horse. Waiting.

I move to Horsey. Brush her down—stroke, stroke, stroke. Normal. Familiar. But my hands won't stop shaking.

Saddle next. I lift it, position it on her back. Check the placement. Is it too far forward? I shift it. Too far back now? Shift again.

The straps. I thread them through, pull tight. Check the tension. Not tight enough? I pull harder. Horsey shifts uncomfortably. Too tight now?

"Is the saddle—" I start, looking over at Milly. "Can you check if—"

"It's fine, Kitt."

"But I can't tell if it's too—"

"It's fine."

I nod. Swallow hard. Check the straps again anyway. They look right. I think they look right.

Saddlebags next. I arrange our supplies, trying to balance the weight evenly. Too heavy on this side? I shift things. Now the other side feels heavier. Shift again.

"Kitt." Milly's mounted now. "We're leaving."

"Right. Yes. Just—" I secure the bag. Open it to check everything's inside. Close it. Open it again because I can't remember if I checked the water skins.

"Kitt."

"Sorry. I'm ready."

I mount Horsey. Miss the stirrup on my first try because my legs are shaking. Second try, I'm up. Settle into the saddle.

We start riding. I stay exactly three horse-lengths back, counting Horsey's steps to maintain the distance. One, two, three, four. Not closer. Not farther. Exactly where I'm supposed to be.

The morning stretches on. The road continues—flatter now, more packed. My hands ache from gripping the reins too tight. I force myself to loosen them. Too loose now? I tighten again.

Around midmorning, I realize I need to adjust my seat in the saddle. But should I? Will it spook Horsey? What if I do it wrong and fall?

I don't adjust. Just sit in increasing discomfort, back starting to ache.

Around noon, Milly pulls off the road into a shaded area. "We'll rest here. Water the horses."

I dismount, legs stiff. Lead Horsey toward a tree at the clearing's edge. Reach for the rope to tie her.

My hands freeze on the rope. Which knot? The one Milly taught me first, or the better one from the book? What if I use the wrong one and she pulls free? What if she gets tangled?

I start with a simple loop. Stop. That's not secure enough. Start over with a different knot. My fingers fumble the rope. Start again.

"Kitt?" Milly's already finished with his horse. "What are you doing?"

"Tying her. I just—I can't remember which knot—"

"Any knot that holds will work."

"But what if it's not right? What if—"

He walks over, gently takes the rope from my shaking hands, and ties a simple, clean knot. Three seconds. Done.

"There," he says quietly. "See? Any tree. Any knot. It doesn't have to be perfect."

I nod, throat tight. Feel like crying over a fucking knot.

We sit in the shade. He eats. I pull out my own rations but my stomach is twisted too tight. I make myself eat anyway. One bite. Chew. Swallow. It tastes like dust.

After a few minutes of silence, Milly sets down his food.

"What are you doing?" His voice is careful. Controlled.

"Eating?" I venture.

"No. This." He gestures at me. "This... freezing. This asking permission for everything. The triple-checking. The—" He stops, visibly controlling frustration. "You're terrified to move."

I stare at my hands. "I'm trying to listen. Like you

said."

"This isn't listening." His voice softens, but there's exhaustion underneath. "This is paralysis."

The word sits in my chest like a stone.

"I don't—" My voice cracks. "I don't know what you want from me."

"I want you to think for yourself. To trust your own judgment." He picks up his water skin, takes a long drink. "But you've swung from ignoring every warning to questioning every breath. Neither of those works, Kitt."

"I'm trying—"

"I know." He cuts me off, not unkindly. "But I can't make every decision for you. And you can't keep asking me to."

Silence stretches. A bird calls somewhere in the trees above us. Normal. Peaceful. Wrong.

"We should keep moving," he says finally, standing. "We need to make the next town by nightfall."

I nod. Force myself to stand. My legs feel weak.

Back to the horses. Milly mounts smoothly. I approach Horsey, reach for her reins.

And freeze.

The leather strap in my hand. Brown. Worn smooth from use.

Just like the reins in the carriage. Before Kanna's Ridge. Before we fell. Before—

My breath catches.

The rope. The leather. Connected to—

*The chains. Heavy iron. Wrapped around the statue's arms. The way they felt under my fingers, cold and corroded—*

"Kitt?" Milly's voice sounds far away. "You coming?"

I blink. Look down. My hands are shaking. The reins feel wrong. Everything feels wrong.

"Yes. Sorry. I—"

I mount Horsey. The saddle creaks.

That sound. Like stone grinding. Like—

The statue rising. The wet scrape of joints moving after centuries of stillness.

My hands tighten on the reins. Too tight. Horsey shifts nervously beneath me.

"Easy," I whisper. To her or to myself, I don't know.

We start riding.

One step. Two. Three. The rhythm should be soothing. Familiar.

Instead, every hoofbeat sounds like footsteps. Heavy. Patient. Following.

*Scrape. Scrape. Scrape.*

I look back. Nothing there. Just the empty road behind us.

But I can still hear it.

We ride for maybe an hour. Maybe less. Time feels strange, elastic.

The hoofbeats won't stop sounding like footsteps.

I try to focus on other things. The road. The trees. Milly's back ahead of me. Normal things. Safe things.

But the rhythm keeps pulling me back.

*Scrape. Scrape. Scrape.*

"It's just Horsey," I whisper to myself. "Just her hooves. That's all."

Except now I'm hearing it behind us too. Like something's following. Something patient.

I glance back again. Still nothing.

My chest feels tight. Breathing is getting harder.

"Stop it," I mutter. "Stop. It's not real. It's not—"

A branch snaps somewhere in the trees to our left.

My whole body locks up. Horsey feels it, tosses her head nervously.

Just a branch. Just an animal. Normal forest sounds.

But my brain supplies the image anyway—the statue, eight pās tall, blank helmet turning toward the sound. Walking between the trees. Stone scraping bark.

"No," I whisper. "No, it's not here. It's back in the tunnel. It went back to its podium."

My hands are shaking so badly the reins slip. I grab them tighter. The leather digs into my palms.

Leather. Rope. Chains.

The chains falling. The metallic clatter echoing through that flesh-stone chamber.

My breathing speeds up. In, in, in, can't get enough air.

"Milly?" My voice comes out thin. Strangled.

He doesn't hear. Or doesn't respond. Just keeps riding ahead.

Three horse-lengths. Always three horse-lengths.

Too far. He's too far. What if the statue comes and he's too far to—

The statue's hand reaching. Ghostly fingers extending toward Milly's chest. About to walk into him. About to materialize inside—

"No—" I choke out.

Horsey stops. I don't remember pulling the reins but she's stopped, ears back, sensing something wrong.

Milly's still riding. Getting farther. Disappearing around a curve in the road.

"Milly—" I try to call out but my throat won't work right.

The trees are too close. The shadows too dark. Anything could be in there. Watching. Waiting.

The statue in the darkness. Walking. Always walking.

I need to get off. I need to—I can't breathe up here. Too high. Too exposed.

I slide off Horsey, hit the ground hard. My legs don't hold. I collapse to my knees on the packed dirt.

Can't breathe. Can't breathe. Can't—

The tunnel. The flesh-stone walls. Pink and white and red. Like the inside of a body. Like Mom's kitchen. Like—

Mom on the floor. Blood spreading. Her eyes watching me. Empty. Fading.

"Mom—"

No. Not Mom. That was—when was that? Days ago? Weeks?

The boat. Dad's boat. Blood everywhere. His entrails collapsing in my hands like overripe fruit. The open slit of his stomach. His dimming eyes finding mine.

"Dad—"

No, that was a dream. That was just a nightmare. He died years ago. I wasn't there. I wasn't—

But I was there for Mom. I was there and I just stood there. Couldn't move. Couldn't help. Just watched her die.

Just like I watched the statue stand. Watched it reach for Milly. Almost watched him die because I unchained it. Because I never listen. Because I—

"I'm sorry—" I'm sobbing now, can't stop. "I'm sorry, I'm sorry—"

The horses. Six horses tied to posts. Six ropes. My wrists, my ankles, my neck. They slap the horses and the ropes go taut and I'm pulled apart, limbs tearing, tendons snapping, still alive, still feeling—

I press my hands over my face. Make it stop. Make it stop.

But it won't stop.

The gorge. Falling. The horse crushed. Blood everywhere. Always blood. Always dying. Always my fault.

"Kitt?"

Milly's voice. Distant. Distorted.

"Kitt, where—"

Footsteps. Running. Coming closer.

The statue. Stone footsteps. Heavy. Patient. It found me. It's coming to finish—

"No—" I try to crawl backward. Away. My hands hit something—a rock, a root, I don't know. "Stay away—"

"Kitt, it's me. It's Milly."

Milly. The statue reached for Milly. I watched it reach. Watched those ghostly fingers extend toward his chest. One second from materializing inside him. One second from—

"I'm sorry—" I can't breathe. Hyperventilating. Vision going dark at the edges. "I'm sorry, I almost—you almost died—"

"Kitt." Hands on my shoulders. Gentle. Firm. "You're not in the tunnel. You're here. On the road. With me."

He crouches in front of me, and I see it clearly now—the exhaustion around his eyes, the way he's bracing himself on one knee like kneeling took effort.

But which Milly? The real one? Or the one with his guts spilling out like Dad? Or the one turning translucent as the statue walks through him?

"Look at me."

I can't. If I look, I'll see—

"Kitt. Eyes on me. Now."

I force my eyes open. Blink through tears.

Milly kneels in front of me. Real. Solid. Not bleeding. Not ghostly. Just Milly, looking at me with something between concern and recognition.

"There you are," he says quietly. "Stay with me. Don't go back there."

But I'm already going back. Can't stop it.

Mom's eyes. Empty. Watching.

Dad's blood. Warm on my hands.

The statue's blank helmet. Turning.

The flesh-stone walls. Pink tissue. White fat. Red veins.

The chains. Always the chains.

"I can't—" My voice breaks. "I can't hold it. I can't—it's all coming—"

"I know." His voice stays steady. Anchor. "Let it come. I'm here."

And it does come. All of it. Everything I've been

holding back since Krandor. Since Mom. Since before Mom.

I sob so hard I can't breathe. My whole body shakes. Milly's hands stay on my shoulders, grounding me, while everything else falls apart.

Minutes pass. Or hours. I don't know.

Eventually, the sobs quiet to ragged breathing. The images fade to gray static.

I'm on my knees in the dirt. Milly's still there, kneeling in front of me. Waiting.

"I'm sorry," I whisper. My throat is raw. "I'm sorry, I didn't mean to—I don't know why—"

"It's alright."

"It's not—I'm falling apart—I can't control it—"

"Kitt." He waits until I look at him. "You're not falling apart. You've been holding too much for too long. This isn't weakness. This is what happens when you can't hold it anymore."

I shake my head. Can't accept that. "You must think I'm—"

"I think you're traumatized," he says simply. "I think you've watched your mother die, nearly died yourself twice, saw things in that tunnel that would break most people. And I think you've been trying to just... keep moving. Keep functioning. Without processing any of it."

He sits back slightly. "That doesn't work, Kitt. Eventually, it comes out anyway."

"I'm sorry," I say again. Seems to be all I can say.

"Stop apologizing for breaking down." His voice is gentle but firm. "You're allowed to break. You're human." The words hit something in my chest. Release something.

I'm allowed to break.

I start crying again, but quieter this time. Exhausted tears, not panicked ones.

Milly doesn't move. Doesn't tell me to pull myself together. Just sits there in the dirt beside me while I fall apart.

After a long while, I manage to speak. "I don't know how to do this."

"Do what?"

"Keep going. Keep... existing. When everything hurts and I can't stop seeing—" My voice breaks. "I don't know how to keep going when I keep destroying everything I touch."

Silence.

Then: "You're not destroying everything, Kitt. You're just... wounded. And wounded things lash out. Make mistakes. That doesn't make you worthless."

"I almost got you killed."

"You did," he agrees. No sugar-coating. "Twice. And that's not okay. But it's also not the whole story."

He shifts, settling more comfortably on the ground like we might be here a while.

"You're fifteen years old. You watched your mother take her own life. You fled your home with nothing. You've been on the road for—what, two months? Three? You've nearly died multiple times. You're dealing with trauma that would hospitalize most adults."

He pauses.

"And despite all of that, you're still here. Still trying. Still getting up every morning and riding even when you're terrified. That's not nothing, Kitt."

"It doesn't feel like enough."

"It never does." Something in his voice suggests personal experience. "But it's what we have."

I wipe my face with shaking hands. Look at him properly for the first time since the breakdown started.

He looks tired. Not angry. Not disappointed. Just... tired. And maybe sad.

"I can't keep doing this," I whisper. "I can't keep making the same mistakes. I can't—"

"I know." He cuts me off gently. "Neither can I."

The words hang between us.

"So what do we do?" I ask.

He's quiet for a long moment. Then: "We get you help. Real help. Dr. Verne in Vestperia—that's why I wrote to him. For you."

I blink. "You... what?"

"I wrote to him weeks ago. From Milldraugh." Milly looks away, jaw tight. "I knew you needed more than I could give. I'm not a healer, Kitt. I'm just... someone trying not to watch another person I care about destroy themselves."

Another person I care about.

The words settle into my chest. Heavy and warm at once.

"You care about me?" My voice is small.

He looks back at me. Something in his expression softens. "Of course I do. You think I'd put up with all this if I didn't?"

A broken laugh escapes me. Not quite humor. Just... release.

"I thought you hated me. After the statue."

"I don't hate you." He sounds almost offended. "I'm furious with you. I'm terrified for you. I'm exhausted by you. But I don't hate you."

He stands, offers his hand.

"Come on. We need to get moving. But—" He pauses. "No more asking permission for every breath. And no more charging ahead without thinking. Somewhere in between, alright?"

I take his hand. Let him pull me up. My legs are shaky but they hold.

"Somewhere in between," I echo.

"That's all I'm asking."

We walk back to the horses. Horsey's waiting patiently, reins trailing. I pick them up with still-trembling hands.

"Kitt?"

I look up.

"If it gets bad again—if you feel it coming—you tell me. Before it breaks you. Understand?"

I nod.

"Say it."

"I'll tell you."

"Good."

We ride for maybe an hour after that. The silence is different now—not angry, not tense. Just... heavy. Processing.

My eyes are swollen from crying. Everything aches. But the storm has passed, leaving behind something quieter. Emptier.

Milly stays closer now. Two horse-lengths instead of three. Checking back more often.

I should feel relieved. He doesn't hate me. He wrote to Dr. Verne. He cares.

But all I feel is the weight of what I've done. What I keep doing.

I'm furious with you. I'm terrified for you. I'm exhausted by you.

The words loop in my head. True words. Honest words.

I'm exhausting him.

The sun starts to sink toward the horizon. The road continues, endless. In the distance, I can see smoke rising—chimneys from a town. Civilization.

Somewhere Milly could leave me.

Somewhere he'd be safer without me.

The thought crystallizes slowly, taking shape as we ride.

He's bound by oath. He can't abandon me on the road. But if I left voluntarily—if I chose to separate—then it's not breaking his oath. It's respecting my choice.

He'd be free. Free of watching me nearly kill him. Free of my constant mistakes. Free of the exhaustion.

Another person I care about destroy themselves.

That's what I'm doing. Destroying myself. And dragging him down with me.

The town grows closer. I can see buildings now, not just smoke. A proper settlement, bigger than a waystation. Big enough to have an inn. Maybe work available. Somewhere I could stay while he continues to Vestperia.

My chest tightens. Not panic this time. Decision.

"Milly?" My voice comes out rougher than I expect.

"Yes?"

"That town ahead. We're stopping there?"

"For the night, yes."

"Good." I swallow hard. "That's... good."

He glances back, something questioning in his

look, but doesn't push.

We enter the town as dusk settles. It's called Brēvast, according to the marker stone. Midsize for Celtor—cobbled streets, two-story buildings, the smell of evening meals cooking. Normal. Safe.

Milly finds an inn. The Sleeping Bear, the sign reads. He handles the arrangements while I tend to the horses at the stable out back.

Horsey nuzzles my shoulder as I brush her down. Patient as ever.

"You'll be okay," I whisper to her. "He'll take good care of you."

Her ear flicks toward me. Listening.

I finish with her care, giving myself time. Thinking through the words. How to say it without him arguing. Without his oath compelling him to refuse.

When I come back inside, Milly's at a corner table with two bowls of stew and bread. Real food, hot and fresh. He gestures me over.

I sit. Pick up the spoon. The stew smells good—meat and vegetables, rich broth. My stomach reminds me I barely ate today.

We eat in silence for a while. The inn's common room is busy but not crowded. Other travelers, local workers ending their day. Normal people living normal lives.

"Kitt?" Milly's watching me. "You're very quiet."

"Just tired."

"Understandably." He tears off a piece of bread. "We'll rest here tomorrow. No traveling. You need it."

My throat tightens. Tomorrow. He's planning for tomorrow. For us continuing together.

"Milly, I need to—" I set down my spoon. "I need to tell you something."

His expression shifts. Wary. "Alright."

I take a breath. Force the words out.

"I think you should continue to Vestperia without me."

Silence. He sets down his bread slowly.

"I'm not abandoning you, Kitt."

"I'm not asking you to." I keep my voice steady. "I'm saying I should stay here. This town. Find work, maybe. Wait for you to send word from Dr. Verne about whether he can help, and then—"

"No."

"You don't understand—"

"I understand perfectly." His voice is controlled but firm. "You're trying to leave because you think you're too much trouble. Too exhausting. Too dangerous."

I flinch at the accuracy.

"You're right," I say quietly. "I am those things. And you said it yourself—you can't keep doing this. So let me make it easier. Let me—"

"Easier?" He leans forward slightly. "You think

leaving you alone in a strange town while I continue on would be easier?"

"For you, yes—"

"For me, it would be abandoning a traumatized fifteen-year-old girl in a place where she knows no one, has no support, and will likely spiral completely. That's not easier, Kitt. That's me failing another—" He stops himself. Takes a breath. "That's me failing you."

"You haven't failed—"

"I won't let you do this." His voice is harder now. "My oath binds me to help you reach Vestperia safely. Your request for aid was accepted. I cannot—will not—leave you behind because you've decided you're not worth the trouble."

"It's not about worth—"

"Then what is it about?" He's not yelling, but there's intensity in his voice now. "Because from where I'm sitting, you just had a complete breakdown, finally started actually processing what you've been through, and now you want to run away again. Except this time you're running from me instead of with me."

The words hit like a physical blow.

"That's not—" I start, then stop. Is that what I'm doing? Running again?

"I'm trying to protect you," I say weakly.

"From what? Yourself?" He sits back. "Kitt, separating won't protect me. It'll just mean you're self-destructing without anyone there to pull you back."

"Maybe I deserve to self-destruct."

"Don't." His voice goes cold. "Don't talk like that."

Silence falls between us. The inn's noise continues around us—conversations, laughter, the clink of dishes. Normal sounds of normal people.

We're not normal.

"I'm exhausting you," I whisper finally. "You said so."

"Yes," he agrees. "You are. And I'm probably exhausting you too. That's what traveling together means. That's what caring about someone means."

He leans forward again, making sure I'm looking at him.

"You made a mistake at the statue. A big one. And yes, I'm furious about it. But that doesn't mean I want you gone, Kitt. It means I want you to do better. To heal. To get help."

"What if I can't?"

"Then we deal with that when it happens. But you don't get to make that decision preemptively." His voice softens slightly. "I've already lost someone because I couldn't reach them in time. I won't lose you because you decided you weren't worth saving."

Sawyer. The name hangs unspoken between us.

"I'm not like him," I say quietly.

"No," Milly agrees. "You're not. You're here. You're trying. And despite everything, you're still standing."

He picks up his spoon again, returns to his stew like the conversation's settled.

"We leave the day after tomorrow," he says, matter-of-fact. "Rest day tomorrow. Then we continue to the coast. Together. Understood?"

I stare at my bowl. The stew's getting cold.

"Understood?" he repeats, firmer.

"...Understood."

"Good." He nods once. "Now eat. You barely had anything today."

I pick up my spoon. Force myself to eat, even though my throat feels tight.

He's not letting me go. Not letting me run. Not letting me separate.

I don't know if that makes me feel relieved or trapped.

Maybe both.

We finish eating in silence. When Milly stands to head upstairs to our rooms, I follow.

At my door, he pauses.

"Kitt?"

I look up.

"If you try to leave in the night, I will find you and drag you back. My oath is absolute. You asked for aid, and I will see you safely to Vestperia. Whether you think you deserve it or not."

His voice isn't cruel. Just certain. Final.

"I won't try to leave," I say quietly.

He studies my face for a long moment. Then nods.

"Good. Sleep well."

He turns toward his door. Pauses, staring at me as if he's thinking about something. His hand on the handle.

"Kitt."

I look up.

"Come with me."

———————◆——◆———————

The hill isn't far. Maybe a quarter-kāl outside the town walls, rising gently above the farmland. Milly doesn't explain why we're here. Just walks, and I follow.

My legs ache from riding. My eyes are swollen from crying. Everything in me wants to collapse into that inn bed and not move for a week.

But he said come with me, so I came.

The grass is longer here, untended. It brushes against my ankles as we climb, damp with evening dew. Brēvast glows faintly below us—lantern light in windows, smoke rising from chimneys. Small. Quiet. Just a town going to sleep.

Milly stops near the top. Sits down in the grass without ceremony.

I stand there for a moment, uncertain. Then sit beside him. Not too close. Not too far.

The silence stretches. Not uncomfortable. Just... present.

"Crickets sound different near towns," Milly says after a while.

I blink. "What?"

"Quieter. More cautious." He tilts his head slightly, listening. "Out in the wild, they're louder. Nothing to hide from."

I listen. He's right—there's a faint chirping, but it's hesitant. Starting and stopping.

"I never noticed that," I say.

"Most people don't."

More silence. The sky is darkening above us, stars appearing one by one. Mün hasn't risen yet—just the deep blue of twilight fading toward black.

"Do you know the constellations?" he asks.

"Some. Dad taught me a few."

"Which ones?"

I scan the sky, searching. Find a familiar pattern—a cluster of stars that curves like a tail. "That one. Mīrrū's Tail."

"Mm." He points to a dim grouping near the horizon. "Fyūnoch's Hearth. The three stars in the center are the coals. The outer ring is the stone."

I squint. It does look like a hearth, if I imagine it. A dying fire, barely glowing.

"The stories say Fyūnoch placed it there to guide travelers home," Milly continues. His voice is quiet. Almost absent. "So they'd always know which way was warm."

"Do you believe that?"

He's quiet for a moment. "I believe it helps to have something to look for."

I pull my knees up to my chest, wrapping my arms around them. The grass is damp against my legs. A breeze moves through, carrying the smell of night and something distant—rain, maybe. Or just the air cooling.

"The crickets stopped," I say.

"They do that. When they sense movement." He doesn't turn his head, but I can tell he's listening to the silence. "Give it a moment."

We wait. The quiet feels different now—expectant, not empty.

Then, slowly, the chirping resumes. Hesitant at first. Then steadier. Then full, like they've decided we're not a threat.

"There," Milly says. Like it matters. Like the crickets coming back is something worth noting.

Maybe it is.

The stars keep appearing. More and more of them, filling the sky until the river of light emerges—that impossible sweep of silver I saw on my first night outside Krandor. Same sky. Same stars.

Different hill.

"You can sleep," Milly says quietly. "I'll keep watch."

"I'm not—" I start to protest, but my eyes are already heavy. The grass is soft beneath me. The air is cool but not cold. The crickets are singing, and Fyūnoch's Hearth is glowing faint on the horizon, pointing the way home.

I don't remember deciding to lean against him. Just that his shoulder is solid, and I'm so tired, and the stars are spinning slowly overhead.

I wake to color.

The sky is shifting—not red, not the terrible red of the tunnel or the kitchen floor. Gold. Soft gold and pale pink, spreading from the horizon like something spilled and beautiful.

I'm still against Milly's shoulder. He hasn't moved.

"Morning," he says. His voice is rough. He didn't sleep.

I sit up slowly, blinking. The world is quiet. Just birds beginning to call, the grass rustling, Brēvast below us catching the first light.

"You should have woken me."

"You needed it more."

That's probably true. I don't argue.

Solis hangs pale in the brightening sky—she rose hours ago, heralding what's coming. Then Astaris crests the horizon, and the world turns gold.

"It's beautiful," I whisper.

"Yes," he agrees. "It is."

We sit there as the world wakes up. Not talking. Just watching.

The crickets have gone quiet now. Daytime sounds instead—buzzing, rustling, the noise of things that aren't afraid of light.

I don't know why he brought me here. Don't know what he wanted me to see.

But I saw it anyway.

The sky ending. The sky beginning again.

And me, still here to watch it.

# PINE & SALT

◆

## WRONGWARD
### CHAPTER XXVIII

The morning is cool and clear when we leave Brēvast.

I wake early, dress quickly, and pack my things without the paralyzing hesitation from two days ago. My hands are steady as I roll my bedding, as I check the straps on my bag. Not because the anxiety is gone—it's still there, humming under my skin—but because I'm choosing to move through it instead of freezing in it.

Somewhere in between, Milly said. Not reckless, not paralyzed. Somewhere in between.

I can do that. I think I can do that.

When I come downstairs, Milly's already settled our bill with the innkeeper. He nods at me once—acknowledgment, not warmth, but not the cold distance from before either. Progress. Maybe.

At the stable, I tend to Horsey with the routine I've built over weeks. Brush, check hooves, saddle. My fingers work through the straps, tightening them to the right tension. Not too loose, not crushing. Just right.

I pause, hand on the leather, waiting for the doubt to creep in. Is this right? Should I check again?

It doesn't come.

The saddle is secure. I know it's secure. I don't need to ask.

"Ready?" Milly's voice behind me.

I turn. He's already mounted, reins loose in one hand. Waiting.

"Yes," I say. And I mean it.

I swing up onto Horsey—one smooth motion, no fumbling—and settle into the saddle. She shifts beneath me, familiar and steady.

We ride out of Brēvast as the town wakes around us. Shopkeepers opening shutters, the smell of fresh bread drifting from a bakery, a dog barking somewhere down a side street. Normal morning sounds. Life continuing.

The road leads west, toward the coast. Toward the Celtian Sea.

Toward what my parents never reached.

The thought sits in my chest, heavy but not crushing. They wanted to see the sea. Dad talked about it like it was a dream—the salt air, the endless water, the way the light looked different near the ocean.

And I'm going to see it.

Not because I'm special. Not because I deserve it more than they did. Just because I'm still here. Still moving forward.

Still alive.

We ride in silence for the first hour. Not the tense, angry silence from after the tunnel. Just... quiet. Companionable, almost.

I stay two horse-lengths behind Milly. Close enough to hear if he speaks, far enough to give him space. The balance feels right.

The landscape continues to flatten as we leave Brēvast behind. The rocky hills of Drūn are long gone now, replaced by Celtor's gentler terrain—rolling fields, scattered trees, stone walls marking property lines. Farmland gives way to wilder grass, and the air tastes different. Sharper. Cleaner.

Salt.

Not strong yet, but there. A promise carried on the wind.

Around mid-morning, we pass a waystation marker. CELTIAN SEA—150 DRŪM.

Three days. Three whole days until the sea.

I glance at Milly ahead of me. His posture is straight as always, shoulders square, every inch the disciplined paladin. He reaches back once to adjust his sword—a habitual check, the kind I've seen him do a hundred times.

The marker disappears behind us. The road continues west.

We stop around noon to rest the horses and eat. Milly dismounts with his usual efficiency, tending to his horse with practiced movements. I follow suit, brushing Horsey down, checking her legs for any signs of strain.

When I pull out the dried meat and cheese from our supplies, I notice my hands don't shake. I portion out food for both of us without asking if I'm doing it right.

Progress.

I hand Milly his share. He takes it with a quiet "Thank you," then moves to sit against a tree at the clearing's edge.

I settle nearby. We eat in silence, watching the road.

The dried meat is tough, the cheese hard. Same food as always. But today I don't mind it as much. Maybe because I'm not choking it down through panic. Maybe because things feel... steadier. Less like everything's about to fall apart.

"The air's different," I say after a while.

Milly glances over. "Salt. We're getting closer."

"Three days."

"If we keep this pace, yes."

He finishes his food methodically, then stands

and brushes dust from his pants. "Ready?"

I nod, gathering my things.

*These aren't my dreams. These are my parents'. Why am I even..?*

We mount up and continue.

The afternoon stretches long and quiet.

We ride through country that gets wilder with every mile. Fewer farms, fewer stone walls. Just open grassland rolling toward the horizon, broken occasionally by clusters of wind-bent trees.

The salt smell grows stronger. Still faint, but persistent now. A constant reminder of where we're heading.

Three days until the sea. Three days until I see what my parents dreamed of seeing.

The thought keeps circling back. Not painful, exactly. Just... heavy. They wanted this so badly. Talked about it like it was paradise. The Celtian Sea, where the water met the sky and everything felt possible.

And they never made it.

But I will.

I glance ahead at Milly. He's riding with that same steady competence he always has, eyes scanning the horizon, hand occasionally resting near his sword hilt. Alert. Prepared.

Always prepared.

We ride for another hour in comfortable quiet before he speaks.

"We'll stop ahead. Water the horses."

"Okay."

We pull off near a scraggly tree, the only shade for miles. I dismount, stretch my legs, lead Horsey to drink from my water skin.

Milly tends to his horse with the same practiced efficiency. Check legs, adjust saddle, brush dust from the coat. Everything correct.

When he's done, he moves to sit against the tree. Pulls out his water skin, takes a few sips, then just... sits. Quiet. Resting.

I portion out food again—easier each time I do it—and bring him his share.

"Thanks," he says, taking it.

We eat. The sun is warm, the breeze cool. Nice weather for traveling.

After a few minutes, I try for conversation. "Do you think it'll look like Dad described? The sea?"

Milly considers. "Probably. The Celtian Sea is known for its clarity. Deep blue water, white sand beaches in some places." He pauses. "Your father had good taste."

Something in my chest loosens at that. "He did."

We finish eating in companionable quiet. When Milly stands to pack up, I notice he's moving a bit slower than usual. Not much—just the slight heaviness that comes from days of riding, from exhaustion that builds gradually.

We're both tired. That's normal.

We mount up and ride on.

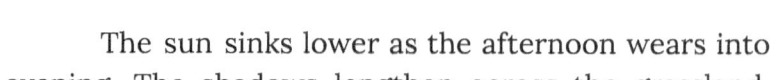

The sun sinks lower as the afternoon wears into evening. The shadows lengthen across the grassland, turning everything gold.

The road continues west. Always west. Toward the coast.

The sound reaches us first.

Not loud. Not yet. Just a low rumble that I feel in my chest before I hear it properly. Like distant thunder that doesn't fade.

"What is that?" I ask.

Milly doesn't answer. Just points ahead.

The road curves, following the natural line of the land. We round a bend and—

The bridge.

It's old. Ancient, maybe. Stone arches spanning a gorge I can't see the bottom of, each block fitted so perfectly there's no mortar, no gaps. Just stone on stone, holding for centuries through nothing but weight and precision.

And beyond it, the waterfall.

I've seen water before. The fountain in Krandor's square. The canals in Celton. The sea itself, endless and blue.

This is different.

The falls are massive—easily fifty pās across, maybe more. Water pours over the cliff edge in a sheet so thick it looks solid from here, white and churning. The sound grows as we approach the bridge, that low rumble becoming a roar that drowns out everything else. Even the horses' hooves on stone are silent beneath it.

Mist rises from where the water hits below, creating a permanent fog that catches the evening light. Rainbows form and dissolve and form again in the spray, shifting colors that refuse to stay still.

"We should keep moving," Milly says, but he's stopped his horse at the bridge's center, same as me.

I lean over Horsey's neck, trying to see the bottom. The gorge is deep—darker than it should be, the mist hiding whatever's down there. The water just... falls. Keeps falling. Disappearing into white and shadow and sound.

My clothes are damp from the spray before I realize we've been standing here long enough for it to reach us. Milly's hair is dark with moisture, sticking to his forehead around the healing cut.

"How long has this been here?" I ask. Have to raise my voice to be heard.

"The bridge? A thousand years, maybe more." He's watching the water too. "Old Empire construction. They knew how to build things that lasted."

"And the falls?"

"Always." He glances at me. "Long before us. Long after."

The words settle strange. Always. This water has been falling since before Krandor existed. Before my parents were born. Before anything I know was real. Just... falling. Constant. Indifferent.

A bird cuts through the mist below—some kind of falcon, wings tucked as it dives. It disappears into the white, then emerges on the other side, climbing back toward the sun. Hunting, probably. Using the falls as cover.

"We should go," Milly says again. This time he means it.

But I take one more moment. Let the sound fill my ears, the mist coat my skin. Let myself be small next to something that doesn't care if I exist or not.

It's... peaceful. In a way nothing else has been.

We cross the rest of the bridge in silence. The sound fades gradually as we ride on, that roar becoming a rumble becoming a memory of a rumble. By the time we're a quarter-kāl away, I can hear the horses' breathing again. Normal sounds. Normal world.

But I keep glancing back until the falls disappear behind the trees.

Milly hasn't said much today. But that's not unusual. Sometimes we ride for hours in comfortable silence. I've gotten used to it—the quiet companionship, the shared purpose of just... moving forward.

Around evening, he pulls off the road near a small grove of trees.

"We'll camp here," he says.

We dismount and fall into the familiar routine. Tents up, horses tended, fire built. Everything practiced and smooth.

When we're settled by the fire with our evening meal, I watch the flames dance. Think about the sea. About being so close now.

"Three days," I say aloud.

"Three days," Milly agrees.

"Do you think..." I pause, not sure how to phrase it. "Do you think they'd be proud? My parents?"

He looks at me across the fire. His expression softens slightly. "Yes. I think they would be."

The words settle warm in my chest.

We eat without a word. The fire crackles. The evening air cools.

After a while, Milly pulls out his whetstone and

sword. The familiar scrape of stone on steel fills the quiet—a sound I've heard countless times on this journey. Soothing in its repetition.

I watch him work for a bit, then stand. "I'm going to get some rest."

"Good idea." He doesn't look up from his blade. "Sleep well."

"You too."

I duck into my tent, settle onto my bedroll. Outside, I can hear the rhythmic scrape of the whetstone. The sound of Milly maintaining his equipment, like he does every night.

Normal. Familiar.

The two wooden horses sit on the small table beside the bedroll. In the lamplight, they almost look alive—one rough-carved, one smooth and deliberate. I pick up Milly's, the newer one, and make it walk across my palm. Then the other. They meet nose to nose, like Horsey greeting Milly's horse on the road.

Stupid. They're just wood.

But I keep them walking anyway. Back and forth. Until my hand stills and sleep finally comes.

Tomorrow we'll ride west again. One day closer to the sea.

One day closer to what my parents dreamed of but never reached.

One day closer to something that feels like both an ending and a beginning.

# GLOWING BEYOND DOUBT

### CHAPTER XXIX

Mün is up.
Solis is down.
Astaris hides.
Milly is sleeping.
I am not.

Three days of riding,
my hair tangled, sliding.
Three days of walking,
my feet are aching.

Three days of living,
my knees are sore.
Three days of wishing,
I wish for more.

Father said Salt.
Mother said Pine.
I said nothing.
They're both in a line.

Salt on my lips,
Pine in my hair.
I taste them together,
under the water's stare.

The wind smells like laughter,
the sky smells like tea.
I close both my eyes,
and wish to be free.

I told him a story,
I made myself small.
I showed him my breaking
so he'd catch my fall.

He did! Isn't that lovely?
He stayed all this time.
Even when I was lying,
even when I wasn't fine.

I'm tired,
I'm sleepy,
I'm too small to fight.
I'm sinking,
I'm scared,
but the red looks so bright.

Tomorrow.
Tomorrow,
the horizon will be
crimson and warm

like it's welcoming me.

Father and Mother
are waiting below.
The water is rising,
it's time now to go.

I'll wade in so gently,
the red at my knees,
then up to my waist,
then I'll finally breathe.

Tomorrow.
Tomorrow,
the ocean will be
full of everyone
waiting for me.

The ships look so pretty
floating above.
Milly is there,
wrapped up in my love.

I did this for them,
for the people who stayed.
I brought them adventure,
I showed them the way.

Into the red,
into the deep,
into the place

where we all go to sleep.

Tomorrow.
Tomorrow.
The horizon will be
*SEA!*

# ... WILL BE *SEA!*

◆

### CHAPTER XXX

Day breaks along with my short rest. We're less than an hour from the Celtian Sea. The pine and salt fill my lungs as the forest seems to get less dense from my little view.

*We're almost there.*

A faint smile appears on my face as I slowly get out of the tent. Milly stands before a smoldering, dead fire, holding a small pot. Plates are scattered everywhere along the logs surrounding the firepit. Smoke curls between us as our eyes connect.

"Breakfast is done."

"I can tell."

He gestures to a plate, which holds an omelet and a small slice of jerky. I walk over, my limbs still sore. My hands shake as the plate's coldness hits my hands.

*Clomp.*
*Thud.*
Fish, salt, pine, wood, ash, sand—all of it hits my nose at once. The sky is a perfect blue as the forest shrinks down, the trees becoming more scattered and tropical. The green is greener, the blue is bluer, the red is blank.

Horsey remains at a steady pace as her hooves gallop along the now-sandy paths made by blazers decades ago.

The trees thin even more, becoming rarer and rarer as sunlight flows into my pupils. Milly's armor seems enchanted because of the glowing light.

Flowers bloom in patches in the sand, their blues and gold reflecting the rays.

I take a breath.

Then another.

It feels wonderful.

Milly signals to his horse to slow down, then hops off the saddle. He leans and stretches back. All of the tension in his back disappears with a loud POP! as he cracks it all.

I do the same—getting off of Horsey, unbuckling the saddle so she can roam without the weight.

Milly takes off his armor, letting only his clothes

remain. He simply stays put, staring out into the turquoise plain.

"This is the Celtian Sea, Kitt. You made it this far."

I stare at it.

Waves break the surface of the blue expanse. The water stretches forever. Blue meeting blue at the horizon, no line between sea and sky. Just endless, perfect blue.

Dad's blue. Salt.

My legs move before my mind can, pushing me into the soft lapping of the shore. One step. Two steps. The sand is soft, then slightly firmer yet more... sinky as I reach where the waves have licked it. Wet. Dark.

I can hear my breathing.

In my ears.

I can hear nothing else, not even Milly's chatter.

The water is right there.

There.

There.

Right there—

My boots hit the surface.

Warm rushes up my ankles as it soaks the leather. I don't care.

Another step. The blue is up to my shins.

Another.

Knees.

The hem of my skirt sinks and rises, flowing.
I stop.
I'm standing in the Celtian Sea.
*I'm standing in the Celtian Sea.*
The water is warm

father?
"Salt and pine, Kitt. That's

SALT

what it smells

PINE

like—"

warm at the same time as Astaris bakes

MOTHER LAUGHS, "We'll see it together
some day. The three of us, no matter what."

so bright I can barely

**"PROMISE?"**

see my chest

THEY'RE NOT HERE

tight I can't

they're not here
they're not here

breathe right—

I did it.

# I DID IT!

*I'm standing at the Celtian Sea.*
The water
laps at my knees.
Warm.
Real.
Real.

they wanted this

for me
for us

## "PROMISE?"

*yes*

yes

yes

yes

I KEPT IT

My chest
not tight with panic
tight with something else

too full
too much
bursting

A sound escapes.
Not a sob.

Laughter?
Another one.
Louder.
LOUDER.
Why am I laughing?
BECAUSE YOU MADE IT
BECAUSE I MADE IT

WHY AM I CRYING?
BECAUSE THEY DIDN'T MAKE IT

Both at once.
Laughing.
Crying.
Sobbing.
Gasping.
Yelling.

My hands cover my face.
Water d
r

K. YUKI | 282

i
p
s
from my fingers.

salt from the sea
salt from my eyes

same salt
different source

"I'm here—" I choke out. "I'm HERE—"

To no one.
To everyone.
To them.
*Mom. Dad. I made it.*

*The blue stretches forever.*
*Perfect.*
*Beautiful.*
*Exactly like Dad said.*

"Salt and pine, Kitt."

I can smell it.
Taste it.

**Feel it.**

*i'm feeling it for all three of us*

My knees buckle
I don't fall

hands catch me
solid
steady.

"Kitt?"

Milly's
V
O
I
C
E
Real
    Real
        Present

I look up at him through tears and laughter and
salty water.
He's waded in.
Boots soaked, not caring.

"I made it," I gasp. "Milly, I—I made it—"

His expression softens.
Something like pride.
Something like relief.
More relief than joy.
Like he's been carrying something heavy and can finally set it down.

"You did." His voice is gentle. Certain. "You made it, Kitt."

"They never—" I can't finish. The joy is too big. The grief is too big. Both happening at once, impossible to separate.
"I know." He steadies me, keeps me upright in the warm water. "But you did. For them. For yourself."
I nod, still laughing, still crying, unable to stop either.
The sun is bright.
The water is warm.
The sea stretches endless and blue and perfect.
And I'm here.
Actually here.
Alive.
Finally, impossibly, overwhelmingly—

*Happy.*

# PLEASURE LETTER

◆

## CHAPTER XXXI

TO DR. ARRONAX VERNE,
*Vestperian Institute of Mind and Healing*

We reached the Celtian Sea.

Kitt stood in the water and wept—not the frozen terror of Byēnwick, not the spiraling panic of Brēvast, but something I have not witnessed before. Joy. Pure, overwhelming, impossible joy.

She laughed. She sobbed. She said "I made it" until the words became a chant, a prayer, a declaration. When her legs gave out, I waded in to steady her, and she looked at me with an expression that made me understand—perhaps for the first time—what it means to survive something you were certain would destroy you.

We have been in Celton three days now. She is… lighter. Not healed—I am not so naive as to believe one moment of catharsis erases months of trauma. But changed. The weight she has carried since Krandor seems, if not lifted, at least shared with something beyond grief.

Celton suits her. The Felidae here walk without fear, and

she watches them with something like wonder. Ryn would have loved this city. Nessa too. Strange, how joy can feel like grief when the people who should share it are gone.

This morning she made a joke about the capital's pigeons being "aggressively incompetent." Yesterday she asked if we could stay an extra day so she could sketch the harbor. Small things, perhaps. But for Kitt, who has spent months merely surviving, these feel significant.

I find myself wanting to believe she is better. That reaching the sea—completing her parents' dream—provided the closure I could not. That perhaps my earlier letter was overly cautious, my assessment too dire.

But I know better.

Yesterday, while watching the ships in the harbor, she went quiet for several minutes—that same distant look I have learned to recognize. When she returned to herself, she said only: "I was thinking about Mom." Not spiraling. Not drowning. Just… remembering. Grief without panic.

She still flinches at unexpected sounds. Still checks and rechecks simple tasks when anxiety rises. The intrusive thoughts she mentioned in Milldraugh—the violent imagery—she has not spoken of them recently, but I suspect they linger. Trauma does not announce its departure.

These are not signs of failure. They are signs that healing is not linear, not complete, not something I can provide alone.

She has asked about Vestperia. Not with dread, as she once might have, but with something approaching curiosity. I believe she is ready to continue. More importantly, I believe she wants to.

We will depart for Kurune's outer settlements within the week. I trust you received my previous correspondence and will see her when we arrive.

Thank you, Dr. Verne. For whatever you did for me two years past, and for whatever you might do for her now.

May the Goddess grant us safe passage.

*Sir Lumber Mills*
*Paladin of Celton*
WRITTEN FROM CELTON, SIXTH DAY AFTER REACHING THE CELTIAN SEA

# THOSE WHO REMAIN

◆

## GONDOLA

CHAPTER XXXII

The gondola rocks gently as we glide through Celton's lower canals.

Water laps against the wooden hull, and the air here is different from any place we've been. Thick. Humid. Every breath feels like drinking—the moisture so heavy it coats your throat, your lungs, makes your clothes cling damper than they should. Salt everywhere, but not clean ocean salt. Canal salt—stagnant, mixed with the funk of trapped water, fish guts rotting in corners, sewage, wet wood slowly molding. And food smells layered over it all: frying oil, garlic, something sweet baking, fermented fish sauce. The air tastes like Celton—complex and alive and slightly rotten all at once.

I lean over the side, watching buildings pass. Houses on stilts, their foundations disappearing into the murky green water. Laundry strung between windows—some of it clearly sized for tails, the telltale loops sewn into pants and skirts. A Felidae kid with tabby-striped ears jumps from one pier to another, his tail streaming behind him for balance. He laughs when he nearly misses, and a human woman—his mother, probably—shouts something worried from a window above.

It's alive. Chaotic. Beautiful. And so completely different from Krandor, where seeing a Felidae was a once-a-month occurrence at best.

I glance back at Milly.

He's sitting ramrod straight in the center of the boat, one hand gripping the edge, the other resting—of course—near his sword hilt. His jaw is tight. His eyes scan the bridges, the windows, the water itself like he's expecting an attack from the canal fish.

I can't help it. I grin.

"You know we're not going to capsize, right?"

He doesn't look at me. "I'm aware."

"Then why do you look like you're about to fall overboard?"

"I don't—" He shifts slightly, the boat rocking with him. His grip tightens. "I'm fine."

"You're white-knuckling a *gondola*, Milly."

"I'm being cautious."

"You're being ridiculous."

That gets him to look at me. His expression is flat, but there's something in his eyes—exasperation, maybe. Or the beginnings of amusement he's trying to suppress.

"This is a main waterway in a major city," he says evenly. "Crowded, unpredictable. Someone could—"

"Someone could *what*?" I interrupt, spreading my arms wide. The boat rocks slightly. He tenses. "Ambush us with a fish? Challenge you to a duel from that bridge?"

"Unlikely, but—"

"Milly." I lean forward, grinning wider. "You need to relax."

"I am relaxed."

"You look like you're about to fight the canal."

The gondolier—a weathered man with sun-dark skin and a knowing smirk—chuckles from his position at the back. "First time in Celton, sir?"

Milly's jaw tightens further. "No."

"First time on a boat?" I ask sweetly.

"No."

"First time enjoying yourself?"

He gives me a look. The kind that says *you're insufferable* but in a way that's almost... fond?

"I enjoy plenty of things," he says.

"Name one."

"Quiet."

I laugh—loud enough that a few people on the nearest bridge glance down. Milly winces slightly, which only makes me laugh harder.

The gondola glides to a stop at a wooden dock in the upper canals. The buildings here are different—taller, cleaner, made of pale stone instead of weathered wood. Marble balustrades line the walkways. Lanterns are already being lit as evening approaches, their warm glow reflecting off the water.

Milly pays the gondolier and helps me onto the dock. My legs feel strange after sitting so long—the ground doesn't rock.

"Where are we going?" I ask, looking around. This district is noticeably quieter. Fewer street vendors, more actual shops with glass windows. People dressed nicer.

"Dinner," Milly says simply.

"We have rations—"

"We're not eating rations tonight." He starts walking, and I have to hurry to keep up.

"Why not?"

He glances back at me. Something in his expression softens. "Because you made it to the Celtian Sea. That deserves better than dried meat and stale bread."

Oh.

I follow him through narrow streets that wind between buildings, across a small bridge where I can see gondolas passing below. The smell of cooking food drifts from open windows—garlic, herbs, something sweet baking.

We stop in front of a restaurant with ivy growing up its stone walls. Small tables are set outside under a canvas awning, candles flickering in glass holders. It looks... nice. The kind of place I'd never think to enter on my own.

"Milly, this is—"

"Come on." He's already heading inside.

The interior is warm and dim, lit by oil lamps hanging from the ceiling. Wood beams, white tablecloths, the quiet murmur of conversation. A woman greets us, shows us to a table near the window overlooking the canal.

I sit, feeling suddenly out of place. My clothes are travel-worn, my hair still tangled from the wind on the water. Everyone else here looks... civilized.

Milly doesn't seem to notice or care. He orders for both of us—some local fish dish I've never heard of, bread, wine for him and cider for me.

When the woman leaves, I lean forward. "This is expensive."

"Probably."

"You don't have to—"

"I know." He meets my eyes across the table. "I want to."

I sit back, not sure what to say to that.

The food arrives faster than expected. White fish in some kind of butter sauce, roasted vegetables, bread that's actually warm and soft. My mouth waters just looking at it.

Milly picks at his meal. Pushes the fish around more than eating it. When I offer him the roasted vegetable, he takes it just to make me stop watching.

I take a bite. It's good. Really good. Not trail rations, not bland inn food. Actual, proper food.

"Oh," I say around the mouthful.

Milly starts eating, but I catch the faint smile at my reaction.

We eat in comfortable silence for a while. I try everything, surprised by how hungry I actually am. The fish flakes apart perfectly. The bread has herbs baked into it. Even the vegetables taste better than they have any right to.

"Try this," I say, pushing my plate toward him slightly. There's a roasted root vegetable I can't identify, golden and caramelized.

He raises an eyebrow but takes one. Chews. Makes a face.

"What?" I grin. "Too sweet?"

"Too sweet," he confirms, but he's not really complaining.

"You have the taste buds of a soldier."

"I am a soldier."

"Former soldier," I correct. "You're a paladin now. That's different."

"Not that different."

"Really? When's the last time you had to sharpen your sword in actual combat?"

He pauses, fork halfway to his mouth. Thinks. "...Vālmarch." Another pause. "Properly, I mean. Skirmishes since then, but nothing that required—" He stops. "A bar fight in Drūn, if that counts."

"A bar fight," I repeat. "You're getting soft."

"Soft," he repeats flatly.

"Domesticated, even."

"I'm sitting across from someone who had a complete breakdown in the middle of the road four days ago."

"And now I'm making fun of you over dinner. Growth." I take another bite, pleased with myself.

He shakes his head, but there's that almost-smile again. The one that says he's exasperated but doesn't actually mind.

We keep eating. The conversation drifts—easier than it's been in weeks. I tell him about the sketch I started of the harbor. He mentions a book he's been reading in the evenings. Small things. Normal things.

At some point, the restaurant gets busier. More tables fill, voices rising in a comfortable hum. Outside the window, I can see people walking along the canal—humans, Felidae, even a few mixed families with children of both kinds playing together. A Felidae gondolier poles past, his tail swishing lazily as he navigates, calling out a greeting in that rolling, purring dialect of Unital. Gondolas pass slowly in the fading light, some carrying couples, others loaded with goods, all part of the city's constant motion.

"What will you do?" I ask suddenly. "After Vestperia, I mean."

Milly sets down his fork. Takes a sip of wine, considering.

"I'm not sure yet," he says finally. 'I haven't thought much past getting you there safely."

"But after?" I press. "You'll have delivered me. Oath complete. What then?"

He's quiet for a moment, turning his wine glass slowly between his fingers. The candlelight catches on the dark liquid.

"There's a grave I need to visit," he says finally. "In northern Celtor. I haven't been since..." He trails off. Doesn't finish.

"I think I'm ready now," he continues, voice quieter. "To say goodbye properly. I wasn't before."

Something in my chest tightens. "That's good. That you're ready."

He nods, still looking at his glass. Then glances up at me. "After that... I don't know. Maybe I'll travel for a while. Actually see places instead of just passing through them."

"Alone?"

He pauses. Something shifts in his expression—considering, uncertain. "I was thinking... maybe not entirely alone."

I blink. "What do you mean?"

"Once you're settled with Dr. Verne. Once you're..." He searches for the word. "Stable. If you wanted company sometime. To see more of the world." He clears his throat slightly, like the offer makes him uncomfortable. "I'd be willing."

Oh.

*Oh.*

"You'd want to travel with me?" My voice comes out smaller than intended.

"If you'd have me along." He picks up his fork again, focusing on his plate like this isn't a significant offer. "No obligations. Just... if you ever wanted a companion. Someone who knows which inns to avoid."

I can't help the smile that spreads across my face. "I'd like that. A lot."

"Good." He takes a bite of fish, but I catch the faint smile he's trying to hide. "Though you're carrying your own pack next time. No exceptions."

"I carried my own pack this whole time!"

"Barely."

"I—that's not—" I stop, realizing he's teasing. "You're the worst."

"You said I was domesticated."

"I take it back. You're still a soldier."

"Thank you."

We finish eating, the conversation flowing easier than it has in... maybe ever. He tells me about a place in western Celtor with hot springs that are supposed to have healing properties. I tell him about a passage in one of Dad's books about floating markets in the eastern islands.

Plans. Futures. Things that feel possible instead of impossible.

The server brings sweet pastries for dessert—thin, crispy things dusted with sugar and filled with cream. I take one bite and immediately understand why Milly made that face at the sweet vegetable earlier. It's almost too sweet.

But I eat it anyway, grinning when he raises an eyebrow at my expression.

"Too sweet?" he asks innocently.

"Perfect," I lie, taking another bite just to prove a point.

When we finally leave, the sun has fully set. Lanterns line the canal walkways, their reflections dancing on the dark water. The air is cooler now, carrying that salt-and-stone smell that means we're near the sea.

Milly leads us back to the dock where gondolas wait.

"We can walk from here," Milly says nodding

toward a nearby bridge. "The hotel's only a few streets over."

I nod, still full from dinner, pleasantly drowsy.

The route takes us through a quieter district—residential, the buildings older. Fewer lanterns here. Our footsteps echo off the close stone walls.

Voices ahead. Sharp. Angry. Speaking Unital too fast for me to follow.

Milly's hand moves to his sword hilt. "Stay close."

Then—that sound. The one I recognize now. Wet. Final.

Footsteps running toward us. A figure stumbles past, gasping, doesn't even glance our way. Gone into the shadows.

"Don't look," Milly says quietly.

But I've already seen. In the alley mouth. A shape on the ground. Not moving. The shadows too dark to see details, but I don't need to see details to know.

"Come on." Milly's hand on my elbow, guiding me forward. Not running. Walking. Steady. "Eyes ahead."

We're two streets away before I can breathe properly again.

"The guard—shouldn't we tell someone—"

"By the time the guard arrives, the body will be in a canal." His voice is matter-of-fact. Tired. "If they bother coming at all. Port cities, Kitt. This is how they work."

The beautiful dinner from an hour ago sits heavy

in my stomach now.

He pays for passage to our hotel—somewhere in the mid-canals, nicer than the inns we've been staying at but not extravagant.

I settle into the gondola more confidently this time, though shaking. Milly still sits carefully, but his grip on the edge is looser. Progress.

The gondolier pushes off, and we slip into the network of waterways. The gondola glides through the mid-canals, quieter now than the lower waterways. Fewer boats, fewer voices. Just the gentle splash of the pole pushing us forward and the distant sounds of the city settling into evening.

I lean back against the cushioned seat, full from dinner and pleasantly tired. The kind of tired that feels earned, not the exhaustion of survival. Just... normal tired.

Milly sits across from me, more relaxed than he was on the ride here. His hand rests loosely on his knee instead of gripping the boat's edge. He's watching the buildings pass, the lantern light reflecting in his eyes.

"Thank you," I say quietly. "For dinner. For all of this."

He glances at me. "You already thanked me."

"I know. But I mean it."

"I know you do." His voice is gentle. "You're welcome."

We fall into comfortable silence. The gondolier hums something under his breath—a melody I don't recognize but find soothing anyway. The water reflects the lanterns above, turning the canal into a river of gold and shadow.

Then the sky cracks open.

Not breaks. Not explodes. *Cracks*—like something immense splitting apart above us.

A sphere of light erupts overhead, white-hot at its center, spreading outward in tendrils of red and gold that reach across the entire sky. Each tendril branches into smaller ones, fracturing into a thousand glowing veins that hang suspended for one impossible moment before beginning to fall.

They don't fall quickly. They drift, lazy and luminous, leaving trails of light that fade like dying embers.

I can't look away.

The gondolier chuckles somewhere behind me. "Festival night. Forgot it was today."

The boat slows. Nearly stops. We drift, rocking gently with the canal's current.

Another one rises. I can see it climbing—a bright point ascending from somewhere in the upper city, trailing sparks. It reaches its apex and detonates.

Milly's hand moves to his temple. Stops. Forces himself to lower it.

Blue this time. Not sky-blue. Deep blue, the color

of the Celtian Sea at dusk. It blooms outward in rings, each one larger than the last, expanding until the whole sky is layered circles of sapphire light. The rings pulse once—twice—before dissolving into falling stars that shower down and vanish before reaching the rooftops.

The water beneath us reflects everything. The black canal surface becomes a mirror, doubling the display. Blue above, blue below. We're floating through the middle of it.

I remember these.

"When I was little," I hear myself say. "Maybe six. There was a festival in Krandor."

Another firework rises. Green this time—spring green, new-leaf green. It spreads like a tree growing in fast-motion, branches extending in all directions, each one blooming with clusters of golden sparks that hang like fruit before falling.

"Mom and Dad took me to the square to watch." My voice sounds distant, dreamlike. "I couldn't see over the crowd, so Dad lifted me onto his shoulders."

The green fades. Purple takes its place—royal purple edged with silver. It spirals as it expands, a galaxy wheeling overhead, pulling my eyes along its curve.

"I remember being so high up. Higher than I'd ever been. And the fireworks felt close enough to touch."

A triple burst—red, white, red again. They

overlap, creating pink where the colors mix. The pink spreads and spreads until it covers half the visible sky.

"I kept reaching for them. Dad told me if I caught one, I could keep it. I believed him."

"Did you catch one?" Milly's voice is quiet. He's not looking at me either. Looking up.

"No. But I tried."

Gold now. Pure, molten gold rising in a column, then fragmenting into a rainfall of golden drops. Each drop splits further as it falls—once, twice, three times—until the sky is filled with thousands of tiny golden lights drifting down like snow.

Milly turns his head away from the brightest bursts. Pretends he's just watching the water's reflection instead.

"Mom said I fell asleep on the walk home. Dad had to carry me the whole way. I don't remember that part." The golden snow fades to nothing. "Just the colors. And feeling safe."

Silence. The gondolier's pole dips into the water. Quiet splash. We drift forward slowly.

Then another rise. Another bloom. White with a green center, spreading in a perfect circle before breaking apart into streaming trails.

"I forgot I could remember them happy," I say softly. "Before everything got complicated."

Milly doesn't respond immediately. We both watch as the white trails fade and something new begins—multiple launches this time. One, two, three, four fireworks rising in sequence. They reach their heights at staggered intervals.

The first one bursts. Orange, bright as a sunset. I catch Milly flinching slightly—just the eyes, squinting against the sudden brightness.

"The day I was knighted," Milly says. "I was nineteen."

The second one. Yellow, with red edges that curl inward.

"It was a small ceremony. Just me, the officiant, a few witnesses. Nothing grand."

The third. Blue-violet, spreading in slow waves.

"But I remember standing there, swearing the oath, and feeling like I'd found something I was supposed to do."

The fourth. Silver-white, so bright it hurts to look at directly. It leaves afterimages when I blink.

"Like everything before that moment had been leading to it."

The afterimages fade. The sky darkens again, waiting.

"Was it what you expected?" I ask.

A pause. Water laps against the gondola's hull.

Another firework climbs. This one moves differently—it corkscrews as it rises, spinning, leaving a spiral trail of sparks behind it. When it reaches its peak, it doesn't burst outward. It bursts downward, like a fountain reversed, pouring light toward the earth.

"No," Milly says. "It was harder. Lonelier, sometimes."

The fountain of light continues falling, falling, endless.

"The oath binds you to help, but it doesn't guarantee you'll succeed. That people will listen. That you'll make a difference."

I think about the Corrupted Well's story. The Colossus—punished for showing mercy, still choosing to protect. Still appearing where the helpless gather.

Like the Colossus. Like a fragment of Death that wouldn't stop serving.

The fountain finally exhausts itself. Darkness rushes back.

"But it mattered." His voice is barely audible over the water. "Even when it was hard. Even when I failed. It mattered that I tried."

Three more rise together. They burst simultaneously—red, blue, green. The colors don't mix. They hang separate in the sky, three distinct flowers blooming side by side.

"Is that why you didn't leave me in Brēvast?" I ask. "When I told you to?"

The flowers begin to wilt. Petals falling.

"Partly." He pauses. Another firework rises—just one this time. Small. It climbs higher than any of the others, a tiny point of light ascending and ascending until I think it might disappear entirely.

Then it detonates.

Massive. The largest yet. Gold and silver and white all at once, a burst so bright the entire city is illuminated for one instant. I can see everything—the buildings, the bridges, the water, Milly's face across from me briefly visible in the flash.

Then it fades, leaving only the afterglow.

"But also because I know what it's like to be drowning and think you're not worth saving," he continues. "And I know what it means when someone refuses to let you drown anyway."

The afterglow dims. Fades. The night returns, darker now in contrast.

"Sawyer?" I ask.

"Sawyer."

More fireworks. Smaller ones now, rapid-fire. Pop-pop-pop. Little bursts of color—pink, orange, yellow, green—like flowers blooming in fast-forward. They don't linger. Just flash and vanish, flash and vanish.

"I couldn't save him. He didn't want to be saved." Milly's voice is steady but soft. "But I should have tried harder. Should have—"

He stops. The rapid-fire bursts stop too. Silence fills the gap.

Then one more rises. Slow. Deliberate. It climbs

through the darkness, trailing gold.

"I couldn't save him," Milly says. "But I could save you."

The firework reaches its apex. Hangs there. Waiting.

"You did save me," I whisper. "You are saving me."

It bursts. Not outward. Inward—collapsing into itself in rings of blue light that contract and contract until there's just a single bright point. Then that point expands again, sudden and violent, throwing out rays of white light in all directions like a star being born.

"We're saving each other, I think," Milly says. "You just don't see it yet."

The star fades. The rays dim. Darkness settles again.

But not for long.

The finale begins.

Milly's jaw is tight. The lights are too much—too bright, too loud, too everything—but he doesn't look away.

I know it's the finale because they all go up at once. Ten, fifteen, twenty fireworks rising together, their trails crossing and weaving as they climb. The sky fills with ascending light.

They reach their heights within seconds of each other.

And then they all burst.

Red. Blue. Green. Gold. Purple. Orange. Silver.

White. Every color at once, overlapping and mixing and creating new colors in the spaces between. The entire sky becomes light. The water becomes light. The buildings, the bridges, everything reflecting and multiplying the brilliance until there's no darkness left anywhere.

It's too much to process. Too much to take in. My eyes don't know where to look—up at the real fireworks or down at their reflections, at the colors bleeding into each other or the individual bursts, at the ones still expanding or the ones already beginning to fall.

So I just watch. All of it. Everything.

The sound is continuous now—not individual booms but a rolling thunder that I feel in my chest. The air itself seems to vibrate.

Beautiful doesn't cover it. Overwhelming doesn't cover it. There's no word for this. Just... light. Color. Sound. The whole world transformed into something that shouldn't be possible but is.

I'm crying. I don't know when I started, but my face is wet.

Not sad crying. Not even happy crying, exactly. Just... crying because there's too much inside me to hold and it has to go somewhere.

The finale reaches its peak. Every firework fully expanded, filling every inch of sky. For one perfect, impossible moment, everything is illuminated.

Then it begins to fade.

Not all at once. Gradually. The colors start to dim, the lights begin falling, the thunder quiets to individual echoes. Piece by piece, the darkness returns.

Until finally, there's just the normal night sky. Stars. Mün's pale glow. The lanterns along the canals.

Silence.

The gondola rocks gently. The gondolier's pole dips into water. We drift forward.

I can still see the afterimages when I blink. Ghosts of color floating in my vision.

"I'm glad you're here," I say. Still not looking at him. Looking at where the fireworks were. "I know I'm difficult. I know I almost got us killed. Multiple times. But I'm glad you didn't give up."

"I'm glad I didn't either."

The gondolier hums his melody again. We float under a bridge, the sound of water echoing briefly before we emerge on the other side.

I finally look at Milly.

He's still watching the sky. Face calm. Peaceful. The lantern light catches in his eyes—not reflected fireworks anymore, just the steady glow of the lamps.

For the first time since Krandor, I think he might actually be okay.

That maybe we both might be.

The gondola carries us forward through the golden water, under stone bridges, past lit windows where people are settling in for the night.

I close my eyes.

Let myself feel it. The gentle rock of the boat. The cool air. The lingering warmth of too much color.

Happy.

I'm happy.

And for once, I don't question it. Don't wait for it to be ripped away.

I just let myself be here.

Safe.

# STRAY

◆

### CHAPTER XXXIII

Morning light filters through the hotel window, soft and golden. I wake slowly this time, not jolted by nightmares or the weight of dread. Just... waking up. Natural.

The room smells faintly of salt air coming through the open window. I can hear Celton stirring below—cart wheels on cobblestones, someone calling out about fresh fish, the distant splash of gondolas in the canals.

I stretch, feeling the familiar ache of travel in my muscles but nothing sharp. Nothing urgent. Just the pleasant soreness of a body that's been moving and is ready to move again.

Milly said we'd explore today. No rush. No schedule. Just... seeing the city. Like Kanne used to say—"rest first, world later." I wonder if she and Kraft are still taking in strays.

I dress in the plaid gray skirt and black shirt—the clothes that have become mine through weeks of wearing them. They're clean now, washed by the hotel staff. The fabric feels soft against my skin.

Downstairs, Milly's already at a corner table with breakfast. He looks up when I approach, something lighter in his expression than I've seen in days.

"Sleep well?" he asks.

He looks like he didn't. The scar on his forehead is more visible in morning light—still red, not quite healed despite the weeks.

"Really well." And it's true. No nightmares. No waking in the middle of the night hearing phantom footsteps. Just... sleep.

He gestures to the plate across from him—eggs, fresh bread (crunchy, he remembered), some kind of sliced fruit I don't recognize.

"Eat first," he says. "Then we'll walk."

The streets of Celton are different in daylight. The lower canals we passed through last night on the gondola look almost cheerful now—the stilted houses painted in faded blues and yellows, laundry bright against weathered wood, children playing on the docks. Three of them are Felidae, their tails held high as they chase two human kids in some complicated game involving a rope and a lot of shrieking. One of the Felidae children—a girl with brown-and-white markings—nearly falls into the canal before her human friend grabs her arm. They both dissolve into laughter.

This is what Milly meant when he said Celton was different. Here, nobody even notices. It's just... normal.

We walk without destination, just moving through the maze of streets and bridges. Milly's not in full armor today—just the padded underclothes and his sword at his hip. He looks more... human. Less like a paladin and more like just a person.

The market district is already busy. The sea breeze offers some relief from the heat, carrying the sharp scent of salt water mixed with spices, grilled fish, and the earthier smell of produce from inland farms. The air is humid but moving, not stagnant like inland cities. Vendors' awnings flap in the wind.

Voices calling out prices—some human, some Felidae with their ears perking forward when customers approach. Fresh bread mingles with the rest. I watch a Felidae merchant haggle with a customer, her tail lashing in mock irritation when he offers too low a price, then curling in satisfaction when they settle on something fair.

At a fruit stall, a Felidae child—maybe seven—stands on a crate to reach the higher displays, her small rounded ears swiveling to track her mother's voice. Her tail, still short and fluffy with youth, wraps around the crate edge for balance.

We turn down a narrow alley between two buildings. The sounds of the market fade slightly, replaced by quieter city noises—someone humming, water dripping from a gutter, a dog barking somewhere distant.

And then I see it.

A cat.

Small, orange-striped, sitting in a patch of sunlight on a stone step. It's grooming itself, one paw raised delicately to clean behind its ear.

I stop walking.

The cat pauses mid-lick, noticing me. Its eyes are huge and green, catching the light.

"Hello," I say quietly.

It tilts its head. Considering.

Milly stops beside me, following my gaze. "Making friends?"

"Maybe."

I crouch slowly, careful not to startle it. The cat watches, wary but not afraid. Its tail flicks once—a question mark in the air.

"Hey there," I murmur. "You're pretty."

The cat blinks slowly. Then, to my surprise, it stands. Stretches. And walks toward me.

Not quickly. Just... approaching. Testing.

I hold out my hand, letting it sniff my fingers. Its nose is tiny and pink, whiskers tickling my skin as it investigates.

Then it bumps its head against my palm.

A small sound escapes me—something between a laugh and a gasp. The cat does it again, more insistent this time. Demanding attention.

I run my hand down its back. The fur is soft, warm from the sun. It arches into the touch, purring so loud I can feel the vibration.

"You like that, huh?"

The cat responds by flopping onto its side, exposing its belly in the universal cat gesture of trust. I scratch gently under its chin, and the purring intensifies.

"Friendly little thing," Milly observes from above.

"Very friendly." I'm grinning now, can't help it. The cat is rolling around on the stones, pawing at my hand when I stop petting it.

A woman appears in the doorway of the nearby house—middle-aged, flour dusting her apron. She sees us and smiles.

"Ah, Cinders found someone new to charm," she says in accented Common.

"Cinders?"

"The cat." She gestures with a floury hand. "Stray. Showed up two weeks ago. Won't leave. I feed her, but she belongs to the whole street now."

"Her?"

"Her. Though she acts like she owns the entire district." The woman chuckles. "You're welcome to pet her. She loves attention."

As if to prove the point, Cinders—because that's her name now, apparently—rolls onto her back again, paws waving in the air.

I laugh. Actually laugh. The sound feels strange coming out of me, but good. Light.

"Can I—" I start, then look up at Milly. "Do we have any food?"

He raises an eyebrow. "For the cat?"

"She might be hungry."

He sighs but reaches into his pack. Pulls out a small piece of dried fish from our rations. "Here."

I take it, break off a tiny piece, offer it to Cinders. She sniffs it once, then snatches it with surprising delicacy. Chews. Swallows. Immediately headbutts my hand for more.

"Spoiled," I tell her. But I give her another piece anyway.

We stay there for longer than we probably should. Me sitting on the stones, Cinders alternating between eating fish bits and demanding pets. Milly standing nearby, watching with that look of patient amusement he gets when I'm being ridiculous.

The woman disappears back inside, leaving us

with the cat.

"We should keep moving," Milly says eventually. But his voice is gentle. Not rushing me.

"I know." I give Cinders one last scratch behind the ears. "Goodbye, girl. Stay out of trouble."

She meows—a tiny, demanding sound—but doesn't try to follow when I stand.

We continue down the alley. I glance back once. Cinders has returned to her patch of sunlight, grooming herself again like we were never there.

But something warm sits in my chest now. Something simple and good.

Just a cat. Just a few minutes in the sun.

But it mattered.

We walk for hours after that, through different districts. The upper canals with their marble buildings. The merchant quarter with its glassblowers and weavers. Past fountains and bridges and narrow streets that wind like mazes.

I keep thinking about Cinders. The way she just... trusted. Walked up to a stranger and demanded affection and got it. No hesitation. No fear.

When was the last time I trusted something that easily?

"You're quiet," Milly observes as we cross another bridge.

"Just thinking."

"About?"

"The cat." I pause. "How simple that was. She wanted attention. I wanted to give it. That was it."

He's quiet for a moment. Then: "Sometimes things can be simple."

"I keep forgetting that."

"I know."

We stop at a baker's stall. Milly buys two sweet rolls—still warm, sugar crystallized on top. We eat them leaning against a wall, watching people pass.

The roll is good. Sweet but not too sweet. Soft in the middle, slightly crispy at the edges. Perfect.

"Thank you," I say. "For today. For letting me pet the cat. For... all of this."

He looks at me. Something shifts in his expression—that same softness from last night. "You don't need to thank me for letting you be happy, Kitt."

The words hit harder than they should.

"I'm not used to it," I say quietly. "Being happy. It feels... fragile."

"It is fragile." He takes another bite of his roll. "But that doesn't make it less real."

We finish eating and keep walking. The afternoon stretches on, warm and lazy. By the time we return to the hotel, the sun is sinking toward the horizon, painting everything gold.

In my room, I sit on the bed, looking out the window at Celton's rooftops. I can see the canal from here, gondolas passing slowly in the evening light.

I think about Cinders. About Milly smiling when the cat flopped over for belly rubs. About sweet rolls and walking without purpose and feeling safe enough to just... exist.

Small things.

Normal things.

Things I thought I'd never feel again.

I close my eyes, hold onto it. This feeling. This moment.

Tomorrow we'll keep exploring. The day after, maybe we'll start thinking about Vestperia again.

But tonight, I'm here. In Celton. With a memory of an orange cat and warm bread and Milly's patient presence.

And for now, that's enough.

# MOTHS TO A FLAME

◆

### CHAPTER XXXIV

I can't sleep.

Again.

It's been three nights in Celton now, and every night is the same. I lie in bed, stare at the ceiling, listen to the city settling around me. Cart wheels fading. Voices quieting. The distant splash of canal water against stone.

From Milly's room next door, I hear his breathing. Steady. Even. The sound of someone who can actually rest.

I count the wooden beams above me. One, two, three, four. Same beams as last night. Same shadows.

My mind won't quiet. Keeps circling back to the same thoughts.

*Mom's kitchen. The blood. Her eyes.*

*The statue's blank helmet turning.*

*Milly's voice: "I cannot make you."*

*The sea. Salt and pine. "I made it."*

Round and round. No pattern. No sense. Just... circling.

I sit up. The floorboards are cool under my bare feet. My traveling clothes are folded on the chair—I pull them on quietly, slowly. Every movement deliberate, trying not to make sound.

Milly's breathing doesn't change. Still steady.

I slip out of my room, close the door with barely a click. The hallway is dark except for one lamp at the far end, its flame guttering low. My boots are in my hands—I don't put them on until I'm downstairs, out of earshot.

The night clerk at the front desk is dozing. Doesn't notice me slip past.

Outside, Celton is a different city. The canals reflect Mün's light, turning the water silver-white. Lanterns still burn along the main walkways, but most of the side streets are dark. Shadowed.

I know where I'm going.

The alley looks the same as it did two days ago. Narrow. Quiet. The stone step where Cinders was grooming herself in the sunlight.

She's there now.

Curled in the shadows, a small orange shape

barely visible in the dark. But I see the gleam of her eyes when she lifts her head. Watching me approach.

"Hey," I whisper. "Remember me?"

She stands. Stretches. That same lazy, deliberate movement. Then walks toward me like we're old friends.

I sink onto the step, and she immediately jumps into my lap. Circles once. Twice. Settles.

The purring starts immediately. Loud and rumbling. I run my hand down her back, feeling the warmth, the softness.

"Couldn't sleep either, huh?" I murmur.

She bumps her head against my palm. Demanding more attention.

I give it. Scratch behind her ears, under her chin. She leans into every touch like it's the best thing that's ever happened to her.

"You're lucky," I tell her. "You don't have to think about anything. Just sleep in the sun. Get pets. Eat fish."

Cinders purrs louder.

My throat tightens.

"I wish it was that simple."

The cat looks up at me with those huge green eyes. Blinks slowly.

And I hear it.

Not a meow. Not a purr.

A voice.

"It can be, sweetheart."

I freeze.

Mom's voice. Soft. Gentle. The way she used to talk when I'd wake up from nightmares as a kid.

"Mom?" I whisper.

Cinders tilts her head. Purrs.

"*I'm here.*"

No. No, that's not—

But I keep petting the cat. Keep looking at her. Because if I look away, the voice might stop.

"I miss you," I choke out.

"*I know. I miss you too, Kitt-y.*"

The old nickname. The one that used to make me groan and roll my eyes. Now it cracks something open in my chest.

"Why did you do it?" The question spills out before I can stop it. "Why did you leave me?"

Cinders shifts in my lap. Gets comfortable again.

"*I was so tired, sweetheart. So, so tired.*"

"But I needed you." Tears are falling now, hot and fast. "I still need you."

"*I know. And I'm sorry. I'm so sorry.*"

"It's not fair." My voice breaks. "It's not fair that you left. That Dad left. That I'm the only one still here."

"*Life isn't fair, Kitt. You're learning that.*"

"I don't want to learn it." I'm sobbing now, trying to keep quiet so I don't wake the whole street. "I want you back. I want Dad back. I want everything to be the way it was before."

"*But it can't be. You know that.*"

"I know." I press my face into Cinders' fur. She tolerates it, purring against my cheek. "I know, but I can't... I can't let go."

"*You don't have to let go. You just have to keep moving forward.*"

"How? How do I do that when everything hurts?"

"*One step at a time. Like you've been doing. You made it to the sea, didn't you?*"

"We did," I whisper. "We made it."

"*I'm so proud of you.*"

The words break me. I sob harder, clutching the cat like she's the only thing keeping me tethered to the earth.

"*I'm so proud of you, Kitt. Your father would be too.*"

"I don't deserve—"

"*You do. You deserve to be happy. To heal. To live.*"

"I don't know how."

"*You're learning. With Milly. With Dr. Verne. You're learning.*"

Footsteps.

Soft. Careful. Coming from the end of the alley.

I look up, tears still streaming.

Milly stands there. No armor. Hair slightly mussed from sleep—or trying to sleep. The scar catches moonlight, pale line across his forehead. Just his underclothes and boots hastily pulled on, like he dressed in a hurry. His expression is... careful. Concerned.

"Kitt."

His voice is gentle. Real.

Not Mom's.

I look back down at Cinders. She's just a cat. Just an orange cat purring in my lap. Not talking. Not answering. Just... being.

"The cat isn't talking back," Milly says quietly. He doesn't move closer. Just stands there, giving me space. "You know that."

I nod. Can't speak. Throat too tight.

"How long have you been out here?"

"I don't know." My voice is hoarse. "An hour? Maybe less."

"I woke up," he says, answering the question I didn't ask. "Heard your door open. Followed to make sure you were safe."

He's quiet for a moment. Then he moves closer, slowly. Sits on the step beside me. Not touching. Just... present.

Cinders looks at him. Meows once—an actual meow, high and questioning.

"I know she's not really talking," I whisper. "I know it's just my brain. Filling in. Making me hear what I need to hear."

"I know you know."

"But I can't—I can't stop." I'm crying again. "I keep hearing her. Mom's voice. Saying things Mom would say. And I know it's not real but I want it to be real so badly."

"That's okay."

"It's not okay. It's—" I stop. Breathe. "It's pathetic."

"It's human," Milly says. "You lost your mother. You're trying to find her anywhere you can. Even in a stray cat."

I laugh. It's a broken, wet sound. "I'm talking to a cat and hearing my dead mother respond. That's... that's not healthy."

"No," he agrees. "It's not. But it's part of grieving. Part of not being ready to let go yet."

"When will I be ready?"

"I don't know." He watches Cinders, who's now grooming herself in my lap, completely unconcerned with our conversation. "Maybe never. Maybe someday. There's no timeline for this, Kitt."

We sit in silence. Cinders purrs. Somewhere distant, a gondola passes through a canal, the water sloshing gently.

"I have to say goodbye," I whisper. "Don't I?"

"Eventually. But not tonight. Not if you're not ready."

"I'm never going to be ready."

"Then say goodbye anyway."

The words sit heavy between us.

I look down at Cinders. At her orange fur and white paws and the way her tail curls around her body. A cat. Nothing more. A sweet, friendly stray who wants attention and food and warmth.

Not Mom.

Never was Mom.

Just... a cat.

"Thank you," I tell her. My voice shakes. "For letting me pretend. For being here."

Cinders looks up at me. Blinks those slow, trusting blinks.

I lift her gently, set her on the step beside me. She protests—a tiny, indignant meow—but settles quickly. Starts grooming her paw.

"Goodbye, Cinders," I whisper.

*Goodbye, Mom.*

I stand. My legs are stiff from sitting so long. Milly stands too, waiting.

I look at the cat one more time. She's already lost interest, focused entirely on cleaning between her toes.

"She'll be okay," Milly says quietly. "The street takes care of her."

"I know."

We start walking back. The alley gives way to the main canal walkway. Lantern light reflects on water. Everything is quiet, peaceful.

"Thank you," I say after a while. "For not... I don't know. Making it weird."

"You were talking to a cat and hearing your mother's voice. It was already weird."

I laugh. An actual laugh. Small, but real.

"Fair."

We walk in comfortable silence. My eyes still burn from crying. My chest still aches. But something feels... lighter. Not healed. Not fixed.

Just... acknowledged.

"Kitt?"

"Yes?"

"I followed you. From the hotel. I wanted to make sure you were safe."

"I know." I glance at him. "Thank you for that too."

He nods once. Doesn't say anything else.

When we reach the hotel, the night clerk is still dozing. We slip past him, up the stairs. At my door, Milly pauses.

"Get some rest," he says. "Tomorrow we'll start looking at passage to Vestperia. We're close now."

"Close," I echo.

He goes to his room. I go to mine.

This time, when I lie in bed and close my eyes, I don't hear Mom's voice.

Just the distant sounds of Celton. The canal water. Milly's steady breathing through the wall.

And slowly, finally, I sleep.

# PLAIN SHEETS OF WIND

◆

### CHAPTER XXXV

Morning light spills through the hotel window, warmer than yesterday. I wake feeling... not rested, exactly. But quieter. Like something that was screaming inside me finally lowered its voice to a whisper.

Milly's already downstairs when I come down. He's at our usual corner table, but today there's a map spread out beside his breakfast. Not a road map—this one shows coastlines, shipping routes, ports marked in careful ink.

"Sleep better?" he asks when I sit.

"A little." I don't mention the dream I had—Mom smiling, waving goodbye, walking into the light. Not sad. Just... leaving. "What's that?"

"Shipping schedules." He taps the map. "We need to book passage. I want to see what's available."

The word *passage* makes it real. We're actually leaving. Getting on a boat. Crossing water to Vestperia.

The end of the journey.

Or the beginning of whatever comes next.

"When?" I ask.

"Tomorrow, if possible. Day after at latest." He folds the map carefully. "The harbor master can tell us more. We'll go this morning."

We eat quickly—bread and cheese, some fruit. The same breakfast we've had for days, but it tastes different now. Final.

The harbor district is chaos.

Ships crowd the docks—massive cargo vessels with holds full of grain and spices, sleek passenger ships with painted hulls, even a few military vessels flying Celtorian colors. The smell is overwhelming: salt and tar and fish and unwashed sailors and cargo rotting in the sun.

People shout in a dozen languages. Unital, Common, others I don't recognize. Dock workers haul crates and barrels. Sailors climb rigging, checking lines. A ship's bell clangs somewhere, sharp and insistent.

But even in the chaos, I notice things: the docks are well-maintained, no rotting wood like I expected. There are public fountains every few streets—free, clean water. A Felidae woman fills buckets while her human neighbor waits his turn, chatting easily. No guards watching them.

In Krandor, guards were everywhere. Here, I've seen maybe three since we arrived, and they're helping an elderly couple with directions rather than watching for trouble.

Milly navigates it all with practiced ease, asking questions in formal Unital, getting pointed from one official to another. I follow, trying not to get separated in the crowd.

Finally, we find the harbor master's office—a wooden building perched on stilts over the water. Inside, a gray-haired woman with ink-stained fingers listens to Milly's request.

"Vestperia?" She consults a massive ledger, flipping pages. "You're in luck. The *Meridian's Grace* departs tomorrow at dawn. Passenger vessel, makes the crossing in three days with good winds."

She pauses, then sighs. "Should be smooth sailing—they're taking the southern route."

"Southern?" Milly asks. "That's longer."

"Mm. Captains prefer it lately. Less... traffic." She doesn't elaborate. Stamps their tickets with finality.

Three days. Three days on the water, then Vestperia.

Then Dr. Verne.

Then... what? Healing? Hope? I don't know.

"We'll take two berths," Milly says.

The woman quotes a price. Milly doesn't haggle, just pays. She marks our names in the ledger with efficient strokes.

"Boarding starts an hour before dawn. Don't be late—Captain Sezane won't wait." She stamps two slips of paper, hands them over. "Fair winds."

Outside, the noise hits again. The bandage on his forehead is still fresh—he adjusted it this morning, fingers careful around the edges. But Milly's smiling—actually smiling, not that careful controlled expression he usually wears.

"Three days," he says. "That's it. Three days and you'll be in Vestperia."

"We'll be in Vestperia," I correct.

"We'll be in Vestperia," he agrees.

He looks lighter than I've seen him in... maybe ever. The tension that's lived in his shoulders since Kanna's Ridge seems eased. Even his voice sounds different—warmer, less guarded.

"What will you do first?" I ask as we walk back through the harbor. "When we get there?"

He considers. "Make sure you're settled with Dr. Verne. That's first."

"And after?"

"After..." He pauses at a stall selling carved wooden tokens—luck charms for sailors. Picks one up, examines it. "After, I'll visit Sawyer's grave. I've been putting it off for two years. Time to stop running from it."

He sets the token down, keeps walking.

"And then?" I press.

"Then maybe I'll take some time. Actually rest. See parts of the world I've only passed through." He glances at me. "Maybe you'll be ready to travel by then. We could see those floating markets you mentioned. The hot springs in western Celtor."

Hope blooms in my chest. Not the desperate, fragile hope from before. Something steadier.

"I'd like that," I say.

"So would I."

We stop at a food stall, buy skewers of grilled fish. Eat them standing at the dock's edge, watching ships come and go. The sun is bright, the breeze cool. Perfect weather.

That evening, we walk through Celton one last time.

The route is familiar now—past the fountain where water trickles over stone, through the market square where vendors are packing up for the night, across the small bridge where I can see our reflections in the canal below.

We don't talk much. Just walk, taking it in.

At one point, Milly stops at a bakery. Buys two of those sweet pastries from our first night. Hands me one.

"For the road," he says.

"The water," I correct.

"The water."

We eat them watching the sun set over the canal district. Orange and pink painting the water, the buildings, everything. Beautiful.

"Thank you," I say quietly.

"For the pastry?"

"For all of it. For not giving up. For getting me this far."

He's quiet for a moment. Then: "You got yourself this far, Kitt. I just... walked beside you."

"That's not true."

"It's true enough." He finishes his pastry, brushes crumbs from his hands. "You made the choice to keep going. Every day. Even when it was hard. Especially when it was hard."

The words sit warm in my chest.

We walk back to the hotel as full darkness falls. Mün rises, round and bright. Lanterns flicker to life along the canals.

We pass a building with a red cross painted above the door—a public physician, the sign says, free for residents. In Krandor, medicine cost coin. Here, it's just... available.

"Celtor spends differently than Orenia," Milly says, noticing me staring. "Your nation builds walls. Mine builds wells."

In my room, I pack the few things I've accumulated. Two carved wooden horses now—the rough one from Byēnwick, the smoother one from Milldraugh. The clothes that have become mine through weeks of wearing them. The small things that mark the journey.

Tomorrow, we board. Tomorrow, the final leg begins.

I should be scared. Should be anxious.

Instead, I feel... ready.

I dream of Krandor.

Not the kitchen. Not Mom. Something older.

I'm at my window, maybe eight years old. It's night, and there's torchlight in the lower districts—guardsmen moving in formation. I can hear shouting, though I can't make out the words. Then screaming. Then sounds I don't have names for yet.

Mom's hand on my shoulder, pulling me back. "Don't watch, Kitt-y. Come away from the window."

But I've already seen. A family running—father, mother, two children, all of them with rounded ears and tails streaming behind them. The guards are faster.

I don't look away fast enough.

In the dream, Mom asks: "Why aren't you

crying?"

I don't have an answer.

I wake up in Celton, where Felidae walk freely, where shrines to Mīrrū stand unmolested, where no one hunts anyone for having fur.

And I think: *How inefficient. How soft. How easy it would be, if someone wanted to.*

Then I get dressed and go downstairs for breakfast, and I don't think about it again.

Morning comes too quickly.

The sky is still dark when we leave the hotel, just the barest hint of gray at the horizon. The streets are mostly empty—just us and a few other early risers heading toward the docks.

At the stable, Horsey nickers when she sees me. That familiar greeting that means *finally, you're here.*

I bury my face in her neck, breathing in the smell of her—hay and warmth and the road we've traveled together.

"I can't take you on the ship," I whisper. "But the stable master will take care of you. He promised."

She huffs against my shoulder.

"You're a good girl. The best girl." My throat

tightens. "Thank you for carrying me this far."

Milly handles the arrangements—selling her to the stable for a fair price, making sure she'll be well treated. I can't watch. Can't see money change hands like she's just a transaction.

When we leave, I don't look back. Can't.

One more goodbye I'm not ready for.

We walk in silence toward the docks. My throat is still tight, eyes still burning. Every step away from the stable feels wrong.

The *Meridian's Grace* is smaller than I expected. Maybe less than a drūm long, two masts, a dozen passengers already boarding. Crew members shout instructions, hauling cargo into the hold, checking rigging.

Milly shows our papers to a sailor at the gangplank. The man nods, waves us aboard.

The deck is crowded—sailors working, passengers finding their berths below, crates and barrels secured against the rails. Everything smells like salt and tar and adventure.

Other passengers are boarding ahead of us—maybe twenty or thirty people total. I watch them navigate the gangplank with varying degrees of confidence.

A merchant family catches my eye. The father—human, broad-shouldered, already sweating in the morning warmth—is directing the loading of several large crates. His wife is Felidae, her longer tail swishing as she counts their luggage, brown fur catching the early light. She calls out to their children in Unital, the purring lilt making the formal language sound almost musical.

Three children. The oldest—a boy, maybe eleven, fully human like his father—is trying to look responsible by carrying a bag almost as big as he is. The middle child—a girl with her mother's rounded ears and a shorter, fluffier tail—is bouncing excitedly, brown braids swinging as she points at the ship's rigging. She can't be more than eight.

But as her mother guides her toward the gangplank, the girl's tail puffs up. She stops, looking down at the water between dock and ship.

"It's deep, Mama," she whispers in Unital, her voice carrying.

Her mother crouches, ears flicking back. "Very deep. But the ship is strong."

"What if I fall in?"

Her mother's tail curls around Yuki's waist like a living safety rope. "Then I jump in after you. And your father jumps after me. And your brothers jump after him. And we all get very wet and have to explain to the captain why we're dripping on his nice deck."

Yuki giggles despite herself, and lets her mother lead her aboard.

The youngest—a boy around six with the same small rounded ears—is more interested in the seagulls than the ship, trying to chase them along the dock until his father scoops him up.

"Klaus, we need you ON the ship, not IN the water," the father says, but he's smiling.

They look happy. Excited. Like they're going on an adventure.

An elderly Felidae couple boards after them, moving slowly, helping each other up the gangplank. The woman's fur has gone gray around her muzzle and ears, and her husband's orange-and-white striped tail moves with the careful deliberation of age. They pause at the top to catch their breath, and the old man says something that makes his wife laugh—that particular rolling sound that Felidae make when they're truly amused.

A young scholar follows—human, maybe mid-twenties, already pulling out a leather journal as he boards, like he can't wait to start documenting the journey.

We're shown to a small cabin below deck. Two narrow bunks, a porthole window, barely enough room to turn around. But it's private, clean, ours for three days.

A sailor leads us down the narrow companion ladder. Our cabin is on the second deck—bunks, porthole, cramped but clean.

As he turns to leave, I notice another ladder continuing down. Darker. The wood looks newer, reinforced.

"What's down there?" I ask.

"Cargo hold, miss." The sailor moves to block the ladder, casual but deliberate. "Passengers aren't permitted below second deck. Captain's rules—safety reasons. Shifting cargo, rats, that sort of thing."

Milly nods, accepting this immediately. I peer past the sailor anyway, curious.

The darkness below smells different. Not like ship-rot or bilge water. Something sharper. Oil, maybe? Metal?

"Miss?" The sailor gestures back toward our cabin. "Best get settled before we cast off."

I follow Milly back, glancing once more at the forbidden ladder.

We stow our packs and come back on deck.

"Cozy," Milly says dryly.

I laugh. Can't help it.

The sun is rising now, painting the sky orange and gold. Celton spreads behind us—the stilted houses, the canals, the upper city with its marble buildings catching first light.

Beautiful.

The captain—a weathered woman with gray hair in a tight braid—calls out orders. Sailors scramble—both human and Felidae working together, the Felidae crew members climbing the rigging with their tails providing extra balance. I watch one of them navigate the ropes with an ease that makes it look effortless, his ears swiveling to track the captain's commands even when he's facing away.

Lines are cast off.

Below us, I can see the merchant family settling near the bow. The little girl—Yuki, her mother called her—has found a ball somewhere and is already bouncing it against the deck. Her brother watches with that particular mix of exasperation and fondness that older siblings perfect. The youngest is being held by their father, pointing at everything, asking questions in a voice that carries even over the harbor noise.

The elderly couple has found a bench near the rail, sitting close together, the woman's tail curled around her husband's hand.

The ship lurches, then settles into motion. Slow at first, then faster as the sails catch wind.

We're moving. Actually moving. Leaving Celton behind.

Milly stands at the rail, watching the city shrink. I stand beside him.

The wind is clean and cool. The water reflects the sunrise—gold and pink and endless blue.

"Next stop, Vestperia," Milly says.

"Next stop, Vestperia," I echo.

He looks at me. Something in his expression is so... peaceful. Content. Like he's finally allowing himself to believe we'll make it.

"We're going to be okay," he says. Not a question. A statement.

"We're going to be okay," I agree.

The sails snap full with wind. The ship picks up speed, cutting through calm water.

Three days. Just three more days.

Behind us, Celton fades to a smudge on the horizon. Ahead, open sea stretches forever.

Fair winds.

Clear skies.

Everything ahead feels possible.

# SPOLIA OPIMA

◆

### CHAPTER XXXVI

The third morning at sea breaks clear and bright.

I wake to the gentle rock of the ship, the creak of wood that's become as familiar as breathing. Through the porthole, I can see endless blue—water meeting sky with no line between them.

Milly's already awake, sitting on his bunk with that book he's been reading. He glances up when I stir.

"Morning. Sleep well?"

The scar is barely visible now. Almost healed. Almost.

"Better than on land." It's true. The constant motion lulls me into something deeper than sleep. No nightmares. No waking in the dark listening for footsteps that aren't there.

"We're making good time," he says, setting the book aside. "Captain thinks we'll reach Vestperia's ports by tomorrow evening. Maybe sooner if the wind holds."

Tomorrow evening. One more day.

The thought should make me nervous. Instead, it feels... right. Like something I've been walking toward for months is finally within reach.

"Come on," Milly says, standing. "Let's get breakfast before the galley runs out of the good bread."

I gather my things from where they've scattered in the night. The wooden horses have fallen over from the ship's rocking. I stand them upright again, adjust them so they're facing the porthole. Toward Vestperia. Like they're looking ahead for us.

Milly catches me doing it. Doesn't comment. Just a slight smile.

On deck, the morning is perfect. The kind of morning that makes you forget anything bad could ever happen.

The sun sits just above the horizon, turning the water gold and pink. The air is cool but not cold, carrying that clean salt smell without any of the fish-rot stench of harbors. The wind is steady, filling the sails with a gentle *whump-whump* that sounds almost like breathing.

The ship's cook has set up a small table near the main mast—wooden bowls of porridge, hard cheese, bread that's only one day old instead of three. Other passengers are already gathering, murmuring good mornings in Common and Unital and languages I don't recognize.

The young scholar—Hiroto, I heard someone call him—is examining the ship with clear fascination, leather journal tucked under his arm. I watch him try one of the lower companion ladders, peering down into the dimness.

A sailor intercepts him before he's down three rungs. "Sorry sir, cargo hold's restricted. Captain's orders."

"I was just curious about the construction—"

"Happy to answer questions up here, sir." The sailor's smile is polite but firm. "But the lower deck's off-limits. Insurance reasons."

Hiroto nods, retreating gracefully. But I catch him glancing back at the ladder as he walks away, that same curious look I probably had on my face yesterday when we boarded.

The merchant family is there—mother, father, and three children who've spent the entire voyage treating the ship like their personal playground. Yuki is still trying to teach her older brother some kind of hand-clapping game. Her tail—short and fluffy, the kind that shows she's only half-Felidae—swishes behind her as she bounces excitedly. She keeps messing up the rhythm and dissolving into giggles.

"No, no, you go *then* I go," she insists in Unital, demonstrating again. One of her ears flicks back in concentration.

Her brother—maybe eleven, human like their father—rolls his eyes but plays along. Patient in the way older siblings learn to be.

Their father is repacking one of their travel bags nearby, muttering. His wife watches, tail tip twitching with amusement.

"We don't need three spare shirts for a three-day voyage," she says in Common.

"What if Klaus spills something? He always spills something."

"Then he wears a dirty shirt for two days. He'll survive."

"He's six. He'll be miserable." He doesn't look up from the bag.

She touches his shoulder—brief, affectionate. "You packed four, didn't you."

His silence is answer enough. She makes that rolling laugh, warm and resigned.

The third child, a boy around six with the same rounded ears as his sister, is more interested in his breakfast, shoveling porridge into his mouth with single-minded focus. His tail drapes over the edge of his seat, tip twitching occasionally.

"Slow down, Klaus, or you'll choke," their mother

says, one of her own ears flicking back in that automatic parental concern. Her tail is longer than her daughter's, more expressive, the brown fur catching morning light. Full Felidae, probably. I've seen a few in Krandor, but they're rarer there. More common in Celtor and Kurune, where the old bloodlines mixed freely centuries ago.

Milly and I get our food and find a spot at the rail, away from the crowd but still able to watch. The porridge is warm and bland and perfect. The bread is crusty on the outside, soft inside. I tear off a piece, offer it to him.

"Want some?"

"I have my own."

"This piece is better."

He takes it, shaking his head but almost-smiling. "You're ridiculous."

"You keep saying that."

"You keep being ridiculous."

I grin, take another bite of my own bread. The crust crunches between my teeth, satisfying in a way that trail rations never were.

The elderly couple emerges from below deck, moving slowly, helping each other up the narrow stairs. They've been kind throughout the journey—offering advice in broken Common, sharing dried fruit from their packs, asking gentle questions about where we're going.

The old woman—Elsa, I think her name is—spots

us and waves. We wave back. Her husband's tail flicks once behind him, the orange-and-white stripes catching the morning light. His ears, also striped, swivel toward us when we acknowledge them. Full Felidae, both of them, probably from the eastern provinces where they're more common.

"One more day," she calls over in accented Common, her ears twitching forward with excitement. "Then we see our daughter!"

"One more day," Milly agrees.

She beams, then makes that clicking sound elderly Felidae make—half-sigh, half-laugh. Her husband's tail intertwines with hers as they move to find seats.

"I told you we should have visited Lirien last year," she says in Unital, loud enough to carry.

"You said it every year for ten years," her husband replies, ears flattening in mock-submission.

"And I was right every year."

"Yes, dear." But his tail curls tighter around hers, and when she laughs—that particular rolling sound—he laughs too.

The young scholar is already at his usual spot near the bow, leather journal open, quill moving across the page. He's been writing the entire voyage—maybe documenting the journey, maybe working on something else entirely. He pauses occasionally to dip his quill in a small inkpot he keeps secured to his belt.

Yesterday he'd asked us about Vestperia, if we'd been there before. When we said no, he'd shared what he knew—the glowing towers (real, apparently, though the glow comes from crystal formations, not magic), the Institute where scholars from across the known world gather to study, the floating gardens in the city's western quarter.

He'd made it sound beautiful. Possible. Real.

A sailor passes by, checking the rigging. He nods to us, calls something cheerful to another sailor who's climbing the ratlines. Normal morning routine. Everything as it should be.

Voices carry from near the helm—Captain Sezane and her first mate, not quite arguing but close.

"—could shave six hours if we angled through the strait—"

"Not with both fleets positioning." The captain's tone is final.

"They're just posturing. They do this twice a year—"

"Not with what we're carrying." A pause. "And not with passengers on board."

"The passengers are exactly why we should look harmless—"

"The passengers are why we're taking the long route, Marcus." Her voice drops. "Families make questions expensive. For everyone involved."

The first mate mutters something about schedules and clients.

"Our client gets their delivery when we dock safely. Not before." The captain's tone sharpens. "We're a passenger vessel on a documented route. That's all anyone needs to see. Understood?"

The first mate mutters something I don't catch. The captain doesn't respond.

I glance at Milly, but he's already looking that direction, jaw slightly tight. When he notices me watching, his expression clears.

"I could get used to this," I say quietly. Trying not to think about what I just heard.

Milly glances at me. "Sea travel?"

"Just... this. Peaceful mornings. Good bread. No one trying to kill us."

He's quiet for a moment. Then: "Me too."

Yuki has abandoned the hand-clapping game. Now she's got a ball, bouncing it against the deck, trying to catch it on the rebound. Each successful catch makes her grin wider, her tail swishing with pride.

Her little brother Klaus, finished with his porridge, toddles over to join her. She bounces the ball to him. He misses, has to chase it as it rolls across the deck, his tail held high behind him as he runs. His laugh is high and bright, the kind of laugh children have before the world teaches them to be afraid.

"Here," Milly says, pulling something from his pack. "I've been meaning to show you this."

It's a length of rope, maybe two pās long. He starts working it with his hands, fingers moving with practiced ease, forming loops and crosses.

"This is a proper bowline," he says. "Different from the one I showed you before. See how the working end comes up through the loop, not down?"

I watch his hands. Try to memorize the pattern.

"Now you try."

He hands me another piece of rope. I copy his movements—awkward at first, fingers fumbling, but gradually finding the rhythm. Under, around, back through. Pull tight.

"Good," he says. Not elaborate praise. Just... acknowledgment. "Again."

I undo it, start over. The rope is rough against my palms, the texture satisfying. Something real and simple and learnable.

On my third attempt, I get it right. The knot holds when I pull, neat and secure.

"There," Milly says. Something in his voice that might be pride. "Now you can tie a proper knot."

"Only took me three months."

"Better late than never."

The scholar looks up from his journal, watches us for a moment. Then closes the book and walks over.

"Practicing knots?" he asks in Common. His

accent is interesting—Vestperian formal, but with edges that suggest somewhere else originally.

"Teaching," Milly corrects.

"Ah. The best kind of practice." The scholar extends his hand to me. "I don't think we've properly introduced ourselves. Hiroto Adler, from the Vestperian Institute."

I shake his hand. "Kitt. This is Milly."

"Just Milly?" Hiroto smiles. "No family name?"

"Just Milly."

"Fair enough." Hiroto leans against the rail beside us. "I was wondering—you said you're going to Vestperia for the first time. Do you have lodging arranged?"

"Working on it," Milly says.

"The Scholar's Quarter has good inns. Reasonable prices, safe. I could recommend a few, if you'd like." He pauses, something fond in his expression. "My brother says I've stayed in half the inns in Vestperia by now. 'Takeshi,' I tell him, 'that's called research.' He doesn't buy it." He chuckles.

His smile fades slightly. "Takeshi thinks I'm chasing romance instead of doing real scholarship. He's not entirely wrong. The Institute is... full of people who've already proven themselves. I'm still trying to figure out what I'm supposed to prove."

Milly nods slowly. "First time presenting?"

"First time presenting research that matters."

Hiroto's hand rests on his journal. "If they don't like it, I go home and teach in Krandor alongside my brother. Which wouldn't be terrible, just..." He doesn't finish. Just looks out at the horizon. "It wouldn't be this."

Hiroto falters for a moment, then continues.

"The Institute doesn't care about poetry or passion," he continues. "They want *results*. Provable, repeatable results. If you can't demonstrate your research through experiment and measurement, you're not a scholar—you're a storyteller." He smiles bitterly. "Kurune has no use for storytellers."

They talk for a few minutes about districts and prices and which streets to avoid after dark. Normal traveler conversation. Friendly and practical and calm.

Yuki's ball bounces past us. She chases it, laughing, nearly crashes into Hiroto. Her tail puffs up slightly in surprise.

"Sorry!" she gasps, scooping up the ball. Her ears flatten apologetically.

"No harm done," Hiroto says, stepping aside with a smile.

She runs back to her family. Her mother is braiding her older brother's hair, trying to tame it into something presentable. He's complaining but sitting still anyway. Klaus is attempting to braid his own tail—a task made difficult by the fact that he keeps having to twist around to reach it.

"They seem like a good family," I say.

"They do," Milly agrees.

The sun climbs higher. The morning stretches on, easy and perfect. Sailors move through their routines, checking lines, adjusting sails. Everything working as it should. No problems. No threats.

Just a ship full of people traveling to somewhere better.

I finish my bread, brush crumbs from my skirt.

Milly's eating mechanically, eyes on the horizon. Still alert. Still watching.

The day feels full of possibility. One more day until Vestperia. One more day until Dr. Verne. One more day until whatever comes next.

"Thank you," I say to Milly. "For getting me this far."

He looks at me. Something shifts in his expression—softer, warmer. "You got yourself this far, Kitt. I just walked beside you."

"That's not—"

"It's true enough." He reaches over, adjusts the knot I tied, making sure it's secure. "You're stronger than you think."

The words settle warm in my chest. I open my mouth to respond—

The lookout shouts.

Not words—just a sharp, urgent sound that makes every sailor on deck freeze and look up.

The lookout is pointing. East and west. Both directions.

# FALL OF *GRACE*

### CHAPTER XXXVII

I follow his gesture.

At first, I don't understand what I'm seeing. Just darkness on the horizon. Like storm clouds gathering on both sides. But the sky is clear, blue and perfect.

Then the darkness resolves into shapes.

Ships.

Two of them.

My brain struggles to process the scale. These aren't vessels like ours. They're... something else entirely. Something that shouldn't exist. Each one rises from the water like a mountain given motion, hull after hull stacked vertically, three full decks visible above the waterline and who knows how many below. Masts pierce the sky—not two like ours, but five, six, maybe more, each hung with canvas the size of buildings. The ships are so long I can't see their ends properly, the perspective playing tricks, making them seem like they go on forever.

A kāl. Each ship must be a kāl long. Maybe more.

Our entire vessel could fit inside one of their cargo holds with room to spare.

"Warships," Milly says. His voice is flat. Empty. The voice of someone who's seen this before and knows what it means.

The eastern ship flies Celtorian colors—blue and white snapping in the wind from a mast so high the flag looks tiny despite being larger than our mainsail. The western vessel bears Orenian red and gold.

Both converging. Both moving fast, impossibly fast for something that massive. The water breaks white at their bows, waves spreading outward like they're carving the ocean itself.

Both heading for the same point.

The same point where we are.

"They're racing," Captain Sezane says from behind us. Her voice is tight. Controlled. "For position. For Vestperia's outer waters. Whoever gets there first controls the shipping lanes."

"We need to move," Milly says.

"We're trying." She's already shouting orders. Sailors scramble to adjust the sails, to turn us, to get us anywhere but here.

But the *Meridian's Grace* is so small. So slow. Built for gentle coastal waters and paying passengers, not for running from giants.

The warships keep coming. Close enough now

that I can see details. The hulls aren't just wood—there's metal plating, riveted steel reinforcing the lower sections. The gun ports lining each deck aren't just holes—they're massive openings, dozens of them, hundreds, each one housing a cannon the size of tree trunks. And the crews—I can see them now, tiny figures moving across decks that stretch longer than Krandor's main street. Hundreds of people. No. Thousands. Each ship carrying thousands.

The shadow of the eastern ship falls across our deck as it passes to starboard. The sun disappears. The temperature drops. The sheer mass of it blocks out the light like an eclipse, turning our little vessel into a toy boat in the shadow of a cliff face.

Then it's closer. Close enough to read the lettering.

Gold letters inlaid with crystal, each character as tall as I am, gleaming in the sunlight that still touches the upper hull.

*EISENHERZ*

Milly goes completely still beside me.

"What?" I ask.

He doesn't answer. Just stares at the ship passing so close I could almost reach out and touch the barnacles clinging to its hull below the waterline.

"Milly?"

"I served on that ship." His voice is barely audible.

"Three years ago. Before... before Sawyer."

The *Eisenherz* glides past us, majestic and terrible and beautiful. Every plank is perfect, maintained by hundreds of crew, polished and painted and cared for like the national treasure it is. The pride of Celtor. The ship Milly once called home.

"They can't see us," someone says behind me. One of the sailors, voice shaking. "We're too small. We're below their sightline."

Then the western ship passes to port. Even larger than the first, or maybe just closer. I can see the grain of the wood where it's been freshly sealed. Can see sailors looking down from their lowest deck—still higher than our masts—pointing at us, but not with concern. With amusement. Look at the little boat.

The wake hits us. Not waves—a wall of water displaced by something that massive moving that fast. The *Meridian's Grace* rocks violently, nearly rolls. I grab the rail to keep from falling. Yuki screams. Klaus's ball goes overboard, lost to the sea. The elderly couple clutch each other, ears flat against their heads.

Then that ship is past too.

And I can read its name.

*SEKIYŌ NO OCHI*

"That's—" My throat closes. "That's from Krandor."

The ship I heard about. The one those soldiers were talking about, back when Mom was still alive. Back when everything was still normal. Back when I thought adventure was something exciting instead of something that kills you.

Both warships are ahead of us now, racing parallel toward Vestperia. Toward whatever strategic advantage they're fighting for.

We're behind them. We're safe. We're—

The *Sekiyō no Ochi* fires first.

Not at us. At the *Eisenherz*. A full broadside—every cannon on the starboard side discharging at once. The sound isn't just loud. It's a physical force that makes the air shudder, makes my chest compress, makes my bones vibrate like they might crack from resonance alone. The *Meridian's Grace* rocks from the shockwave, and we're a hundred pās away.

Smoke blooms from the Orenian hull, white and thick, rolling across the water like fog.

The cannonballs scream through the air. I can hear them—high whistles like wind through a narrow canyon, but wronger, more violent. Some hit. Most hit. Wood explodes from the *Eisenherz*'s hull. Even from here I can see the splinters flying, massive chunks of timber—each piece larger than our entire ship—torn away like paper.

The *Eisenherz* returns fire. Another broadside. More thunder that I feel in my teeth. More smoke. More screaming metal tearing through wood and canvas and rope.

The Celtorian flag on our mast snaps in the wind. Blue and white.

The same colors as the *Eisenherz*.

One of the Orenian shots adjusts.

Turns toward us.

I see it. Actually see it. A dark sphere the size of a man's torso, spinning as it flies, trailing smoke.

Time doesn't slow. I just notice more. The way the cannonball moves—not straight but arcing slightly, dropping as it comes. The way it catches sunlight, the metal glowing dull red from the heat of firing. The way it sounds like something tearing, like the air itself is being ripped apart.

"DOWN—" Captain Sezane screams.

The cannonball hits our main mast eight pās above the deck.

Wood doesn't break. It explodes. The mast is there—solid, whole, thick as three men standing together, holding our largest sail—and then it's not. It's splinters and dust and pieces flying in every direction, each piece as dangerous as the cannonball itself. Shrapnel made from what was holding us up.

The sound is wrong. Not a crack or snap. A wet crunch, like the mast was never wood at all but something softer, something that could be pulverized into pulp and mist.

The top half of the mast falls. Still connected to

the sail, the rigging, everything. Falls like a tree but faster, no resistance, just weight and momentum and gravity.

It hits the deck where the merchant family was standing.

Was standing.

The mast doesn't land the way falling things should. It hits at an angle, and the father is there and then he's not—not whole, anyway. Something fundamental about his shape changes, becomes wrong in a way my brain struggles to process. The deck beneath him turns dark so quickly, spreading like spilled wine but thicker, warmer when the spray hits my face.

Yuki is pinned under the edge. Her mouth opens—that same mouth that was laughing moments ago—but the sound that comes out is wet, wrong, like she's trying to breathe through water that shouldn't be there. I watch her tail twitch. Once. Twice. The brown fur darkening as the deck drinks something it shouldn't hold. The twitching slows. Stops. But her eyes stay open, still reflecting the morning light.

Klaus disappears beneath the timber. Just gone. But I can see where he was—the planks bowing, splitting, something dark seeping up through gaps too narrow to show what's making them widen.

The mother's head is still there. Just her head. The rest hidden by wood that's settling, creaking, finding its final resting place. Her eyes move—searching, finding her children, her mouth working like she's calling for them. But there's nothing below to make the sounds with. Nothing to push air through. Just movement without voice, recognition without response.

The older brother almost made it. Almost. The rigging caught him, wrapped around his legs and held him suspended between sky and deck, bent in a shape that makes my spine hurt to look at. His mouth is open too—everyone's mouth is open—but he's making sounds I've never heard a person make. Sounds that aren't screams or cries but something more fundamental. The sound of a body realizing it's broken in ways it can't survive.

Then the sounds stop.

All of them.

The twitching stops.

The deck where they were is no longer brown wood. It's dark and slick and spreading, the planks warped from sudden weight and sudden wetness, and I can smell it—copper and salt and something underneath that's worse, something organic and wrong that makes my stomach clench.

Everything tilts. The *whole* ship tilts. The mast is heavy, pulling us sideways, dragging us down. Water starts coming over the port rail, not in waves but in a steady pour, like the ocean is impatient.

Sailors are screaming. Running. Trying to cut the

rigging, to free the fallen mast before it drags us under. Their axes rise and fall, hacking at rope thick as my arm, but there's too much of it. Too much weight.

The warships keep firing. At each other, not at us. We don't matter. We're not even a consideration. Just something small that got in the way.

Another cannonball screams past—so close I feel the wind of it, hot and wrong, smelling like sulfur and burning. It hits the water off our starboard side. The plume of water that erupts is taller than our remaining mast, crashes down across the deck like a wave, like the ocean itself is trying to swallow us.

I'm on my hands and knees. Don't remember falling. The deck is wet—water from the ocean, water from leaks, other wetness that's darker and thicker and spreading from where the mast fell.

Milly grabs my arm, hauls me up. "Move—we need to—"

The *Eisenherz* and *Sekiyō no Ochi* are still firing. The smoke between them is so thick I can barely see the ships anymore. Just muzzle flashes. Just the continuous thunder of cannons that won't stop, can't stop, because this is war and war doesn't care about the people caught between.

Our ship is sinking. The port rail is almost underwater now, the mast dragging us down by degrees. Sailors have given up trying to cut it free, are just abandoning ship, jumping into water that's churning with debris and bodies.

"We need to go," Milly says. He's pulling me toward the starboard rail, away from the sinking side. "Kitt, we need to—"

Another impact. This one I don't see coming. Just suddenly the deck beneath us isn't there anymore, replaced by a hole as wide as I am tall, splintered edges smoking. Another stray shot. Another miss aimed at a real target that found us instead.

The elderly couple—Elsa and her husband—are gone. Just gone. The hole is where they were standing.

Hiroto is at the rail, trying to help people into the water. His journal is still tucked into his belt, the leather already soaked. He sees us, waves frantically. "Jump! You have to—"

A piece of burning canvas falls from somewhere above. I watch it drift down, almost gentle, and land across Hiroto's shoulders. For a heartbeat nothing happens.

Then his shirt catches. The flame spreads faster than thought—across his back, up his neck, into his hair. He screams and starts beating at himself, hands slapping at fire that moves quicker than his hands can follow. The smell hits me—something sweet and wrong that shouldn't smell sweet, shouldn't smell like cooking meat but does.

His skin starts changing color. Not burning black

like I expected. Darkening, yes, but in shades—red to brown to something blistered and wrong that peels away when his hands touch it.

He jumps. Still burning. Hits the water.

The flames go out.

The water where he went in is dark with ash and things I don't want to name.

He doesn't surface.

"Kitt—" Milly's voice is urgent. "Kitt, look at me—"

But I can't look away from the water. From the debris floating everywhere. From the bodies—some moving, some not. From the *Meridian's Grace* tilting further, further, the mast almost vertical now as we sink.

A cannonball hits our remaining mast.

This one doesn't explode the wood. Just punches through it like it's not even there. The mast stands for one more second, swaying. Then falls. Not toward the deck. Toward the starboard rail.

Toward us.

"MOVE—" Milly shoves me. Hard. I stumble, fall, hit the tilting deck and slide toward the water.

The mast falls where I was standing.

Where Milly is still standing.

Not the whole mast. Just a section. Just timber as thick around as a barrel, longer than our entire cabin, rigging and canvas still attached and dragging.

It catches him across the chest.

The sound is wet. Like something soft giving way under pressure, like fabric tearing but deeper, more complete. The timber rolls off him but the wrongness stays—his chest doesn't rise the way it should. There's a hollow where roundness belongs, a depression that shouldn't exist in something living.

I drop to my knees beside him and my hands go to his chest automatically, trying to understand through touch what my eyes can't accept. My palms sink slightly. There's nothing solid underneath anymore—just pieces that shift independently, fragments floating in something warm and thick that's trying to escape through the gaps between my fingers.

Something grinds when I press down. Something that shouldn't move sideways moves sideways.

His mouth fills with darkness. Not bleeding—filling. Like a cup under a tap, steady and unstoppable. It spills over his lips, down his chin, pools in the hollow of his throat where his pulse should be visible. Each breath brings more, bubbling up from somewhere deep inside that should be separate from his lungs but isn't anymore. His lips are red, his teeth are red, his chin is red and it won't stop coming.

I press my hands to his chest, trying to feel where, trying to understand what's broken so I can fix it. But my hands sink slightly. The chest isn't solid anymore. It gives under pressure like a bag of water, like all the hard things that should be holding him together are just floating pieces now.

Something shifts under my palms. Something that grinds. Something that shouldn't move independently but does, and each movement brings more of that dark wetness from his mouth.

Dread... Wounded—mana arrow through the chest, armor cracked, bleeding black-red.

No. Not the Colossus. Milly. This is Milly. The image won't leave. Fragment of Death, still protecting. Still holding the line.

"You're okay," I say. "You're okay, you're—"

He tries to speak. The effort brings a fresh rush from his mouth, spilling over his lips, down his chin, spreading across the deck beneath his head. I can see it pooling in the hollow of his throat, filling the space where his pulse should be visible.

His eyes find mine. Still conscious. Still here. Still trapped inside a body that's breaking in ways I can't unsee.

"Kitt—" His voice is wet. Wrong. Like he's drowning on dry land. On a sinking ship. On the deck of a vessel that's dying just like he is.

"Don't talk. Don't—I'll fix it. I'll—" But I don't know what I'll do. Don't know how to fix this. Don't know anything except that he's bleeding and I can't stop it.

The ship groans. A sound like a dying animal. The

port side is underwater now. We're sliding. Both of us. Toward the ocean that's rising to meet us.

Milly's hand finds mine. Grips it. His fingers are cold. Too cold. Wrong.

"You made it this far," he says. Each word costs him. Each word comes with more blood. "Dr. Verne... he'll help..."

"You're coming with me," I say. "We're both—we're both going to—"

"Kitt." He squeezes my hand. "You're stronger... than you think."

Those words. The same words from five minutes ago. From when everything was safe and normal and good.

"No—" I'm crying. When did I start crying? "No, you can't—you can't leave—"

The *Meridian's Grace* rolls. Fully rolls. Capsizes.

We hit the water together.

Cold. So cold. Salt in my mouth, in my eyes, burning. I'm underwater. Can't see. Can't breathe. Can't—

I surface. Gasping. Choking on seawater and terror.

Milly surfaces beside me. Barely. His face is pale, lips blue. Blood spreads in the water around us, mixing with the salt, with the foam, with everything.

"Stay with me," I beg. "Milly, stay with me—"

Something large floats nearby. Part of the deck. A

door, maybe, torn from its hinges. Big enough for one person. Maybe two if they don't move.

I grab it. Pull it closer. Get Milly's arms over it.

"Hold on," I tell him. "Just hold on—"

His eyes find mine. Still conscious. Still here. But fading. I can see him fading.

The warships are still fighting. The *Eisenherz* and *Sekiyō no Ochi* are so close now they're almost touching, firing into each other at point-blank range. The smoke. The thunder. The screaming of metal and wood and people I can't see but know are dying by the hundreds, by the thousands.

I look away from the battle. Look for anything. Any hope.

There.

The *Eisenherz*. Maybe two hundred pās away. Listing slightly from the Orenian hits, but still afloat. Still fighting. Still there.

"That ship," I gasp. "Milly, that ship—we can get to that ship—"

He doesn't respond. His eyes are closed.

"NO—" I shake him. "No, stay awake. Stay with me. We're going to—we're going to get help—"

I start paddling. One arm around Milly, one arm pushing the debris-door through the water. Kicking. Moving. Toward the *Eisenherz*. Toward salvation. Toward people who can help, who can save him, who can fix this.

"HELP!" I scream. "PLEASE! WE'RE HERE!"

My voice is nothing. Swallowed by the cannon fire. By the screams of other survivors. By the roar of battle.

I keep paddling.

My bag splits. The wooden horses, the grimoire—slipping into red water. I grab them back one-handed, shove them against my chest with the arm that should be paddling. Slower now. Heavier.

The *Eisenherz* is so tall. So impossibly tall. Even listing, even damaged, it towers above the water like a cliff face. I can see sailors on the lowest deck, tiny figures running, fighting fires, manning guns.

They don't look down.

They can't see us.

We're too small.

"PLEASE!" I'm screaming and crying and paddling. "HELP US! HE'S DYING!"

Three hundred pās.

Milly's breathing is wrong. Shallow. Wet. Each breath rattles in his chest like something's broken inside that can't be fixed.

"Stay with me," I beg. "Just stay with me. We're almost there. Almost—"

Two-fifty pās.

The *Eisenherz* is so close. I can see the rivets in the steel plating. Can see the names of cannons carved into their barrels. Can see faces of sailors through gun ports.

Can't make them hear me.

Thirty pās.

"HELP! PLEASE, GODDESS, SOMEONE HELP US!"

Milly's eyes open. Just barely. He looks at me.

"Kitt," he whispers. So quiet I barely hear it over the battle. "It's okay..."

"It's not okay! Nothing's okay! Just hold on—"

Two-twenty pās.

The *Sekiyō no Ochi* fires again. Another broadside. Another symphony of thunder and smoke and death.

I see the impacts hit the *Eisenherz*. See the wood explode. See fires start spreading across the deck.

See one cannonball punch through the hull at the waterline.

Right at the magazine.

Where they store the powder.

The *Eisenherz* doesn't explode.

It detonates.

The entire ship—all three thousand people, all that timber and steel and pride—becomes light and heat and violence in an instant.

The sound isn't sound. It's feeling. It's the world ending. It's every nightmare I've ever had made real and loud and impossible.

The fireball rises. Climbs. Reaches toward the sky like it's trying to tear heaven down.

The shockwave hits the water before the sound finishes echoing.

Hits me.

Hits Milly.

Throws us back.

Away from the ship.

Away from help.

Away from everything.

I'm underwater again. Don't remember going under. Just suddenly I'm drowning, lungs burning, pressure in my ears.

I surface.

The door-debris is gone. Milly is—

There. Still floating. But not moving. Not holding on. Just there.

I grab him. Pull him close. Tread water for both of us.

Where the *Eisenherz* was, there's nothing.

Just burning water.

Oil spreading across the surface, on fire. Wood debris, some pieces as large as houses, some small enough to be kindling. Metal bent and twisted into shapes metal shouldn't make.

And the people.

Three thousand people.

Parts of three thousand people.

The ocean can't hide them. There are too many. Too much. Bodies floating face-down, face-up. Bodies that are no longer whole, that the explosion or the fire or the impact with water separated into pieces that float independently.

An arm here, still in a uniform sleeve, the hand clenched like it's still trying to hold a rope. The fabric is Celtorian blue. The sleeve ends too soon.

A torso there, bobbing gently. The head missing, the neck showing cross-sections that should never see daylight. The uniform jacket is still buttoned. Name tag still pinned to the breast: LARS TORSTEN.

A face floating past. Just a face. The back of it gone, but the front perfect—eyes still open, expression frozen in something between surprise and nothing. Young. Maybe twenty.

Legs still in boots, severed clean and floating separate. The boots are polished. Someone polished those this morning.

Hands everywhere. So many hands. Some still gripping things—rope, tools, pieces of railing. All of them alone now.

Things that should be inside bodies, outside instead. Dark shapes, wet shapes, shapes I recognize from Mom's kitchen and shapes I don't. All of it drifting like debris because that's what it is now. Not people.

Just pieces. Just matter that used to be people.

The water isn't blue anymore.

It's deep crimson, spreading from the *Eisenherz's* grave in every direction. Not a stain. Not a patch. The whole ocean as far as I can see, turned dark and wrong, waves carrying it further, mixing it with salt but never diluting it enough to forget what it is.

I'm floating in it. Treading water in it. It coats my skin, my clothes, my hair. It gets in my mouth when I gasp, tastes like copper and salt and something more, something that used to be inside people and should have stayed there.

Milly floats beside me. His eyes are open, staring at the sky. The same sky we watched turn gold this morning. The same sky that held nothing but possibility.

His chest isn't moving. Hasn't been moving for—I don't know. Time stopped working somewhere between the explosion and now.

The dark wetness that was coming from his mouth has stopped. Not because it's fixed. Because there's nothing left to come out. It's all in the water now. All mixed with the three thousand others. All the same.

The blood of three thousand people turns the ocean red for kāls in every direction.

I'm floating in red water, holding Milly, watching debris rain down from the sky.

Watching pieces of the ship he served on fall like

snow.

Like ash.

Like the end of everything.

The *Sekiyō no Ochi* sails past.

Victorious.

Proud.

Doesn't slow down.

Doesn't stop to rescue survivors.

Can't stop. Would make them vulnerable.

Just... continues toward Kurune.

Toward the strategic position they were fighting for.

Toward the shipping lanes.

Toward what matters.

Individual lives don't matter.

Three thousand people dead.

Thirty more from the *Meridian's Grace*.

Just numbers.

Just collateral.

Just the cost of controlling trade routes.

I float in red water, holding Milly.

He's not breathing anymore.

Hasn't been breathing for—I don't know how long.

"Milly?" My voice sounds far away. "Milly, please..."

His eyes are open. Staring at nothing.

Still. Empty. Gone.

I hold him anyway.

Hold him while debris keeps falling.

While fires burn on water that shouldn't burn.

While the red spreads and spreads and spreads.

I don't know how long I float there.

Time doesn't work anymore.

Just me and Milly and the red water and the burning and the silence after all that noise.

Eventually, there's a ship.

Not a warship. Something smaller. Merchant vessel, maybe. Neutral flags.

Picking up survivors.

Hands reaching down.

Pulling me out of the water.

Trying to take Milly.

"No," I say. Or try to say. My voice doesn't work right.

"Miss, he's—"

"No."

But they take him anyway.

Take him because they have to.

Because there are other survivors.

Because the dead need to be... I don't know. Accounted for. Respected. Something.

They wrap him in canvas.

Other bodies too. So many bodies.

They lay them on the deck in rows.

I sit beside him. Beside the canvas that used to be Milly.

The ship starts moving. Away from the burning water. Away from the debris. Toward Vestperia.

Toward the place we were trying to reach.

The place we almost made it to.

Someone drapes a blanket around my shoulders.

I don't remember being cold.

Don't remember anything except the red water and Milly's eyes and the sound of the *Eisenherz* dying.

Three thousand people dead.

Thirty more from our ship.

One of them was mine.

The only one who mattered.

And the war continues.

The *Sekiyō no Ochi* controls the shipping lanes now.

Victory.

Strategy.

Success.

I sit beside canvas that used to be a person.

Used to be someone who saved me.

Used to be someone who believed I was strong.

The ship sails toward Vestperia.

I don't move.

Can't move.

Just sit there in wet clothes and a borrowed

blanket while the sun sets and the sky turns red like the water and everything that was supposed to matter doesn't matter at all.

# NOTHING WANTS

◆

The horizon is crimson today.

I've been at this window since dawn, watching it meet the sky. Solis has barely risen—her smaller disc climbing ahead of Astaris the way she always does, the scout-moon racing the sun. The light catches the water and throws it back the color of the kitchen floor.

The knife is warm in my hand. It's always warm now.

They used to argue about what it would smell like. Dad said salt. Mom said pine.

"Still watching?"

Mom's voice behind me. I turn around. She's standing in the doorway, leaning against the frame like she needs it for support. Her blond hair is matted—darker where it sticks to her neck, to her shoulders, to the places where it shouldn't stick at all. Her apron is wrong. Too torn to hang properly, the fabric parted where it should cover her, the strings dangling loose where they should tie.

Underneath it, her chest is open. Deep cuts. The kind that take.

"It's beautiful," I say, meaning the sea.

"It is." She moves to the windowsill. Something wet trails behind her across the floor—thick, heavy, following her like a hem she's forgotten to lift. She doesn't seem to notice. Her hand goes to her apron pocket—that automatic gesture I've seen a thousand times. Her fingers find the hole first. The hole in the pocket. The hole in her. Her hand comes out red and trembling.

She shakes her palm like she's trying to dislodge a pill. Nothing falls.

"For the headaches," she says, though I didn't ask.

Behind her, I can see them on the floor. The pills. Scattered in their familiar pattern. The label facing up so anyone would see. The tape beside them, still coiled, still clean. I don't look at the tape.

"Mom?"

"Lunch is on the table," she says brightly. Too brightly. "You've been up here for hours."

Hours. I glance at the window. The sun has moved. When did that happen?

"I was just—"

"Getting ready?" She looks at me. Her eyes are the same as always—warm, tired, full of something I can't name. The cuts don't reach her eyes. "That's not your uniform, Kitt."

I don't have an answer. She doesn't push for one. Instead, she moves closer to the windowsill, looking down at the crimson waves. Her hand goes to her chest—that new gesture, the one she's learning. Holding herself in.

Dad comes in from the kitchen.

He's carrying a plate—eggs, the ones with peppers—and he sets it on the table with the particular care of someone who can't see what he's doing. I set the knife beside the plate. Pick up the fork. The knife stays where I put it, waiting.

His head is somewhere else. Has been for years. The absence starts just above the jaw, a clean horizon where the rest of him should continue but doesn't. I can see the wall behind him through it. The window. The red light coming through.

His stomach, too—open, hollowed, the chair visible through the bowl of his middle where breakfast should be going.

He hums while he moves. The sound comes from his chest now. Wet. Resonant. Like something caught in a drain trying to sing itself free.

"Smells good," I say.

He nods. The shoulders move in a way that means agreement. He's learned to speak with what's left—the tilt of his torso, the angle of his collar, the way his hands rest on the table beside the plate he made for me.

I pick the knife back up. It fits my hand the way it always has.

"Your father was right," Mom says, still watching the red horizon. "It does smell like salt."

"And pine," I add.

"And pine." She smiles at me. It reaches her eyes. It doesn't reach beyond them—there's nothing left for it to reach. "Both. He would have liked knowing that."

I almost reach for her hand. Almost. My fingers twitch toward hers and then I stop—not because of the knife, I've forgotten I'm holding it—but because she's holding herself together, and I don't want to make her drop anything.

Before long, Milly comes up from below deck.

His armor is clean. I polished it this morning, the way he taught me—every piece gleaming, the Celtorian crest bright on his shoulder. But the breastplate sits wrong now. Flatter. Pressed in where it should curve out, the metal remembering the shape of what broke it. When he moves, there's a sound like things settling in a space too small for them.

He opens his mouth.

What comes out is dark. Thick. It spills over his chin, down the front of the armor I just polished, catching in the grooves of the crest. He keeps trying—his jaw working, his tongue moving behind his teeth—but there's nothing left to shape the air with. Just the gurgle. Just the wet, rhythmic sound of someone drowning upright.

"Good morning to you too," I say.

He gurgles again. Nods. The movement makes more of it come up. It runs down his neck, finds the gap where his gorget should meet his breastplate, disappears inside.

"I know," I tell him. "I slept well too."

He reaches out—slowly, carefully, the way he always does when he's not sure if touch is welcome. His gauntlet finds my shoulder. The hand beneath it holds the knife. He doesn't look at it. No one looks at it anymore.

The metal is warm. It's always warm now, no matter the weather. Something to do with what's still happening inside him.

His chest makes a sound like water in a closed container. I think he's laughing.

"That's good," I say. "You deserve the rest."

His eyes are the same. Warm. Tired. Looking at me the way he always does—like I'm something worth protecting. Like I'm something that could still be saved.

There are others, too.

A girl with brown braids sits on the deck, bouncing a ball against the railing. Her tail doesn't move—it trails behind her, flat and still, the fur matted where it shouldn't be matted. She keeps missing the catch. The ball rolls toward the edge, toward the red water, and she watches it go with eyes that don't track quite right.

Her brother is beside her. Smaller. Six, maybe. He's looking for something—hands patting the deck, the railing, the space where his chest should be. He can't seem to find it.

An elderly couple sits near the bow, heads close together. The man's fur has gone gray around his muzzle. His wife's orange-and-white stripes are duller than they should be—waterlogged, maybe. They're holding hands. They're always holding hands now. I don't think they can let go.

"One more day," the woman is saying. "One more day and we'll see her."

"One more day," the man agrees.

They've been saying that since I pulled them aboard. I don't tell them we've arrived. I don't think it matters.

"Kitt?"

Mom's voice. She's behind me again. I don't remember her moving.

"You know I love you, right?"

The question comes out of nowhere. Too sudden. Too serious. Her hand is on my shoulder—wet, warm, leaving a print I'll have to wash out later.

"I know."

"Good." She nods, like she's confirming something to herself. The movement makes her sway. Makes things shift. "Good. That's... good."

She doesn't leave. Just stands there, looking at me. Looking through me. Her eyes asking the same thing they were asking on the kitchen floor.

"Mom?"

"I worry about you," she says. "The way you look at that water. The way you talk about being part of something." She pauses. Takes a breath. It rattles. "This isn't a story, Kitt. It's not grand."

"I know that."

"Do you?" She leans forward. There's something in her eyes now—not the drifting absence from before, but something sharper. Desperate. "Because your father knew. He knew, and he went anyway, and—"

She stops. Her hand goes to her chest, pressing flat against where her sternum should be. Her fingers sink slightly.

"Mom?"

"I'm fine." But she's not fine. I can see her fighting something—tears, maybe, or something worse. Something that wants to come out of her that shouldn't.

"I just need you to understand. People die out there, Kitt. Not heroically. Not meaningfully. They just... stop."

She's looking at Dad when she says it. At the space where his head should be. At the hum still coming from his chest.

"And the people who love them have to keep going," she continues. "Have to keep waking up every morning and making breakfast and pretending the world still makes sense when it doesn't."

Her hand finds the edge of herself. Holds it closed.

"When nothing makes sense."

"I just want to matter," I say finally. Quietly. "I want to be part of something."

Mom stares at me across the deck. The crimson laps at the hull beneath us. The girl with the braids has stopped bouncing her ball. Everyone is listening, or would be, if they still could.

"You matter to me." Her voice cracks. Something dark wells up in the cracks. "Isn't that enough?"

The question hangs there.

I should say yes. I should tell her of course it's enough, she's my mother, her love is everything.

But something in me—something small and

terrible and honest—doesn't say that.

"I don't know," I whisper.

Her face does something complicated. Pain, yes. But also something like recognition. Like she understands exactly what I mean. Like she understood it then, too, on the kitchen floor, when she was watching me watch her.

"Go to your room, Kitt."

"Mom—"

"Please. Just... go."

I go.

Behind me, I hear the wet sound of her breathing. The gurgle of Milly trying to say something. The hum from Dad's chest, still trying to find its melody. The ball rolling across the deck, no one catching it.

I climb below. The knife comes with me. Find my bunk. Close my eyes.

The room is small. Bed, porthole, barely enough space to turn around. Mine for however long this lasts.

I should wash. Should eat. Should do something.

Instead I lie there, listening to the ship creak around me. To the red water lapping at the hull. To the sounds of my family above, still moving, still trying, still here.

I lie in bed and dream of adventure.

The canvas beside my bunk doesn't move. Hasn't moved since I dragged it down here. The shape inside it is familiar—the shoulders, the chest that's too flat, the place where his voice used to be.

I reach out. Touch the fabric with my free hand. The other hand holds what it always holds. It's warm. It's always warm.

"Goodnight, Milly," I say.

The canvas doesn't answer.

But I know what he would say. I've learned his language now.

Goodnight, Kitt. Sleep well.

The knife rests on my chest, rising and falling with my breath. I don't remember putting it there.

I close my eyes.

I fall asleep.

In my dreams, someone sees me. Someone needs me. Someone reaches out their hand and says: *you belong here, Kitt. You're exactly who we needed.*

I can't tell if I'm smiling.

I can't tell if any of this is real.

I can't tell if it matters.

The horizon is still crimson when I wake.

It will be crimson tomorrow, too.

And the day after.

And the day after that.

One morning at a time.

www.ingramcontent.com/pod-product-compliance
Lightning Source LLC
Chambersburg PA
CBHW030221120726
47903CB00005B/1318